Unexpected
Beginning

Alissia Roswell: Book Four

Tianna Holley

Unexpected Beginning

ISBN 978-0-9894908-5-6

Published by:
Canton Walk Publishing

Other Books in the Alissia Roswell Series

The words of those closest to us have the power to discourage us the most.

I thank each person who has reached out over social media to let me know how much they enjoy my writing—complete strangers from around the globe. When I get discouraged about my art, your words help to pull me back.

I'm extremely grateful for my readers' support, and I'm continuously surprised by it. Please forgive me for the delay in getting *Unexpected Beginning* out. The last couple of years have been chaotic—both, in a good and bad way. Stay tuned. Chaos wreaks havoc, but it also gifts us with great stories!

Chapter 1

"No one's here!" Alissia hurled a knife, and as soon as it hit the practice target, she spun around to face Selona, sitting at the base of a large tree. "Gore was wrong, and it'll soon be winter. Is that your plan? Get us stuck out here, so we'll freeze to death?"

Strange eyes resembling polished, black onyx stared back at Alissia. Selona gave a smug grin, revealing sharp, slimy teeth. With her dark hair matted wildly atop her head, filth and animal blood covered her body and clothing, although a clear stream flowed nearby.

The swamp creature let out a sickly cough before responding in her natural, raspy voice, "They're here somewhere, and our task is to find them."

Alissia snatched another knife from her boot and briefly turned as she slung it at the block of wood lined with knives. She barely noticed it land within an inch of the last one she had thrown before directing her gaze to Salvatore.

Ignoring Luke's request to only speak in the ancient language, in order to help with his teaching, she griped, "We've been searching this forest for weeks and haven't found anything. How long are we planning to stay?"

Salvatore's weather-beaten face crinkled with unease, and Alissia thought she noticed more grey streaks in his shaggy, brown hair. His broad chest filled with air, and he let out a heavy sigh.

"I've been assigned to find these people, and we have to do a thorough search." He stood from his seat on one of the large roots protruding from the ground and stretched.

Alissia could not remember if it had been three or four weeks since they had entered the dark forest. Her healing body kept her muscles free from pain, but she could tell the strenuous hiking took its toll on Salvatore. Although he refused any special treatment, he recently began to stay behind more with Selona. No one trusted her alone, and she appeared too weak to help search the forest.

The creature showed signs of sickness from being away from her homeland, where her body thrived on the unique bacteria and algae found in the black, swampy water. Having eaten all the plants and animals she had packed from her bog, she now filled her stomach with food foraged from the forest. She often used her mental choking ability to catch small prey, and to the others' dismay, she enjoyed devouring the animals alive.

At the sound of Lita's laughter coming from behind a large tree, Alissia's frown deepened. She reached into her other boot to retrieve a knife, only to find it missing.

"Looking for this?"

Her face softened at the sight of Luke carrying her knives from the target. Placing them at her feet, he remarked, "I see you lost count." Straightening, he held out a knife. "I thought I told you to count your throws, especially while distracted. In a heated battle, you'll always need to know how many you have left."

Smiling sweetly, Alissia took the knife from his hand and responded, "I see you're doing an amazing job at learning the old language. I'm impressed with your fellziag myandar."

"You're right. I know enough to know when you're trying to confuse me, and it won't work this time." Shaking his head, he added, "You have a sadistic side to you. You know that, don't you?"

Having an assassin for a boyfriend often made it difficult to get the upper hand, especially when it came to anything physical. Although Alissia had always been one to work out and Luke started giving her self-defense lessons shortly after they met, she still found herself completely powerless against him.

It had nothing to do with the fact that he stood a foot taller than her five feet, as she learned early in life that a fighting spirit could often overpower someone bigger in size.

Luke spent his childhood training for his elite position within the league, and while only a teenager, they gave him his first secret mission as a killer. Every part of his olive-toned, lean body was pure muscle, and his dark, penetrating eyes and unruly black hair greatly matched his personality. Without saying a word, his presence easily dominated those around him.

Alissia grinned, reveling in her past accomplishments of tricking Luke. "I prefer to think of it as extra training. Having you learn fake words broadened your memory capacity and helped to prepare you for the real ones."

They both turned at the sound of Santo's laughter. He stood from the fire he tended and shook his head, staring at Alissia.

Although Santo could easily be recognized as Salvatore's son, with his brown eyes and shaggy hair, along with his chiseled facial features, he did not have the same broad frame as his father. He also had a playful disposition.

As he opened his mouth to speak, his younger sister, Lita, ran into the clearing. Her husband, Duff, followed but stopped near the tree line. The younger woman grabbed her sword and turned to face him, a grin filling her face. "I think it's time I take you down today."

"Is that a challenge?"

"Yes! Get ready to battle."

Duff grinned, his blue eyes twinkling with mischief. He strolled over and put his hand over Lita's, covering the sword's grip. With his blond, shoulder-length hair in a bun, he only stood a few inches taller.

Since becoming a bride, Lita had changed in many ways. At first, while aboard her father-in-law's ship, she wore a bit of makeup and sported her long, honey-colored hair down. However, as soon as they began to travel by horse, she resumed dressing in riding clothing, with her hair pulled into a braid.

Like Alissia, Lita hid many knives beneath her clothing, and since they spent most of their time trudging through the forest with backpacks, neither bothered to look into a mirror.

Lita raised her brows, as if daring Duff to make another move. When he began to lean toward her, Alissia sighed in frustration and threw the knife in her hand. It zipped past the young couple, landing in a tree behind them.

Duff released his grip on Lita's hand, and they both turned to face Alissia.

"You could have hit us!" Lita accused.

"But I didn't."

The young woman set the sword against the tree and stomped over to Alissia. "That was overdone!"

Unfazed, Alissia responded coolly, "No PDA, remember? We've talked about this."

"We weren't even going to kiss!" Lita pointed to Salvatore. "My father's standing right there."

Alissia gave a tight smile. "Then consider my knife a reminder."

Lita fumed, her chest rising and falling rapidly beneath her shirt.

"Can't the two of you get your women under control?" Santo asked, glancing between Luke and Duff.

Lita swung around to face her brother. "What did you just say?"

"I said you two need to be tamed."

"Really?" Alissia asked, crossing her arms. "And you want to show us how that's done?"

Lita smiled over her shoulder at Alissia. "It has been a while since we've given my brother a lesson." She took a step toward Santo.

Alissia grinned and uncrossed her arms, challenging Santo with her eyes. "A good fight does sound like something I could use."

Santo glanced expectantly between Duff and Luke.

Duff held up his hands, shaking his head. "You did this to yourself. Again."

"It's fun to watch Alissia in action," Luke replied, grinning eagerly.

Alissia turned to him. "Should I try one of the new moves you taught me?"

He nodded. "But not the one involving the throat. It could kill him."

"The groin one then?"

Eyeing Santo, Luke asked, "Do you think he deserves that much pain?"

She passed her sunglasses to him and shrugged. "He's the one that thinks he can tame me." Grinning, she turned back to Santo. "So, you think you can break me like a horse?"

"Father?" he asked, looking desperate.

Salvatore chuckled and shook his head. "You'll learn one day not to open your mouth around these two." To Alissia, he warned, "Just remember his body doesn't heal like yours, and he needs to be able to hike tomorrow."

Alissia nodded. Then she and Lita began to roll up their sleeves, both eyeing their prey. Santo let out a resigned sigh and took off his shirt, revealing his tribal tattoos. After throwing the shirt on top of his pack, he stepped away from the fire, staring back at them.

"I'll go first," Alissia replied, as she stepped toward him. Stopping in front of him, she cocked her head. "Hmm… Where have I not hit you?" Looking thoughtful, she frowned. "Luke taught me how to break a leg, but I guess I can't do that." When she poked him in the chest for more taunting, he grabbed her wrist.

Alissia's other hand immediately flew up to Santo's face, and the heel of her palm slammed into his nose. He let go of her wrist and tried to take a step back, but she quickly tucked her leg around his and yanked. With both of her hands pushing on the side of his face, she forced his body to the ground.

"Am I tame yet?" she asked smugly.

Santo sat up, and she stepped back. His fingers went to the blood trickling from his nose, and he frowned, just as a cloth hit his chest.

"Thought you'd need that," Luke replied.

Alissia turned around and grinned with excitement. "It worked!" She sprinted over to Luke. "I can't believe it was so easy. Did you see that?"

He nodded, pride covering his face. "Feel better?"

"Definitely!"

"You're not done yet," Lita warned, holding out her hand to her brother. "I want to spar, so grab your sword."

"Alissia, I'd like to talk to you," Salvatore replied, stepping forward, "if you don't mind."

"Okay," she answered, with a nod.

The two of them walked from the clearing and found a seat on one of the many strange trees in the forest. Instead of standing upright, the small tree developed in an arched position, with both ends growing into the ground.

"What's up?" she asked, reverting back to her natural language. She smiled expectantly, with her feet dangling beneath her.

Salvatore gave one of his fatherly smiles. "You seem stressed lately."

She looked down and began to chew on her bottom lip, knowing he was right. Once they left the Medicians on the island, they traveled by ship, where Captain Blackwell oversaw the marriage of his youngest son to Lita. Then they traveled to the northern border by carriages during the hot summer months.

They left the carriages behind when they reached the forest and followed a stream as far as their horses could take them. After setting up a base camp in a clearing by the stream, they spent the past few weeks in groups of two backpacking through the forest. Every three days they returned to the base camp, hoping someone had found the creatures supposedly living in the forest.

But no one had found anything, not even Salvatore's two large dogs or Mia, the resourceful, little creature sent by the Medicians from the mountains.

While spending time with Luke on the island, Alissia got a taste of what life could be like for the two of them once they reached the mountains, where she would finally meet the Medicians who saved her life—changing her in the process.

The Medicians Alissia met on the island answered many of her questions about her transformation. They explained that she accidently triggered a special bond between her and Luke when she saved his life, gifting them with the ability to mind speak to each other. It also meant they could not live without each other, and they would die together.

Although she loved her connection with Luke, it made things difficult for them. Like a magnet, the unfinished bond pulled them together, their bodies longing to finish the connection.

The last time they had kissed, Luke could barely pull away from Alissia. Heat had risen within her body, causing her veins to glow as the bond began to ignite between them.

Since then, they took extra precautions and avoided affectionate touch. Mia seemed to enjoy helping, as her sharp teeth constantly bit into them if they even looked at each other the wrong way.

If they completed the bond, Luke's jet-black hair would change into a dark shade of purple, unlike her plum-colored, long curls. His eyes would turn purple and glow slightly. Like her, he would have purple blood, shimmery skin, and his body would naturally heal itself from wounds.

Alissia also acquired special abilities with her change. She could bond with animals, healing them in the process, and she could summon them to do her bidding. Plants thrived from her touch, and she could charge the many types of solar-powered stones this reality greatly depended upon.

Night vision was an interesting side effect to the change, along with her inability to eat or even smell meat without getting sick. Sunlight burned her eyes, making dark glasses a daily necessity, except under the cover of deep shade—like the forest.

With the Eldership guards searching for Alissia along the roads, she and Selona had to constantly hide in the secret compartments in the carriages. The swamp creature continuously taunted Alissia, provoking resentment and anger throughout each day.

As young newlyweds, Lita and Duff spent most of their time with each other, and although Alissia truly enjoyed seeing them happy, she could not help but feel envious of them as well.

Looking up to meet Salvatore's gaze, she responded, "I just don't think we're going to find anything here."

He nodded. "Is that all that's bothering you? How are you and Luke?"

"We're fine." She smiled slightly. "Since entering the forest, we talk more than ever, and he's taught me how to forage for food and shown me a variety of animal tracks." Her smile grew, and she added, "I've even gotten to interact with animals I've never seen before."

Salvatore chuckled, and she continued, "We finish most nights with a self-defense or knife throwing lesson, and except for the rainy days, it's been great sleeping in the hammock. The sound of leaves beneath my feet and the beauty of this forest have a calming effect."

He dropped his gaze and brushed his hands over his legs before clasping them in his lap. Then he looked up at her with a solemn expression, his eyes probing. "So you're not overly stressed or upset?"

Alissia looked down at her feet, not wanting to complain about her primitive lifestyle, which required a lot of work. She yearned for a soft bed, appetizing food, and shelter from the cold and rain. With all the traveling, she now considered a bathroom a luxury item, and she swore she would never take simple things for granted again.

"I'm just tired of all the traveling," she answered, turning back to Salvatore, "and I still haven't met the Medicians who saved me. I've been in this reality for a year now, and it feels like all I ever do is fight and hide. I just want it all to be over with, so my life with Luke can finally begin."

He nodded. "Is there anything I can do to help?"

"Get us out of here," Alissia implored.

"We won't be here much longer, but we do have to do a thorough search." Salvatore smiled reassuringly and put his hand on her shoulder. "I know you and Luke have been through a lot, but it'll only make your relationship stronger. One day all of this will a be distant memory, and it'll prompt the two of you to never take each other for granted."

He gently squeezed her shoulder and added, "I know it bothers you that Lita and Duff get to be together, but you have to remember that you and Luke will probably live to be over three hundred years. The two of you will have much longer to enjoy each other's company. You just have to be patient."

Alissia sighed as Salvatore let go of her shoulder. "I know. I guess I'm just worried about traveling through the winter. I hate cold weather."

She yelped in surprise and nearly fell from her seat when a grey and black furball suddenly landed beside her.

"Mia, you've got to stop doing that!"

As usual, the tiny creature seemed unfazed by Alissia's scowl. Staring back with round, grey eyes, she blinked before lifting a raccoon-like paw to a pointy ear. Her nose twitched as she scratched.

Only two feet tall when standing on her hind legs, Mia's adorable appearance easily deceived. The tiny creature took her role as Alissia's protector seriously, having already viciously killed a man threatening her ward.

Alissia let out a frustrated sigh and turned to Salvatore. "Sorry about that. I think she gets bored easily."

He hopped to the ground and held out his hand. "Shall we join the others?"

She nodded, and as she reached out, a smooth, masculine voice startled her from overhead, causing her to stumble clumsily into Salvatore's chest.

"I believe you've been looking for us," the voice replied, in the ancient language.

Chapter *2*

*A*fter regaining her balance, Alissia took a step back and looked up to find a glowing figure standing on a branch in a nearby tree. About four feet tall, the creature resembled a luminous ice statue, with a variety of colors swirling within its body.

It glided toward them, barely touching each branch along the way, and without making a sound, it landed where Alissia recently sat. Sitting next to it, Mia cocked her head, watching.

Its eyes looked like etched glass, and Alissia could barely make out its facial features. With the details of its body a blur, she could not even tell if it wore clothing. Tentacles, giving the appearance of long hair, flowed from its head in an upward manner.

"I am Prince Veer," he stated, in an assertive tone. "My father, the king, would like to meet you. Alissia and Mia can go to him tomorrow, but everyone else must stay behind."

"We prefer to stay together," Salvatore replied protectively.

The prince gave a nod. "I understand, but your people are too large to enter our kingdom. Alissia will barely fit through the entrance."

"Can the entrance be widened?" she asked, trying to hide her fear. Memories of the horrifying bog filled her mind, and she dreaded the idea of meeting more creatures. The thought of going without the others scared her even more.

At the sound of crushing leaves, she turned around to see Luke walking briskly toward them. Although he appeared to look at the creature with minor curiosity, Alissia knew he attentively assessed their situation, searching for danger. Stopping beside her, he held out her dark glasses.

The sun barely showed through the branches of the trees in the thick forest, but she accepted them and put them on.

"I see your zeer feels threatened by my presence." Turning to Luke, he placed his fist over his chest and replied solemnly, "I mean no harm, and I'm only here in response to your continuous search for my people."

Lowering his hand to his side, he continued in a less formal tone, "At first, we thought you would tire of your search, but it seems you're a determined group. My father's curiosity has been roused, and he would like to meet with you."

Alissia smiled at Luke. "The prince informed us that the entrance is too small for everyone but Mia and me."

"Why can't the king come to us," Luke asked, dropping his polite smile. He put his arm around Alissia, gripping her shoulder.

"The king is dying. Otherwise, he would love to leave his private chambers and stroll through the forest, as he often did in his youth."

Prince Veer paused before adding, "There's no obligation to enter our kingdom, and I understand your concern. If you decide to leave—"

"We won't be leaving," Selona replied from behind.

Alissia turned around and glared as she wondered how long the creature had been eavesdropping. Then a sly grin spread to her face, and she said, "It seems you can't meet the king."

Selona stopped in front of the arched tree and gave a formal bow to the prince. After straightening, she said, "My name is Selona Gulzinger, and I'm a medicine woman. At the high cost of my health, I left my home to fulfill the greatest desire of my people, and I bring a gift from our leader, along with a letter."

Motioning toward the camp, she said, "I apologize, as I'm caught by surprise, and they're with my belongings at the moment."

The prince lifted his hand to his chest. "It is an honor to meet you, Selona, and your immense sacrifice shows you're not just a woman of medicine, but a great warrior among your people."

Luke's grip tightened on Alissia's shoulder. *"Think logically, not emotionally,"* he mentally warned.

"He just called her a warrior. She's not a warrior, Luke! She's a rotten, sneaky, lying, devious . . . cunning . . . She's a snake!"

The prince lowered his hand from his chest. "We've not welcomed guests for many years and never imagined we would have that honor again. Our ancestors built the entrances into our kingdom so that humans could not find or enter them. It's only because of Alissia's size that allows her passage, and I apologize for this inconvenience."

Selona smiled and gave a nod. "I understand. However, I ask that I have a moment alone with you to explain things in more detail." Motioning to Alissia, she added, "I'm afraid my escorts are ignorant as to the true meaning of our quest. As you can imagine, there's only so much a human can be trusted with."

"She's trying to provoke you," Luke mentally warned. *"Don't let her win. You control how you react."*

Alissia focused on her breathing, forcing herself to appear calm as the prince turned his attention to her.

"If you decide to meet with my father, you'll need to hike to the underwater entrance. Can you swim and hold your breath long?"

"I can," she answered, nodding. The thought of plunging into cold water heightened her dread, and she forced a smile onto her face.

"I completely understand your trepidation and distrust of the unknown, and there'll be no anger if you choose not to meet with my father. I don't ask for an answer now and will come to you again in the morning."

He lifted his gaze and motioned upward, where hundreds of glowing figures, in a variety of colors, materialized in the branches of the surrounding trees. Then he lowered his hand and turned his attention back to them.

"If you choose not to enter our kingdom, I ask that you end your visit to our forest. Although we've enjoyed watching you, it's time my attention returns to Father, as I can no longer be distracted."

"I understand," Selona replied. "There's truly no reason for Alissia to take any more of your attention, as I also have a sealed message from the elders of the Medicians." She smiled as her gaze went to Alissia. "I must warn you that this former human is considered a mistake and burden to them—as you can imagine. She wasn't planned and isn't the reason for our meeting." Locking eyes with Alissia, she added, "She's merely a convenient pawn, or tool, to help achieve certain goals."

"Unlike Selona would have you believe," Alissia retorted, "I'm an ambassador for the Medicians, and I'm here out of our distrust for her people. Their barbaric lifestyle, along with their simple minds, gives rise to questions of whether they can truly be trusted."

She looked at Selona with contempt. "I've visited the bog she calls home and dined with her leader, and I'm a witness to the true nature of her people." Turning back to the prince, she warned, "You and your father need to be aware of all the facts before entering into any agreement with her people."

As soon as the words left Alissia's mouth, she mentally gloated to Luke, *"Ha! Yes! How did that sound? Enough logic for you?"*

He gently squeezed her shoulder. *"Much better than I imagined. I'll admit I was ready to grab you."*

"Before or after I hit her?"

"I never quite decided."

The prince seemed to consider Alissia's words before responding, "I shall listen to what Selona has to say, and tomorrow Alissia has the choice to meet with my father. He's a wise leader and will be the one to make any decisions."

"I'll retrieve the letters and gift," Selona replied. She turned and made her way back to the camp.

"I'm guessing you and your people have been watching us for quite some time," Luke replied. "We're greatly outnumbered, and you could have easily harmed us already. The fact that you're giving Alissia the choice to enter your kingdom increases my belief that you mean her no harm. However, you must understand that I've witnessed her suffering greatly at the hands of many, and it's difficult to allow her to leave without me."

"I give you my word that no danger shall come to your zeer," the prince assured. "We've lived peacefully for many years in this forest and have only killed out of necessity."

His hand glided through the air as he motioned toward his people above. "If we wanted to cause harm, we could have easily poisoned your food or placed something in your bedding. Toxic plants and animals abound in this forest, and they've taken the lives of many without any help from our kind.

"Out of curiosity for the reason you search for us, we've already saved the lives of some of the humans within your group. More than once and without your knowledge, we've deterred certain deaths."

"I am humbled in learning this," Luke replied, sounding sincere.

"My father desires to meet with you, as we've not shown ourselves since making this forest our home. It's with great sadness that he cannot come to you, and it would be an honor if Alissia chose to be the first outsider to enter our kingdom. However, it's completely her choice."

Alissia smiled. "I would love to meet with your father, and it would be an honor."

Luke's hand left her shoulder, and she felt his anger toward her.

"Then I shall come to you after breakfast, and we'll hike to the entrance." Turning to Luke, the prince added, "The entrance we'll be using isn't close or convenient to reach my father, and we'll be traveling farther once inside the kingdom. I don't know much about your zeer bond, but I can have my men lead you through the forest as we travel underground. That way your bond may continue to work, but I have no guarantees to this. I can only be certain that your location will be directly above her."

"Your kingdom's underground?" Alissia asked.

"It is."

Selona joined them, holding a small, locked chest, and the prince sat down on the arched tree, his movements light and nimble, as if weightless.

Feeling Luke's anger growing, Alissia bowed. "I look forward to meeting the king and will be ready for travel tomorrow morning."

Without waiting for a response, she turned and headed back to the camp, with Luke close behind.

"You didn't even consider talking to me before making your decision," he snapped, as soon as they stepped into the clearing.

Alissia wondered if he spoke in the modern language so the creatures could not understand them or if he did it out of frustration, not wanting to take the time to interpret his words into the ancient language.

Seeing Lita, Duff, and Santo watching from their seats by the fire, Alissia marched through the camp and entered the woodland on the opposite side. Although she assumed the toxic plants would not affect her, she maintained caution while trampling through the thick vegetation.

After a while, she stopped, and as she turned around, she reminded herself that she felt his anger, not hers.

"Selona doesn't want me to meet the king," Alissia calmly replied.

"This isn't about Selona! You didn't even consider talking to me before making the decision!"

"Like you would have asked me for permission if it were you!" she retorted. Letting his anger take its hold, she crossed her arms and scowled back.

"I don't need to ask for your permission, Alissia. I'm the one who's been trained to make these types of decisions. You haven't."

She flung her hands from her chest, wanting to slap the smug look from his face. "Just because I didn't go to school to learn how to kill people doesn't mean I can't make decisions for myself! I don't *need* your permission for anything."

Fury flashed in Luke's eyes, and his thoughts shouted into her mind—calling her stubborn, difficult, untrained, and obstinate. Suddenly fierce and dominating, part of Alissia feared him in that moment, but she instinctively lifted her chin and glared back at him, refusing to back down.

They stared at each other for a moment before he turned around and let out a long, shaky breath, with his fists clenching and unclenching at his sides.

Seeing Luke struggle to regain control over his anger, Alissia's face softened. She stepped in front of him and put her arms around his waist. With her head resting against his chest, she closed her eyes and began to will soothing emotions into him.

His heartbeat eventually steadied, and he put his arms around her. "I only want you to be safe."

Alissia pulled her head from his chest to look up at him. She gave an encouraging smile as she lifted her hand and began to caress his beard. "I know you do, and I should have talked to you before making a decision that could put us both in danger. Selona just gets me so angry, and it feels good that I get to meet with the king when she can't."

Dropping her hand to his waist, she gripped the top of his pants and smirked. "You have no idea how it makes me feel that she can't enter the kingdom when I can."

"I believe I know how you feel," Luke responded, smiling slightly.

Alissia frowned and let out a harsh breath as her gaze drifted to the side. "She's just so mean. I've tried to be nice to her. I know she's going to die young because she left her bog. Maybe she even blames me, but . . . she brings out the worst in me."

She shook her head to rid herself of the negativity and looked back up at him. Cocking her head, she smiled playfully. "Besides, you should be proud of me."

"And why's that?"

"I didn't let my emotions get the best of me. Instead of punching her like I wanted, I smiled and ignored her."

Luke's chest trembled with laughter. "You didn't ignore her. You just found another way to get to her."

"I remained calm," Alissia replied, feigning offense. "You should give me some credit."

He stared down at her for a moment, amused by her pout, but Alissia soon recognized a flash of sadness in his eyes. She instinctively pulled out of his arms and stepped back.

"So, what do you think about the prince?" she asked, glancing around for a place to sit. By now, it seemed they had both mastered the art of distraction when it came to their desire for each other.

"I think he's telling the truth."

"Why do you say that?" she asked, taking a seat at the base of a large tree. She watched as Luke sat down beside her.

"If he wanted us dead, we'd be dead by now," he answered matter-of-factly. "They've been watching us and haven't done anything. You know what the locals say about this place."

"You think they killed that group of researchers?"

"I think they'd be reckless not to. This place is filled with plants that our people know nothing about, and I imagine many researchers have ventured here. Yet, none of them have been able to take anything out."

Alissia nodded, remembering what Salvatore had learned from a nearby village. The locals believed deadly plants and animals filled the forest, while some even feared ghosts and demons. They never entered it—not even for hunting.

"Think they're watching us now?" she asked, scanning the overhead branches.

Luke shrugged. "I believe it's best we don't use the ancient language when we want privacy."

She cringed at the thought of the creatures secretly watching her during the past few weeks, and she barely noticed when Luke took her hand and set it on his leg, threading his fingers through hers.

"After you meet with the king, we can leave."

Alissia nodded, eager for their journey to end, and the two of them sat in contented silence—as they often did—until Mia scurried into Alissia's lap.

"She's smiling at me," Luke replied.

"She's not smiling."

"I think she likes me." He stroked Mia's back, causing her to purr. "See. She likes me."

A prank came to mind, and Alissia looked down to conceal her smile.

"Luke," she said softly, "I'm worried about leaving in the morning." She furrowed her brows and looked up at him, staring into his eyes for emphasis.

Luke stopped petting Mia and turned his full attention to Alissia. While studying her face, a look of surprise came over him, but he quickly recovered and gave a reassuring smile.

"I have faith in you."

"But, what if I mess up?"

He squeezed her hand. "You'll do fine."

The creases on her forehead deepened.

Luke let go of her hand and turned toward her. He cupped her chin and lifted it. "No one's forcing you to go." Looking hard into her eyes, he added, "But I know you can do this. I have faith in you."

Alissia drew her bottom lip between her teeth and tried to turn away, but his grip held her head in place. In an effort to hide from his probing eyes, she dropped her gaze to his chest.

"No one's ever believed in me like you," she whispered.

Losing patience, she met his gaze and lifted her hand to his neck. She lightly rubbed her thumb over his skin and said, "If something happens to me tomorrow, you know that I love you, don't you?"

He smiled slightly and nodded, and she could barely contain her grin as he lowered his mouth to her cheek. As soon as he cried out in pain, she jumped from her seat and gave a triumphant laugh.

Luke grumbled as he wiped the blood from the back of his hand. The fresh wound would soon match the two nearby scabs.

"I thought she liked you," Alissia gloated.

He scowled up at her for a moment before glancing at Mia. "I'm surrounded by pixets. You're both evil!"

Alissia looked up and eyed Mia as Luke stood and walked by. Lounging like a cat on a nearby branch, the tiny furball yawned before turning her gaze to Alissia. Although she looked bored and uninterested with her surroundings, something within Alissia told her the creature had known about her little game, as an innocent kiss to the cheek did not often provoke her to attack.

A smile spread across Alissia's face, and she gave a wink before turning away. As she began to follow Luke's footsteps, a song Salvatore occasionally sang came to mind.

In the lively ballad, a husband bemoans his insubordinate wife. Each section gives a humorous account of how she skillfully outwits him, but in the last line, he concedes he would not have it any other way.

Although Alissia could not recall the words, she remembered the tune clearly, and with a mischievous glint in her eyes, she quickened her pace and began humming aloud.

Chapter 3

"*I* got this," Alissia said, with an edge in her voice.

Luke turned to the prince. "Are you certain it's safe?"

"I know it looks daunting," Prince Veer responded, "but we'll be with her. As soon as she plunges into the water, she'll be rushed through a hole in the rocks and will only be in the stream momentarily. My men have already checked the opening, and it's big enough for her to fit through."

"And it's at the bottom of those rocks?" Salvatore questioned, pointing.

"It is."

Alissia fumbled with one of her boots, and Salvatore caught her arm, steadying her. She ignored Luke's interrogation of the prince as she hastily removed both boots and tossed her pack to the ground.

She took off her glasses and outer shirt, and with a heavy sigh, she stared down at the swift current. Shivering, she ran her hands over her arms, and when she glimpsed Selona watching her, she glared back for a brief moment.

"Are we ready?" she asked, turning to the prince. Seeing Luke step toward her, she mentally warned, *"I got this."*

With his back to the others, he gave a worried look, and she smiled and lifted her hand to his beard.

"I'll be back soon," she said softly, wishing they could have a moment alone.

"I love you," he mentally responded. *"Go do what needs to be done, and I'll be here when you return."* He placed a kiss on her forehead and stepped back.

"Do I need to hold Mia?" she asked, turning her attention to the prince.

"No, it's best she jumps alone. My men will grab her as soon as she hits the water."

Alissia nodded and walked over to the ledge, where a group of glowing figures awaited. Mia and the prince followed, both stepping in front of her.

"Are you ready?" he asked.

She nodded.

The prince and his men dove into the water, and once their heads broke the surface, Mia jumped.

"Alissia!" Luke called out.

She turned slightly, looking over her shoulder.

"Stay out of trouble this time."

Alissia grinned. Then she threw herself over the ledge.

As soon as she plummeted into the frigid water, two glowing figures appeared at her side and grabbed each of her wrists. They towed her farther down, fighting against the current, and then they shoved her hands through a small hole in a cluster of rocks.

A new set of glowing figures from the other side grabbed her hands and pulled her through the cramped tunnel. They hauled her upward, and just when she thought she could no longer hold her breath, her head shot from the water.

After gasping for air, she began to swim to the shallows of the dark cavern, and as she waded toward the shore, she spotted Mia vigorously shaking out her fur near the entrance of a tunnel.

Alissia flicked her arms through the air and shook out her legs before joining Mia, and then she scanned the cavern in search of the prince. All the creatures seemed to change colors on a whim, and with their blurry features, they looked exactly the same—except for the various lengths of their tentacle-like hair.

Two of the creatures stepped out of the water carrying glowing orbs, and Alissia struggled to keep her eyes on them as they walked toward her. Although they dimmed the glow of their bodies as they neared, the darkness amplified their radiance, forcing her gaze to the ground.

"You'll want to put on your glasses while we dry you," one of the creatures said.

Alissia nodded without looking up.

"I apologize," he said. "Let me give you your glasses."

He set the orb at her feet, and it disappeared as soon as his hands left it, leaving behind her outer shirt and dark glasses. She quickly retrieved them and placed her glasses on her face.

"Is that better?" Prince Veer asked.

She nodded, and the two creatures stepped aside as the prince stopped in front of her.

"While above, you didn't notice our glow as much, but it may be too bright for you down here. I'll try to dim my light while near you. However, you'll need to completely cover your eyes as we travel through the capital. We're creatures of light, and that may be a problem for you."

He motioned to the two beside him. "If you close your eyes, we'll dry you."

Alissia nodded and dropped her outer shirt to the ground. She closed her eyes, and for extra protection, she placed her fingers over them, beneath her glasses.

"We'll be careful, but please let us know if we begin to burn you," Prince Veer said.

A sudden heat covered her body, and although pleasant at first, she soon began to sweat and feel uncomfortable. As soon as the heat ended, she smiled in relief and dropped her hands from her eyes.

"Thank you," she said, looking down at her dry clothing. She felt of her braid to find it nearly dry.

"You're welcome."

"Alissia, are you safe?"

Luke's voice sounded distant in her head, but his words remained clear. She picked up her outer shirt and began to put it on. *"I'm fine. I'm in an underground cave."*

"Any surprises?"

"No, I'm putting on my boots right now, and the prince and two of his men just dried me off with their heat. The only problem I know of right now is how bright they are. He says their capital will be even brighter, and I may have to cover my eyes. I didn't foresee that, as I imagined it to be dark underground."

"I'll be traveling above you, but I was just told you'll be moving much faster. There may be a period of time we can't reach each other. I don't know how far this mental bond works."

Alissia grabbed her pack and straightened. *"My boots don't feel right without my knives. I feel naked without them."*

"I recall you laughing at me for giving them to you."

Not one for compliments, she decided to ignore his smug reply. *"I'll try to reach out to you while traveling."*

"Are you ready?" Prince Veer asked, as she finished putting on her backpack.

"Ready!" As she began to follow the prince, she mentally said, *"They're gathering at a tunnel entrance, and I'm about to join them."*

"Let me know if you get a bad feeling."

"Everything seems fine. You wouldn't have let me come down here if you suspected danger. Besides, Mia's with me."

"Don't get too comfortable and confident," he said firmly. *"Always look for danger. And trust no one!"*

Alissia grinned. *"I don't."*

"I believe we're ready," the prince said, stopping at the entrance. "It's only a short walk through the tunnel, and then we'll ride the rest of the way."

She nodded, suddenly feeling like a giant compared to those around her.

While walking through the tunnel, she wondered if the creatures were weightless. Nearly two dozen of them, along with Mia, walked with her, yet she could only hear the sound of her own boots hitting the ground.

The tunnel led to another cavern, with even more glowing creatures and a line of large orbs positioned along a wall. Although intrigued by the orbs, which looked like frosted glass, Alissia kept her eyes on the prince when he left her side. Not able to distinguish him from the others, she did not want to lose sight of him in the crowd of dimly glowing creatures.

Shortly after meeting with a yellow figure, the prince's blue glow suddenly exploded in bright colors, causing Alissia to close her eyes. She waited for a moment before opening them again to find the prince back to his dim, blue glow. He snapped out orders, while his men dashed about in various directions. Then he rushed to her side.

"I apologize, but we must hurry. My father's not doing well today, and I fear it may be too late."

"I understand," Alissia replied. She winced as Mia scurried up her body.

He led her to one of the large orbs and entered it, as if walking through a hologram. Then he sat down on a matching, glass-like bench and motioned for her to join him.

Alissia clutched Mia to her chest and cautiously stepped through the wall of the orb, and to her surprise, she felt nothing unusual as she passed. After she sat down beside him, the prince placed his palm on the bench between them, and the orb immediately began to glow brightly, causing her to close her eyes in discomfort.

"You may want to take a nap," he said. "I'll need to focus on driving, and the glow could be too much for you. Now that we're hovering, you can lean against the side."

She nodded and took off her backpack, placing it between her feet. Then she slowly reached out and touched the orb's wall. Finding it solid, she leaned against it, and Mia repositioned herself in her lap.

The lack of sound seemed odd, especially when Alissia could feel the orb occasionally lurching to the left or right. Out of curiosity, she risked a peek, but the bright light instantly forced her eyes shut.

She wanted to ask questions, but she sensed the prince's distress over his father and did not know how much attention he needed to give the orb. Reaching out to Luke proved unsuccessful, leaving her resigned to her own thoughts.

The orb resembled something from a science fiction movie, and she began to imagine what the capital would look like. After a while, she fell asleep.

*****

"We're here. You need to sit up before I remove my hand."

Alissia opened her eyes at the sound of Prince Veer's voice, only to cry out in pain and close them again. Grimacing, she pulled away from the wall.

"I apologize, as I should have warned you of how bright things are. Your room's been prepared with dim lighting, but it's not possible to do that in any of our main areas. You'll need to keep your eyes closed."

Mia hopped down, and Alissia blindly reached out for her.

"She's fine," the prince said. "She can see and has already walked out."

Alissia frowned, feeling helpless and betrayed by her little guardian. She lifted her pack and hefted it over her shoulder.

"Here, let me help you," he said, slipping his small, warm hand into hers. Once on her feet, he led her from the orb, where warmth filled the air, reminding her of a hot, summer day.

"Everything's so quiet," she marveled. "I can't even hear your footsteps."

The prince chuckled. "I do hope it's not too unsettling." He passed her hand to someone else. "I must see my father, but these two escorts will take you to your room. I believe you'll find it quite pleasing."

The second escort took Alissia's free hand, and the prince continued, "I'm certain my sister will want to meet you, but I expect she'll be detained as well. Please forgive the inconvenience and understand that this is a sensitive time for my family."

She smiled, hoping to hide how awkward she felt from having her eyes closed. "Don't worry about me. I hope your father improves."

"Thank you for understanding."

The guides introduced themselves and started forward, and as they began to describe their surroundings, Alissia could not help but wonder about a subtle odor lingering in the air.

Once she determined the warm air held the scent of some kind of mineral, she listened with interest as the guides explained how they could see more hues of color than others. This caused them to see things much differently and explained how they could see each other's features when she could not.

When Alissia asked how they could appear invisible, they explained they could only do that from a distance by bending the light around them, and if they got too close, she could easily see them. They also could not hide themselves at night, in the darkness. Laughing, they assured her no one would be hiding in her room, concealed by invisibility.

"We're almost there, and your handler's waiting for you."

"My handler?" she asked.

"Yes, Kizzy will be taking care of you during your visit."

The escorts stopped and wished her a pleasant stay in the capital before saying their goodbyes. Then Kizzy, with a velvety, feminine voice, guided Alissia into her room.

"You can open your eyes now."

Alissia opened her eyes and looked around. Unlike a crude, underground cave she had envisioned, she found herself in a square room with smooth, glass-like walls, where a breathtaking mural of a forest glowed from within.

Full of rich, earthy tones and intricately detailed, the magnificent display appeared to have a life of its own, with birds darting about the trees and small animals scurrying to and fro.

While watching a tiny beetle make its way up a tree, Alissia noticed an owl with round, curious eyes watching her, nearly hidden by leaves trembling in an unseen breeze.

She glimpsed glowing creatures flitting about the woodland, hopping along the branches and jumping from tree to tree. As if playing a game of hide-and-seek, they popped into view and disappeared behind a tree or into a thick cluster of leaves. Leaving behind temporary sparks of glitter, they reminded Alissia of mischievous pixies, but she soon realized they portrayed the glowing creatures hiding in the forest above.

Although she could stare at the walls for hours and still see something new, she looked up and discovered the ceiling presented a sparkly, night sky in deep colors of blue and purple, complete with a full moon and occasional falling stars.

The bed, made from the same smooth material and topped with dark, silky bedding, blended with the walls' art display, while in one corner of the room, a grey mist moved along the bottom of a matching table with chairs.

Alissia turned to Kizzy. With her tentacle-like hair floating behind her, the small creature shimmered in hues of deep green and purple.

"It's amazing!"

"It's not too bright, is it?"

Alissia shook her head and reached up to touch the smooth ceiling. "No, it's perfect. I've never seen anything like it. Is this glass?"

"Similar, but not quite." She glided over to the table and pointed to a bowl. "I brought some food, but I . . . uh . . . we've never had guests outside our people, and I don't quite know what you eat. I included a variety of fruits and vegetables we grow underground, along with some from the forest above."

When Alissia joined Kizzy, Mia hopped onto the table and grabbed something resembling an avocado. Without hesitation, she began to devour her selection.

"How do you grow food down here?" Alissia asked. "I mean, I imagined caves and tunnels when I was told I'd be going underground."

Kizzy chuckled, a pleasant, high-trilled sound, causing the green and purple hues of her body to swirl around. "This room's been modified for you and doesn't fully represent the way we live. We produce enough light down here to grow our own vegetation." Running her fingers along the top of the table, she added, "And we use dirt and the natural resources available to us."

She crossed the small room and stopped in front of a flowing stream on the mural. Putting her hand through the wall, she turned to Alissia. "The lavatory is through here."

She stepped through the mural, and Alissia walked over and passed her hand through the wall. Following it, she entered a tiny room with glowing waterfalls depicted along the walls.

"We don't need water for cleansing, but I believe your people do." Kizzy pointed to a large basin of water made from the same glass-like material. Like everything else in the room, it looked like a piece of art, with beautiful, glowing fish swimming along. Except for a small, matching toilet extending from the wall, nothing else occupied the room—not even a towel.

"Do you require anything else in here?"

Alissia shook her head. "No, it's perfect."

"If the lighting's too bright, we can modify it."

"Thank you, but it's really fine."

Kizzy turned and disappeared through the unseen door, depicted by a path between the waterfalls, and Alissia followed.

"I understand you had a long hike this morning, and I should let you rest," Kizzy replied, gliding across the room. She stopped and turned around near a path in the mural. "If you need anything, you can put your hand through here, and one of the guards standing outside will check on you. They can lower the lighting, if needed.

"I apologize for the inconvenience, as most of our devices are built to work with the light and heat from our bodies, and you're not able to use them."

Kizzy watched Mia hop onto the bed before glancing around the room. "Shall I lower the lighting? I don't know if you need complete darkness to sleep."

Alissia smiled reassuringly. "I'm fine, and the lighting's perfect."

"Then I shall see you in the morning. I know the princess is excited to meet you, but she may be delayed with her father."

"How is the king?"

"His time with us is nearing an end, and he'll soon be leaving this world for the hereafter." She stepped toward the path on the wall. "I hope you sleep well, and I'll see you in the morning."

As soon as Kizzy disappeared through the wall, Alissia reached out with her mind, but she neither felt nor heard anything from Luke in return. She stared at the art along the walls, searching for hidden creatures in the forest. Then she walked into the bathroom, where she felt along the walls and strained to see past them. Finding them solid and too thick to see beyond, she told herself no one secretly watched, but the suspicion lingered.

Once finished in the bathroom, she sat down at the table and began to taste the food. Thoughts of leaving the forest and dumping Selona near the bog gave her comfort her as she ate, and she continued with those thoughts while readying for bed.

Exhausted, she crawled into the bed and drew Mia close. As she pulled the silky bedding over her shoulder, she looked up and glimpsed a falling star on the ceiling. She smiled, turning her head on the pillow before closing her eyes, and for the first time in months, she allowed herself to imagine a future with Luke as she drifted to sleep.

Chapter 4

"**I** apologize, but you must send a letter to your zeer."

Alissia opened her eyes and rolled over. Her face twisted in confusion, and she squinted to see Kizzy standing in the middle of the room.

"Is it morning?" she asked, her voice thick with sleep.

"I apologize for waking you in the middle of the night, but your zeer is demanding to know you're safe." Holding up a small piece of paper and pencil, Kizzy added, "He wants you to write him."

She set the writing material on the table as Alissia sat up.

"I thought we'd be able to speak to each other once he was above me."

"I was told that he's somewhere above us, but he hasn't been able to get a response from you. Maybe you can reach out to him."

Not feeling his presence, Alissia closed her eyes and mentally called out to Luke. After a while, she shook her head and opened her eyes. "It's not working."

"Maybe we're too far underground. I don't know, but you need to write to him." Kizzy paused before adding, "I was told he's quite upset at the moment."

Alissia imagined Luke causing trouble, and she smiled as she stood and walked over to the table. She sat down and picked up the pencil, and in the modern language, she wrote:

Dear Luke,

I hear you're missing me! You should see my room. I feel like I'm back in my reality at an expensive hotel, and I can't wait to describe it to you when I return. Don't worry about me. I'm safe, and everyone seems nice. Be sure to tell Selona and the others that I'm enjoying my visit down here. These creatures are nothing like the ones in the bog.

Just so you know, I was completely asleep in a soft bed just a moment ago, and you still found a way to wake me. Thanks for that!

Stay out of trouble, and I'll see you again soon. Now I'm going to crawl back into that cozy bed and snuggle up to Mia. You should find a nice, hard spot on the ground or wrap up in your hammock to get some sleep as well.

Love,
Your pixet

(Only writing that so you'll know it's me. Don't get used to it!)

Alissia stood and held out the note. "How long before he'll get it?"

"It shouldn't take long for the guards to take it up to him." Kizzy accepted the note and started toward the path on the mural. "Goodnight, Alissia."

"Goodnight."

After Kizzy disappeared through the mural, Alissia walked to the bed and grinned down at Mia. "He's worried about me."

The tiny creature answered with a mix of grumbling and growling, and she rolled over.

"You know you like him," Alissia teased, crawling under the cover. "You went into the bog with him when I was kidnapped. And after we're married, he'll be the one sleeping with me, so you can have your own little bed."

Mia responded with a low growl, and Alissia chuckled as she put her arm around her and pulled her close.

When she woke the following morning, she smiled at the sight of Mia still sleeping soundly beside her. The tiny guardian distrusted everyone, yet she seemed relaxed around the glowing creatures. That confidence helped to ease Alissia's apprehension, and she rolled over and let out a contented breath. Then she closed her eyes and nestled her head into her pillow, savoring the soft bedding and chance to sleep late.

Hours later, while finishing a lengthy yoga session, a tinkling chime sounded in the room. Opening her eyes, Alissia straightened from her child's pose to look at the path on the mural.

Earlier, Kizzy had sounded the chime before entering the room with more food and water, and Alissia expected to see her handler again. When two glowing figures—one turquoise and the other sparkling fuchsia—glided through the mural, she quickly stood and grabbed her overshirt. Ignoring the sweat from her workout, she slipped it over her head and pulled it down before buttoning the top buttons.

"Hello, Alissia," the sparkling fuchsia one replied, her voice soft and feminine. "I'm Princess Ferne." Motioning to the other figure, she said, "This is our head recorder, Izar. I hope you don't mind our prying, but since hearing about you, Izar and I can barely contain our curiosity."

Alissia smiled politely. "I don't mind."

Princess Ferne and Izar sat down, and Alissia joined them at the table. Feeling awkward and oversized, she leaned back and clasped her hands in her lap.

"My brother said you're from another reality, and you were saved by the Medicians," the princess replied. "It seems you've done much traveling and have had quite the adventure."

Alissia nodded, wondering how much Prince Veer had learned from watching her and the others, along with the letters Selona had given to him. "Yes, it's been an adventure." Hearing sarcasm in her voice, she smiled and added, "Some have been more understanding and accepting of me than others."

"You bring change and opportunity with you," Izar said. He sounded excited, and Alissia wished she could see his facial features. "The great races have been in hiding for nearly two thousand years, and without you, we'd still be lost to each other."

"I agree," Princess Ferne replied. "I was raised on the stories of our ancestors and can barely conceive how they could live and survive above ground. We've thrived down here, and our cities have grown and flourished into something our ancestors could never have imagined."

She watched Mia jump into the last empty chair before continuing, "Although we don't need anything else for our survival, the idea of reconnecting the great races arouses my curiosity in what the future could bring."

"Yes," Izar agreed, nodding, "it's all very intriguing."

Alissia frowned. "It may be intriguing, but it could also be dangerous for your people."

"How so?" he asked.

Alissia's gaze drifted to Mia as she considered how much to tell them. The sight of her tiny friend taking small bites from a root, instead of devouring it in her usual manner, surprised her. However, the distraction only lasted briefly before she turned to the princess and began to speak about the creatures in the bog.

She told how they kidnapped her, and she described their gruesome tattoos and matching lifestyle. Hoping to expose their barbaric nature, she detailed her and Luke's torture before talking about their chief.

"I just wouldn't trust them if I were you," she warned. "The Medicians are great, and your people seem kind as well. Just be careful."

"That sounds horrifying," the princess responded. "Does my brother know?"

Alissia shrugged. "I don't think the Medicians I met on the island took my warning seriously. I don't know what they wrote in the letters, but not all of them accepted me." She added resentfully, "I think some of them accepted Selona but saw me as a threat and a mistake. They aren't the ones who changed me."

"Well, that doesn't sound right," Princess Ferne replied.

"I understand why they don't like me," Alissia said, trying to smile. "I heard what the humans did, and I know what people are capable of—even in my old reality. But, not all humans are bad. I mean, look at the people that have protected the Medicians on the island all these years. They're human, yet they would die to keep the Medicians' secrets."

"We understand," Princess Ferne responded. "Although we must keep the forest above uninhabited, our guards do not take pleasure in ending a human life. In a way, we actually owe them for our great city. Because of them, our ancestors were forced underground." Motioning to one of the walls, she added, "And look what they found. An abundant supply of raw materials we learned to manipulate."

"It's beautiful," Alissia replied, eyeing the glowing wall.

"I wish you could see more," Princess Ferne said, "or see it as we do. Has your vision been affected much since your change?"

Alissia nodded. "I go through a lot of dark glasses, but I can see more clearly than ever." She added gently, "How is your father?"

"He can only stay awake for short periods of time, but Izar and Veer met with him and the advisors this morning to discuss you and the letters."

"Yes," Izar added. "He seems more alert in the morning, and that's why we plan for you to meet with him tomorrow morning. Prince Veer understands you're eager to leave due to the impending cold weather."

"Will I see the prince today?"

"I'm afraid not," the princess answered. "My brother's quite busy preparing to become the next king, and he has much to do."

"I'm sorry to hear about your loss."

"Thank you. It's our loss but Father's gain." Seeing Alissia's confusion, she explained, "My Father remained faithful to the Creator and has served Him well. Now it's time for him to move on, but I'll see him again. He's just getting there before me."

Alissia smiled and nodded. "The Medicians said your people are great inventors. This room and the machine I rode in remind me somewhat of my old reality."

"We'd love to hear more about where you're from," the princess replied. "Do you mind sharing with us?"

Soon after she began describing her former reality, Alissia regretted never taking an interest in science and technology. Many of their questions focused on mechanics, forcing her to continuously admit her lack of knowledge on how things worked.

She learned the creatures lived in an advanced society consisting of subways, with radiant murals transforming their underground cities into bright, scenic landscapes. Known by the other great races as Lustrodems for their light from within, the glowing creatures could not effectively harness their power and share it with others like the Medicians with their jades.

Izar said their ancestors called the bog creatures Eremitagens for their secluded lifestyle. He also revealed the records documented the great races dwelling across the land in harmony, with each having something to contribute, before humans brought war to their world.

They talked for hours, until the princess needed to help with her father's feeding, and Alissia enjoyed the company and rare acceptance of her. After a relaxing evening, she went to bed early, and shortly after breakfast on the following day, escorts arrived to take her to the king.

She put on her dark glasses and closed her eyes before stepping through the mural, and hot, stuffy air immediately greeted her on the other side. She asked the escorts to describe her surroundings as they walked, and a bright and colorful world soon came to life in her mind. Although she occasionally heard voices and laughter as they passed populated areas, her footsteps remained the only other sound to penetrate the thick silence.

Her guides told her the king was too sick to leave his bed, but his room had been modified to accommodate her eyes. When she asked about his health, they both believed his life would soon come to an end.

In the king's chambers, Alissia opened her eyes and looked around to admire the glowing mural encompassing the room. The ceiling's cloudy night sky blended into a moss-covered, stone garden depicted along the walls and flooring. With lifelike expressions revealing their personalities, mythological statues moved about the enchanted garden, while tiny winged creatures flitted around them.

Numerous fresh plants adorned the room, and it even contained a small tree growing upside down through the glass-like ceiling. A bright, red snake stretched out along the winding branches, contrasting the green leaves filling the tree.

One end of the large room contained an elaborate bed and nightstands. The opposite end of the room held a small table and chairs, with a cluttered desk nearby. A sitting area arranged in the center of the room matched the rest of the sleek, glass-like furniture.

Many luminous figures filled the room, dimming themselves for her sake. They all stared in silence, and she wished she could see more of their features to determine their expressions and tell them apart.

"Please join us," Prince Veer said, motioning from his father's bedside. He currently presented himself in yellow and blue tones.

Mia scurried up Alissia's body, demanding to be held, before Alissia joined the prince and looked down at the king, surprised by what she saw.

Hardly any light came from his pale, green body, and she could see his wrinkled skin clearly, along with the shimmery, thin gown he wore. An oily sheen covered his skin and tentacle-like hair.

"You're the chosen one," he rasped, looking up at her with round, black eyes.

The prince seemed to notice her confusion, and he clarified, "My father believes you're a blessing to the great races, and you've been sent to reconnect us."

Alissia gave a polite smile, not knowing how to respond. She had planned to warn the king of Selona's people, but it suddenly seemed out of place. "I . . . uh . . . thank you for welcoming me. I find your kingdom beautiful, full of technology that reminds me of my true home, but much more magnificent."

The king's lips curled into a tired smile. "My son will make it even greater. Will you tell us about your former home?"

Alissia glanced around at her audience and nodded. She hoped no one would ask any technical questions as she began to talk about her former reality, and she soon noticed those across the room had gathered closer to hear.

Seeing the king listening with a smile on his face, she tried to think of the most outrageous gadgets to describe. Although she could not discern the expressions in the room, despair lingered in the air, and she hoped her words momentarily distracted everyone from their pain. After a while, she noticed the king falling asleep, and she gave the prince a questioning look as she finished her sentence.

He reached out and fumbled with his father's covers before turning to her. "We can talk over here."

She and a few others followed Prince Veer to the sitting area, and she sat down beside him with Mia in her lap.

"Thank you, Alissia, for letting my father be a part of history today. He wants us to reestablish trade among the great races, and my men are already gathering the items Selona requested. She should have them soon."

"About that," she said hesitantly. "I've already told your sister and Izar about Selona's people kidnapping me, and I don't want to take up your time with the details. However, you should be aware that there's an extremely dark side to them. I don't think they can be trusted, and I feel the need to warn you to be very careful with them."

Prince Veer nodded. "Thank you for the warning. I'll have my sister and Izar explain things more when I have a chance to sit down with them." He stood, and Alissia followed his lead, positioning Mia on her hip. "I know you're eager to leave the forest before winter sets in, so I won't keep you any longer."

He motioned to a glowing figure standing near the table and said, "I apologize I'm not able to accompany you, but I'm afraid I mustn't leave my father at this time."

After accepting a large, leather box from the one who had been standing by the table, Prince Veer turned back to her. "I have a parting gift for you."

He set the box down on the glass-like sofa and opened it to reveal an orb, similar to the one Salvatore had used shortly after they met.

"I'm giving you two of these. Our ancestors built them and often gifted them to the Medicians. They each require a jade to work, and although we no longer have access to jades, I believe the Medicians will be able to help you with that."

As he pulled the globe from the box, Alissia said, "I think I've seen one before. Salvatore used it to contact the Medicians on the island, but the jade was low on power. We couldn't hear any sounds, but it's used to talk to others, isn't it?"

"They're still using them?" the prince asked, sounding pleased.

Alissia nodded. "They're extremely rare, but I have seen one."

He placed the orb back in its container and turned to her. "Well, now you have your own. Please accept them as gifts from the king, and I hope to hear from you again—once we start the trade process. It'll give me something to look forward to."

A sparkly, light green figure joined them and said, "It's been a pleasure meeting you, and I—"

"His glow is leaving him!" someone near the king cried out, interrupting the princess.

Prince Veer and his sister shot to their father's side, and the two escorts darted to Alissia. One of them grabbed her hand and told her they needed to leave, but before she could respond, a burst of light exploded in the room. She closed her eyes, wincing, and Mia jumped from her grasp as the escorts rushed her out of the king's chambers.

Alissia and Mia ate lunch in their room, and after a short wait, the escorts arrived to take them to a pod. A guard introduced himself before helping her inside, and as he took her pack, he told her the king's gifts had already been loaded.

Although surprised by his silence during the ride, she enjoyed not having to talk, and she began to reflect on her time with the glowing creatures. Those thoughts soon led to the realization that she was finally free of the burden she had carried since leaving the Medicians in the mountains.

Her anticipation grew as she walked through the tunnels, and when she emerged from the stream, she wondered if she shivered from the cold or from her excitement.

"Where are you?" she mentally called out, as two guards began to dry her with their heat.

"We're on our way. Any problems?"

"Nope." Alissia told Luke about her time underground as a group of guards led her to a small clearing. They built a fire as she set up her hammock, and then they surprised her with food. She thanked them before sitting down alone by the fire, where she began to eat.

"Miss me?"

Alissia glanced over her shoulder at Luke and a few glowing creatures standing near the edge of the clearing. She grinned and set her bowl down. Ignoring Salvatore and Selona as they stepped into view, she stood and flung herself into Luke's arms. He lifted her off her feet and grinned, turning his back to the others.

"I knew you'd miss me."

She shook her head, laughing, before looking into his eyes. "We're done. We can leave now."

He gave a playful wink. "You must really love your little compartment beneath the wagon."

"Ugh!" she groaned, squirming. He set her down, and she pushed him away and began to walk past him. "You really know how to suck the life out of my happiness."

After Salvatore gave her a hug, he asked, "How was it?"

"It was amazing! I met the king and princess and slept in a beautiful room. It was *nothing* like the bog. They have manners, and they're nice. A very modern society." Locking eyes with Selona, she added snidely, "They're not barbarians."

Selona stared back at her with her usual look of contempt.

"So, what's the plan now?" Alissia asked, smiling at Salvatore.

"Well, we can spend a few more days resting in the forest, or we can begin our journey toward the bog first thing in the morning."

She immediately clapped her hands together and looked from Luke to Selona. "All right, hurry up and get ready for bed," she commanded. "We leave first thing in the morning, and you'll need plenty of sleep."

Chapter 5

"He doesn't need to control his horse," Alissia asserted. She and the others stood hunched over Duff, eyeing his oversized face as he sat leaning against a large tree. His swollen cheeks forced his eyes closed. "I can tell the horse to follow us. How soon before the venom leaves his body?"

"He should be able to open his eyes within a few days," Luke responded, "but he won't be completely healed for a few weeks. It'll be a while before he gets his energy back, depending on his body's reaction to the dalinger."

"You should see his toe. It looks horrible," Lita replied.

Alissia glanced at the bandage wrapped around Duff's left foot. She knew from a book she had read that a dalinger resembles a large spider with bat wings. "How did it happen?"

"My sea-loving husband forgot to check his boots before he put them on."

"This forest is cursed," Duff mumbled, his puffy lips making his words difficult to understand.

Alissia turned to Salvatore, her eyes pleading. "We can still travel." He sighed thoughtfully.

"I want out of this place," Duff muttered.

Salvatore gave Luke a questioning look.

"He can travel," Luke replied, nodding.

"It sounds unanimous," Salvatore announced. He straightened and turned to Santo. "Prepare his horse. We need to leave as soon as possible."

Everyone but Duff rushed through their chores, as they all seemed eager to leave. Alissia focused on her duty to the Medicians by preparing some of the birds that followed them from the island. She called them from the trees and attached the notes Selona gave her. A small parcel fit on one of the birds, and although Alissia wondered about it, she refused to ask questions, knowing Selona would only gloat over her lack of knowledge.

As she sent the birds on their way, she regarded Selona with distrust. The creature stared back at her, sneering, and Alissia turned away, hoping to hide her unease.

While traveling through the forest on horseback, Alissia often looked up at the branches, wondering if the glowing creatures still watched from afar.

They made it out of the forest the following day, and Salvatore, Lita, and Santo left to retrieve their carriages from a nearby village. They returned the next day with supplies, and Alissia straightaway devoured a portion of fresh pastries they had bought.

They spent the next couple of months traveling away from the northern border. Duff fully recovered from his dalinger bite, but he continued to get teased about being a sea lover not able to take care of himself on land.

Selona and Alissia stayed in separate carriages each day, and they easily slipped into the hidden compartments when the others noticed guards nearby. Alissia often rode in the covered wagon with her head sticking out so she could talk to the drivers, which were usually Salvatore and Luke.

At one point, Selona and Alissia, along with Mia and the dogs, hid in the brush along the road, while the others ventured into a city to update their traveling papers. By now, Luke sported a beard, and his hair had grown past his shoulders. Lita decorated his hands and neck with temporary tribal tattoos, giving him a wild look to go along with his nomadic lifestyle as a trader.

Although traveling on the main roads saved a lot of time, they often passed other carriages and saw many troops along the way. Whenever Salvatore and the others talked to someone, they usually heard about the growing unrest among the people, and the fear of war seemed to be increasing.

Selona coughed a lot, and she visibly appeared sick. Although the Medicians had said she sacrificed herself for the journey, Alissia wondered if the creature would get better when she returned to her bog.

No matter how much respect Alissia wanted to feel toward Selona for her bravery, she only felt contempt, and the feeling seemed mutual.

The day finally arrived when they stopped near Selona's bog, and Alissia hopped out of the carriage and looked around. Although she could barely see the skull-shaped trees in the distance, she scanned the nearby woodland in search of feliums. The others seemed to share her concern, as she noticed them looking around as they set Selona's belongings near the edge of the trail. She walked over and joined them at the back of the other carriage, where Selona stood frowning while peering into the distance.

"Where are we?"

"You're home," Alissia replied curtly. She wanted to say more but decided to be nice.

"But I don't see our markers."

"If you continue walking along the trail, you'll soon see the skull-shaped trees," Salvatore responded, pointing ahead of the carriages.

Selona turned to Alissia and sneered. "You're scared."

"You're darn right I'm scared! Your people are crazy!" Alissia motioned to the pile of boxes containing plants and insects Selona collected while traveling. "No need for goodbyes. You should gather whatever you can carry and be on your way. We're ready to get on with our lives and forget about you and your backwoods people."

Selona gave Alissia her usual look of disdain. "I need you to send a note to my people, so they can help carry my things. You'll need to instruct the birds to lead them back to me."

"I can't direct birds specifically to Gore's location."

Selona coughed before rasping, "That won't be a problem. Whoever reads the message will get word to Gore and send help."

Alissia shrugged. "Fine with me. I'll get a carrier on one of the birds while you write the note."

She turned to walk away, and Selona added, "You'll need to instruct the birds to stay away from the water."

"I hear you," Alissia answered, forcing the images of the terrifying merpeople from her mind. The traumatic events from the past year frequently plagued her thoughts, and although she could usually set aside her memories while awake, they often held her captive when she slept.

Luke explained how he taught himself to discern a dream from reality, and that awareness allowed him to take control of his dreams before they turned into nightmares. She hoped to learn that skill one day as well.

After Alissia finished attaching the note to the bird, she turned to Selona. "What about the feliums and all the other crazy animals in the bog? Will they attack them?"

"Feliums only bite humans, and if they notice the carrier, they'll protect the birds and lead them to Gore. You should instruct them to trust the feliums."

Alissia's expression turned skeptical, but she turned her attention back to the birds and selected another one to travel with the messenger. She mentally gave them their instructions and described the tiny, stick-like creatures before sending them toward the bog.

"Now what?" she asked, turning back to Selona.

"Some of the birds need to follow me, and then they'll need to fly back to the island to learn the route. Take the rest of them to the other Medicians, and they'll know what to do with them after reading the letters." Selona sneered and added, "The sealed letters."

Alissia almost responded with a snide remark, but when Selona began to cough, she grinned instead. "You should probably see about that when you get home. You haven't been looking well lately."

Ignoring the tinge of guilt she felt, she turned her attention back to the birds and began giving them instructions. When finished, she grinned at Selona and clapped her hands together. "Done! You can leave now, and I hope you enjoy your walk."

She waved at the others gathered beneath a tree, where they had eaten lunch, and called out, "We're ready."

Salvatore and Luke walked toward Alissia and Selona, while the others headed to the carriages.

"I hope your time with us has given you a new perspective of humans," Salvatore replied, smiling at Selona. "We're not all evil."

Selona smiled slightly and gave a nod. Then she turned to Alissia and grinned. "I want to thank you."

"Why?" Alissia asked, staring back with narrowed eyes. The creature's smiles usually came at her expense.

Selona cocked her head, her eyes never leaving Alissia's. "Without you, none of this would be possible."

Alissia shrugged. Sensing the usual disdain, she asked coolly, "You mean opening the trade again?"

While coughing, Selona picked up her pack from the ground. Then she locked eyes with Alissia and said solemnly, "Your name will go down in the historical scrolls of all the great races, and you'll forever be known as the one responsible for making this happen." She smiled. "Thank you, Alissia Roswell."

Without waiting for a response, she began walking toward the bog, leaving the three of them staring at her back in disbelief.

"Um, did anyone else find that a bit strange?" Alissia asked, breaking the confused silence. She still stared ahead, as if waiting for Selona to turn around and call out something demeaning.

"No, it was definitely odd," Salvatore noted.

Luke started toward the carriage. "We should leave."

Salvatore and Alissia both asserted their agreements and rushed past him. Without wasting any time, she jumped into the back, and they began the task of turning the wagon around.

While seated on one of the beanbags, she pondered Selona's words as she ate lunch. When finished, she set the food cloth aside and wiped the corners of her mouth with her fingertips, absent-mindedly staring ahead.

Mia crawled into her lap, and Alissia looked down and began petting her behind the ear. "Something doesn't feel right, little one."

She sighed heavily and reached out to Luke, asking, *"Why would she say something nice?"*

"Maybe she grew a conscience around us."

"You really believe that?"

"Not really," he responded, *"but I don't know what else to believe."*

Alissia rested her hand on Mia's back and frowned deeply, ignoring the tiny creature as she pawed for more attention. *"Think they'll attack whoever the Medicians use to handle the trading?"*

"No. Why would Selona go through all the trouble of leaving the bog and giving up her own health, just so they could kill a few humans?"

"I don't know, but it doesn't feel right. There's no way she just gave me a compliment." Alissia began to chew on her bottom lip, her forehead creased in thought.

"Maybe she knew you'd worry and wonder about it," Luke responded. *"And this is another way to irritate you."*

Alissia nodded to herself. *"You're right. She's just doing what Gafeen did when we left him. He acted like we'd see each other again and tried to intimidate me."* She smiled and relaxed in her seat. *"I'm not going to let it bother me. They're all evil, and we'll never see them again."*

*****

The temperature dropped over the next couple of weeks, and they began to pass fewer travelers along the roads. Although they carried proper documentation and the carriages contained some rare goods, Salvatore thought they needed a better excuse for risking the cold.

When stopped for a search, they began telling the patrols they were rushing to Salvatore's eldest daughter, hoping to see her before she died of a terminal illness. Many of the soldiers gave their condolences, while some even shared sad stories of their own.

Alissia desperately wanted to get to the mountains without stopping, and her ability to charge heat stones and pour energy into the horses helped fight against the cold. When they only had about two weeks left of travel, a group of soldiers along the road warned of a harsh, winter storm heading their way. Salvatore decided to stop in a nearby village to search for a private place to stay, but with the amount of soldiers traveling toward the northern border, he and Luke worried they would not find anything available.

The two of them, along with Lita, visited the village, and as they sought out rental property, she shopped for supplies. Their visit proved successful, and they returned a few hours later, happy and eager to lead the others to a log cabin on the outskirts of the village.

"It's not much," Salvatore said, unlocking the door, "but it's private and will keep out the cold."

"It's also all we could find," Luke added.

Alissia kept her head down as she fidgeted behind him on the porch. "There's cold, and then there's cold wind," she complained. "I feel like I'm back in Jersey, but at least there, I wasn't crazy enough to go camping in this kind of weather." Her scowl grew at the sound of Luke's laughter, and she added, "I swear we better not be traveling this time next year, or you'll be doing it alone."

Alissia followed him through the door, into an open kitchen and sitting area, where stagnant air filled her nostrils. Frail bella flowers, barely sparkling, clung loosely to the walls, leaving the glow stones in lamps and sconces responsible for the dim lighting.

"How long has it been since the old man died?" Lita asked, eyeing the cobwebs.

Duff walked past her and set his packs on the wooden floor behind the sheet-covered sofa before a bout of sneezing overtook him.

"Don't tell me you're allergic to dust, sea lover," Santo teased.

Salvatore placed his packs on the sofa and turned his attention to everyone in the kitchen area. "I'll admit it's a bit small, but we can fix everything else." Glancing up at the tinted ceiling, he smiled and added, "Luckily, the new owners came out here a couple months ago and cleaned the roof so the sun could get through, and they watered and treated the bella flowers. They also prepared the plumbing for the cold weather, and they did some other maintenance work around here."

Looking at Alissia, he asked, "Can you help with the bella flowers?"

She nodded and set her belongings on top of the sheet-covered, round table as Salvatore continued with his optimism.

"Santo, you'll need to check the fireplace before building a fire, and you may need Alissia's eyes to see up the chimney. Lita and Duff, you two pull the sheets from the furniture, but try to do it without killing the sea lover with the dust."

As they started toward the sitting area, Salvatore held up his hand and shook his head. "Wait. Duff, it may be best if you do another job."

"I'm not allergic to dust, sir."

"It's all right, son. We bought a fresh purifying flower and cleaning supplies, and somebody needs to clean the pool in the bathroom." Turning to Luke, he asked, "Want to help me bring things in?"

Alissia inspected the ivy along a wall before squatting to check one of the bases for water. Finding it empty, she wrapped her hand around a group of strands near the roots and whispered, "There's still some life left in you."

Remembering how she had fainted when healing Fang and the attacking wolves, she closed her eyes and dispensed a little energy into the ivy—only enough to affect the roots. Then she moved on to another grouping of strands and continued along the walls in the sitting and kitchen area, stopping briefly to look up the chimney for Santo.

Shortly after she began in the bedroom, she started to feel drained and lightheaded, but she continued with her task.

"You need to stop," Luke mentally warned.

Alissia sat down on the bed and nodded to herself. *"I am."* A smile crept to her face and she added, *"I can make you faint."*

"You can make us both faint, but I don't believe Salvatore will be pleased if I can't help him."

"And what about my help? He needs me, too."

"Do you want to take my place and do maintenance?"

She frowned, letting him have the last word.

Hours later, the smell of fresh pie and spices, along with a warm fire, soothed the weary travelers. After a savory meal Lita purchased from the local innkeeper, everyone ended their evening in the sitting area.

At one end of the sofa, Lita and Duff piled together, leaving barely enough room for Santo at the other end. Salvatore stared at the fire from his place on the oversized chair filling a corner of the room, while his two menacing dogs rested on the floor at his feet. Alissia and Luke reclined in separate beanbags they brought in from the carriages, and although the fire and heat stones warmed the cabin perfectly, everyone nestled beneath their personal blankets for extra comfort.

All the dusty sheets from the cabin were piled near the door, ready for tomorrow's washing, and all the containers holding bella flower roots held fresh water. Cobwebs no longer decorated the rooms, and Alissia made sure to instruct all the small critters living there to stay hidden beneath the floors.

Mia scurried into Alissia's lap and turned to face Lita, and Alissia laughed at the grin on her tiny friend's face. "She's still happy about dinner."

"The former resident was an avid hunter," Luke replied, sharing a knowing look with Salvatore. "You should see all the outside cooking gear." Santo chuckled, staring at Alissia, and Luke continued, "You know what that means, don't you?"

Alissia shook her head, too relaxed to exert any energy into thinking.

"That means I plan to do a lot of hunting," Luke said.

"Meat! We get meat!" Santo exclaimed, grinning at Alissia.

"I've missed that," Duff added.

Alissia frowned. "Y'all've been eating meat strips this whole time. Don't act like I've been keeping y'all from it."

Luke shook his head. "There's a difference between a dried strip of meat and a fresh, grilled roast."

She stared back at him in disbelief. "Says the man who spent last year torturing me with murdock root, and I watched you eat bugs you found in the forest. Since when do you even taste food—as fast as you eat—much less enjoy it?"

"There's a time and place for everything," Luke replied, pointing in the air for emphasis. "I was too busy trying to survive traveling alone with you."

"You're the one who kidnapped me."

"I didn't kidnap you," Luke responded, lowering his hand back into his lap. "I was protecting you."

"You kidnapped her," Salvatore stated, with his eyes closed and hands clasped over his belly.

"You did kidnap her," Santo agreed.

Luke turned to Lita and Duff, and he frowned when they both nodded. "I was protecting her."

"Yeah, a big, scary man—assassin—tackled me to the ground, drugged me, and then forced me to travel with him." Alissia shook her head. "That was some *great* protecting."

He glanced down and pulled his blanket up higher, his expression obstinate.

"Besides," she added, "you can't go hunting."

"Why can't I?"

"We're on our way to the Medicians, and you'll soon be like me."

"That's exactly why I need to hunt," he countered. "Go on a final binge for the last time in my life." Cocking his head, he grinned. "You know, you can help. Don't you have a way to locate the animals around you?"

Alissia looked back at him in disbelief. "The Medicians didn't give me this ability to help you kill animals. In fact, it's unnatural and goes against who they are."

"Don't go acting like you haven't hunted before. I know your past," Luke said with smug satisfaction. His gaze went to Mia. "I bet you'll want to go hunting with me."

"Don't drag her into this," Alissia fussed, pulling Mia into her arms. "She lives with the Medicians, and they probably have rules about killing certain animals."

"You want to go hunting, don't you, Mia?" he coaxed.

Alissia put her hands over Mia's ears. "We should never have taught you the old language. You're trying to lure an innocent into your world."

"Hah! I've seen her teeth," Luke exclaimed, "and we both saw what she did to the man in Pallen. She was born to hunt. She's a pixet, just like you. She may look sweet and innocent, but she's a beast on the inside."

Ignoring Santo's laughter, Alissia frowned and let go of Mia's ears. "Are you calling me a beast?"

Luke sat up partially and leaned toward Mia, staring into her eyes. "You want to go hunting with me, don't you?"

The tiny creature growled and bared her sharp teeth.

"You want fresh meat," he pressed, "and I know you're a skilled hunter."

"Stop corrupting her, Luke," Alissia warned.

Mia unexpectedly jumped into his lap and rubbed her furry head across his chest.

"I bet you're an expert at tracking, aren't you," Luke sweet-talked. Leaning back in the beanbag, he scratched behind her ear.

Alissia rolled her eyes, ignoring everyone's laughter. "It's winter, and you'll have a hard time finding anything, anyways."

"Not when I have our little pixet." He gave a wink before looking back down at Mia. Using both hands, he stroked his fingers through her fur, and the tiny creature closed her eyes and purred as he continued with his show of flattery.

"We'll show her, won't we? She thinks you can't hunt, but I know you're a master huntress and warrior. She can just stay inside while we brave the snow to bring home some meat."

Luke looked up abruptly. "Who's with us?"

"I'm not much for snow," Santo answered lazily.

"I may go a few times with you," Salvatore replied, "but I doubt I'll be much help in the snow."

"I'm in," Lita exclaimed, raising her hand.

"I thought you hated snow," Duff remarked.

She shrugged. "I do, but it's been a while since I've been on a good hunt." Looking at Alissia, she mumbled, "I'm sick of meat strips and vegetable soups." To Duff, she added, "You don't have to go with me. You've never really done much hunting, especially in the snow."

"I can hunt," he asserted defensively. His frown deepened at Santo's sarcastic laugh.

"Leave the boy alone, Santo," Salvatore said. "He's fresh off the boat, and I don't see you wanting to get out in the snow."

"I may be a drifter now," Santo responded, "but my heart's never left the island."

Alissia thought she noticed a touch of sadness in Salvatore's eyes, although he smiled lightly and nodded. "I know. Maybe we'll return home after we visit your cousins and meet the baby."

"You mean that?" Lita asked eagerly.

Salvatore nodded. "I do. I think it's time we go back to the island. We need to help your brother find a wife."

Lita gave a loud, sarcastic laugh. "Good luck with that."

Santo lifted her blanket off her feet, and she fussed while kicking it back into place.

A touch of sadness tugged at Alissia's heart as she watched the playful siblings. A year ago she lived with Grady, Langley, and Anika, and she thought they'd always be a part of her life. Yet, now they were gone, and she doubted she would ever see them again.

Looking around the room, she knew she would soon have to say goodbye to everyone but Luke and Mia, and that thought bothered her. She nestled into the beanbag and closed her eyes in an effort to conceal her sudden melancholy.

"Who's sleeping in the bed?" Santo asked.

"Too comfortable to move," Lita answered.

"I'll probably go there at some point in the night," Salvatore mumbled.

"Then I'm going there now," Santo announced as he stood. Alissia opened her eyes and watched him add more wood to the fire before disappearing into the bedroom.

She smiled contentedly and closed her eyes. *Maybe it's a good thing we stopped here,* she thought to herself. *We'll make memories before we have to say goodbye.*

Chapter 6

A winter storm moved through the area, causing heavy snow, and Luke, Santo, and Duff worked hard to maintain a clear path to the small barn. Being from the North, Luke shoveled the snow with ease, while Santo continually expressed his hatred for the cold. Although Duff tried to conceal his discomfort—most likely out of fear of more teasing—he seemed just as miserable.

Alissia continued to heal the ivy along the walls, and since the sun could not shine through the snow-covered ceiling, she frequently charged the heat and glow stones. She enjoyed the freedom of doing yoga and Pilates any time of the day, and she intensified her workouts.

True to his word, Luke soon began to wake before dawn each morning, eager to track and kill a wild animal. Alissia occasionally woke from her makeshift bed by the fireplace, where she silently watched him get ready. Although her bond with animals ended her desire for hunting, she secretly took pleasure in Luke's happiness.

It reminded her of some of her best childhood memories, before her father became violent. During hunting season, he occasionally woke her before sunrise, and she would rush to dress in her warmest camouflage clothing. After a quick breakfast, she would hop into his truck, and as they made their way to their tree stand, she would imagine the great deer they would bring home.

Luke always came back with a fresh kill, thanks to Mia's exceptional tracking skills. He said she enjoyed hunting a little too much, as she often ripped apart small game and completely devoured it. When he targeted a shot with the bow and arrow or crossbow—whichever one he chose to use that day—Mia would watch with great anticipation, and she celebrated each kill by jumping into the air and running around in circles.

Salvatore joined them once, and Lita went often. Everyone except Alissia spent a lot of time outside servicing the carriages or prepping and cooking the wild game. With all the attention on food, a cooking competition soon arose between Luke and Salvatore, and although Alissia could not participate in tasting and judging their main courses, she enjoyed their frequent bantering.

The aroma of cooking meat often found a way into the cabin, but Alissia refused to complain and ruin everyone's joy. She learned to simmer herbs and flowers in the kitchen during the day, and she rubbed spices under her nose to distract her sense of smell when the scent became too strong.

Everyone usually ended their day playing cards or relaxing in the sitting area, and Salvatore's family often entertained with music. Duff's rich voice blended perfectly with the others, and he played more than one musical instrument as well.

Their routine continued for nearly three weeks without any surprises, and only a thin layer of snow remained when Salvatore and Santo rode into the nearby village to buy some needed supplies and parts for the carriages. They also sold their collection of furs and took frozen meat to the church to help feed the local widows and orphans.

During an intense yoga session a few days later, Alissia stretched into a backbend and closed her eyes, focusing on her breathing. Alone in the cabin, she inhaled deeply and smiled, appreciating the pleasant smell of spiced fruit. Along with Salvatore's gift of fresh potpourri from the village, she relished the feel of sunlight on her skin after weeks of gloomy, winter weather.

A sense of peace filled her as she deepened her backbend, and her thoughts went to the fresh bag of herbal chet Salvatore recently bought. Looking forward to a pot of the warm drink after her yoga session, she took a few more breaths before she began to slowly come out of her stretch.

"Hide! Hide now! Soldiers are coming!"

Luke's mental commands shattered Alissia's tranquil thoughts, and she lost control of her balance and collapsed onto her mat.

"Do you hear me? Get to the sofa!"

"I hear ya. Now stop yelling at me, so I can pick up my things."

"Don't forget to hide your boots. They're too small for Lita."

Grabbing her mat, Alissia stood, and her gaze swept the kitchen and sitting area before she bounded toward the bedroom. She heard voices outside as she flung her mat into the nearest corner. Glancing around the small room, she saw nothing that would alert anyone to her presence, so she snatched her boots from the floor and rushed back to the sitting area.

The door flew open, and Alissia nearly screamed as she shot to the wall and pressed her back against it.

"Get under the sofa!" Lita whispered harshly. She closed the door and set a platter on the table.

"What's . . . oh, geez." Alissia gagged and began to fan the air in desperation. "I can smell it. Why'd you bring it in here when it's still steaming?"

Lita grabbed a spice tin from the counter and quickly opened it before holding it out. "Here! The guards will be here soon. We need to hurry."

Alissia's eyes darted around the room as she accepted the tin and took a long whiff. She dropped her boots and jabbed the tip of her finger into the powder. Liberally brushing it under her nose, she grimaced as the pungent odor filled her nostrils.

Mia darted from the bedroom and stopped behind the sofa. Pointing at the base, she growled.

"I'm coming." Alissia set the spice on the table before grabbing her boots and rushing to the sofa.

Lita lifted one end, and Alissia squatted.

"Great!" Alissia complained. "We never cleaned it." She cringed at the sight of a thick, white spider web filling the hollow base.

"What are you waiting for? Get in!"

"I need something to move the spider web."

"There's no time! Get in!" Lita shook the sofa in frustration. "Get in!"

"They're going to search the cabin," Luke mentally warned.

Alissia scowled and slid her boots toward the opposite end before throwing herself onto the floor and curling into a tight ball. *At least we moved the couch and mopped under it,* she thought to herself, remembering how much filth she and Lita had found.

She felt Mia's fur against her bare feet as Lita began to lower the sofa, and she watched in horror as the massive web grew closer. *There's no way a small spider made that.*

Her pulse flew into a frenzy when she spotted a shiny, black spider with red fangs in the midst of the web.

In that moment, Lita released her grip on the sofa, and Alissia clamped her eyes shut and mentally screamed as it landed on the wooden floor. Choking on the unsettled dust, she held her breath and tucked her nose into her shirt, and after a few short breaths, her body froze in terror.

Peering to the side instantly confirmed one of her worst nightmares. The web now covered her body, touching her skin.

In her youth, she had watched a horror show on television that instilled a certain fear in her, and while staring at the mass of white at her face, a flashback of the most haunting scene played clearly in her mind.

Somewhere in an underground crypt, a man woke to find himself tightly wrapped in a shroud. As he began to struggle, a few black beetles crept out of holes along the dirt walls and slowly made their way to the ground. Then, as if a floodgate had opened, beetles began to burst from countless holes along the walls.

The man frantically screamed as the insects swarmed the underground prison, soon covering every inch of the crypt—devouring him alive.

Chaotic screams filled Alissia's thoughts as she drew her chin to her chest and pulled herself into a tighter ball. Worried about the skin exposed by her undershirt, she covered her neck with her hands and tried to pull in her arms. When her breathing became struggled, her silent screams died, and she began to focus on her breaths.

"Alissia, stop!" Luke mentally commanded. *"You're a Medician, and the spiders won't hurt you. Get control of yourself! I can barely move or breathe, and this will only make the guards think I'm stalling or scared."*

Instantly realizing her mistake, Alissia winced. Not only had she allowed one of her biggest fears to control her, but she also let Luke see her weak. She chided herself for forgetting about her ability with animals, and her body gradually began to relax, along with her breathing.

"I've seen you handle much more dangerous animals. How are you terrified of spiders?"

*"*I wasn't terrified,*"* she contended, annoyed he knew the truth. *"Snakes and other animals don't scare me. It's just that the spider I saw had big, red fangs, and red usually signifies danger. Besides, spiders remind me of cockroaches, and I don't like cockroaches."*

Ready to change the subject, she added, *"I'm also feeling claustrophobic from being stuffed under an old couch, full of dirt and bugs. You couldn't even fit under here, and I'm sure you have your own phobias. Now where y'all at?"*

"I've convinced everyone I'm all right and capable of walking on my own, and the guards are ready to search the cabin. Get ready for their dogs."

No longer gripped by fear, Alissia noticed a board digging into her shoulder, causing some pain. She tried to find a better position in the cramped space as she mentally reached out to the dogs, instructing them to ignore her presence.

Hearing footsteps, she stopped moving, and her frustration grew when she felt the board pressing even deeper into her shoulder than before. She reached out to the spiders around her and released a quick, mental command for them to remain still. Then she closed her eyes and listened intently, but with her ear so close to the floor, she could barely hear the muffled voices over the sound of heavy footsteps. Her shoulder began to ache, but she dared not move, except to rub her nose in an attempt to find relief from the dust.

Forced to remain still, time passed slowly for Alissia. She told herself she should be used to it by now, with all the times she had hidden in the secret compartments beneath the carriages.

Her usual, cramped hiding places suddenly seemed appealing, as she could at least move her feet and tap her fingers on her chest.

"For goodness' sake! What's taking so long?" she mentally complained. *"It's not like there's much to search. Y'all invite them to dinner or something?"*

"They're about to leave. They're just—"

A scream filled Alissia's mind when someone plopped onto the sofa, directly above her. Her claustrophobia increased as the frame and cushion pressed down, causing the board to cut into her shoulder.

"Who's sitting on me?" she mentally demanded.

"Santo. The guards are about to leave. It's almost over."

The wooden frame creaked and shifted under Santo's weight, and Alissia squeezed her eyes shut, holding back tears of pain.

I'm going to kill him. I'm going to kill him. I'm really going to kill him, she mentally swore.

He eventually stood, and Alissia sighed in relief when someone lifted the end of the sofa and set it down beside her.

She pulled herself from the floor, and with trembling hands, she swiped at the dust and webbing along her arms. When her efforts proved useless, her scowl deepened, and she looked up, searching for the one deserving her wrath.

"You sat on me and nearly smooshed me to death!" she whispered harshly, not knowing if any soldiers lingered in the yard.

"You should be thanking me. One of the guards looked like he was considering the sofa, so I sat down and started eating to deter him." Santo frowned and glanced at the plate in his hand. "It was undercooked, too."

Luke grabbed Alissia from behind as she began to climb over the sofa. Although her conscious told her not to overreact, she desperately wanted to rid Santo of the smug look on his face.

Intent on getting over the sofa, she soon found herself in Luke's arms, and when he began to carry her toward the bathroom, she looked back at Santo with a spiteful grin.

"I wouldn't fall asleep tonight if I were you," she taunted. Her eyes remained locked on his until she passed through the bathroom door.

"Did that make you feel better?" Luke asked, nudging the door closed.

"Yes!"

Luke shook his head and set her on her feet. "You're bleeding. Let me look at it."

"You know it'll heal, if it already hasn't."

He chuckled, causing her frown to deepen. "I know, but it'll keep you from killing Santo."

Alissia crossed her arms and continued to scowl as Luke pulled a small hand towel from a hook on the wall. After wiping the blood from her shoulder, he set the towel on the edge of the sink and stepped in front of her. Crossing his arms, he leaned back against the wall, watching her.

Still feeling indignant, she stared back at him for a moment. Then she stepped in front of the sink and grumbled at her reflection in the mirror. After swiping at the dirt on her face and picking a few pieces of webbing from her braided hair, she let out a frustrated sigh and turned to Luke.

"Great! Now I need a bath, and I just washed my hair last night."

He took her hand and gently pulled her back in front of him, his expression troubled. "Alissia, I apologize for how I reacted about the spiders."

"No problem," she said lightly. Uncomfortable by his sudden show of emotion, she forced a smile and tried to pull her hand away, but he tightened his grip.

"I thought I saw all of your worst experiences in life when we bonded," he said softly. Pulling away from the wall, he drew her into his arms and began to caress her back. "Who was the man in your memory, and how did you witness his kidnapping and death?"

Alissia's confusion only lasted briefly before her mouth curled upward. Wanting to trick him, she tried to think of a morbid story, but she could not stop herself from laughing. When he pulled away, the sight of his bewildered expression heightened her amusement, and she leaned against the door, her body shaking with laughter.

Luke frowned. "What am I missing?"

She laughed a bit longer before wiping a tear from her eye and stepping away from the door.

"Remember when I told you about television and movies?" She waited expectantly and began to giggle when understanding dawned across his face.

"But it looked real. I saw it. I saw your memory."

Alissia shook her head. "You saw a scene from a show I watched in my youth. It was a memory of the movie. A movie I watched safely from my couch. With one of my cousins. While eating pizza."

Luke's gaze fell briefly as he considered her words. Then he looked up in horror. "A man died so you and others could take pleasure in watching a movie? And that's what people in your reality deem fun?"

She grinned and stared back at him for a moment, enjoying the look of shock on his face. "You know," she replied, stepping close and wrapping her arms around his waist, "I could *really* mess with you right now." She lifted her hand and rubbed her finger along the side of his neck, stopping at his throat. "Has anyone ever told you how adorable you look when you get all weird?"

His scowl deepened, and she laughed, stepping away. "Nobody got hurt in the movie, and I doubt they even used real bugs. It's against the law to even hurt an animal, so you can relax. I don't know how they do it, but they make things look real by using fake blood and computers, and other things y'all don't have in this reality."

Although Luke's expression softened, Alissia could tell he did not fully believe her, and she frowned. "Really? I already told you I wouldn't be considered some kind of weird creature in my reality. People would just think I colored my hair and wore strange contacts."

She placed her hand over her heart, suddenly serious. "I promise. No one got hurt, and it was just an actor, just like the ones they have in Pallen."

Luke nodded, seemingly appeased, and Alissia leaned against the side of the sink, crossing her arms.

"Why did the soldiers come?" she asked.

"It was just a random search. They heard about us in the village."

"Still looking for me?"

"Not just you. The questions they're asking lead me to believe they're searching for spies."

"Spies?"

Luke nodded. "The threat of war is growing, and that's why we're seeing so many patrols along the roads." He paused before adding thoughtfully, "I just wish I knew where everyone's alliances are at the moment. I usually know these things."

"You miss the Eldership?"

"Not when I have you to keep me busy," he quipped.

Alissia responded with a dirty look before asking, "How soon until we leave? It shouldn't take long to get to the mountains, and the snow's already melting."

"It's melting here, but it'll be worse toward the mountains."

She frowned, and Luke stepped in front of her and pulled her hands from her chest. Holding them down at her sides, he glanced around the room. "You know she's lurking around here somewhere, peeking through a crack in the wall."

"I'm sure she is," Alissia agreed, chuckling. She looked up, knowing her resourceful, little guardian loved to surprise them from above.

"I know you're wanting to get there," Luke replied, his voice serious, "but I suspect there'll be more security checks around the mountains. We have to act as if we're going to cross them, and people aren't doing that with the weather we're getting. We're going to have to wait until the mountains are clear enough to travel, which means we shouldn't leave here until early spring."

Alissia nodded. "I know. And this'll probably be our last time to ever see Salvatore and the others. I guess it's not so bad taking a break." A mischievous grin spread to her face, and she added, "Enjoy your last days as a carnivore."

"Oh, I am." He risked giving her a quick peck on the cheek and stepped toward the door. "I need to get out there and help Santo replace the shocks."

"How many repairs are y'all going to do? Y'all've been working on them almost every day."

"Better to work on them now than to have a carriage break down while we're traveling. You should come out there and learn some things."

"I would if I didn't get sick every time the door opened. Y'all spend the entire day playing with your food."

Luke chuckled. "It's called cooking."

"I think y'all are getting too competitive with it."

"Oh, there's no competition. I plan to win."

Alissia shook her head. "I've tasted your cooking. Remember?"

"Yes, but that was different. We were traveling." He turned and grabbed the handle of the door. Looking back over his shoulder, he grinned and gave a wink.

"You may want to help Lita do something with that spider in the sofa. If it had red fangs, it's quite venomous and could be a hazard."

She stared incredulously as he opened the door and stepped out. When he turned back to see her reaction, she grabbed the hand towel from the sink and threw it, only to have it slam against the closing door. Hearing his laughter from the other side, she rolled her eyes.

Chapter **7**

*A*fter a few weeks, Alissia began to feel restless in the small cabin, and although she hated mornings and cold weather, she began to get up early so she could spend time outside before the cooking started.

Behind the cabin, she practiced shooting a crossbow, along with throwing her knives, and she taught Lita some of the fighting skills she learned from Luke.

By now, the thrill of slow-cooked meat had worn off somewhat for the others, and they mostly cooked over an open fire. This allowed Alissia to spend more time outside, and she and Luke began to spar again.

While checking on the horses in the barn one morning, she heard the faint sound of child-like laughter, and she walked outside to look around. Hoping to find a tiny, glowing creature similar to the one that had gifted her with the power of extra healing, she eagerly scanned the edge of the woodland before letting out a sigh.

"It's just your imagination," she muttered. Not ready to give up hope, she cocked her head and listened intently, but after a while, she shook her head and turned back toward the barn. She took a few steps, but she spun around when she heard a playful giggle from close behind.

Alissia looked from side to side. She turned back toward the barn, and then she turned around again. Doubt began to creep in, but she immediately shook her head, certain of what she had heard.

She focused on a patch of bella flowers growing along the outside of the cabin. Barely able to discern their glow in the sunlight, she squinted, and her gaze moved on to another cluster of the flowers.

A wisp of light suddenly whizzed by, giggling and only inches from Alissia's face. She shot after it, running into the woodland, where she ignored the clawing branches while trampling through the brush, desperately trying to keep sight of it.

The creature laughed as it flitted through the air, circling trees and zipping back and forth. When it disappeared through a tight group of evergreens without returning, Alissia raced forward, fearing it had flown away.

"There you are," she panted, stepping into a small, shaded clearing. She placed her hand over her heart as she took a few breaths, eyeing the translucent being hovering in front of her. Unlike the one she had met while traveling with Luke, this one's inner glow appeared blue, instead of green.

"I never thought I'd see another guardian. I guess I should thank you or one of your friends for gifting me with the ability to save Luke's life. I understand he would have died without it."

The tiny guardian flew down to Alissia's left hand and tugged on her glove.

"Need help?" Alissia pulled off her glove and held up her hand.

The guardian flew up and touched her palm with hers, and a blue glow surrounded them. A great feeling of euphoria came over Alissia, and she closed her eyes, losing herself in the moment, until the guardian pulled away. Giggling softly, it flew to the other side of Alissia's hand.

"This is going to hurt, isn't it?" She bent her wrist so her palm faced the ground, and her body tensed when the guardian laughed, hovering near her thumb. As soon as the stinging began, she closed her eyes, absorbing the pain in silence.

"I guess that wasn't too bad," she said, opening her eyes. She smiled up at the guardian, now hovering in front of her, and slipped her glove into her back pocket. Then she began to rub the puncture dot on her hand.

"Thank you. Will you at least tell me why I need this? The Medicians told me you only show up when needed."

The creature flew around Alissia's head, giggling. Then it shot away, disappearing through the trees.

Alissia waited a few seconds before glancing around the tight clearing. Looking up, she frowned and asked loudly, "Really? Not a single answer?" She gave a frustrated sigh and turned around. "Just another thing I have to figure out on my on."

Grumbling to herself, she struggled through the thick growth of evergreens, and on the other side, her frown deepened as she looked around. "Great! Now I'm lost."

She thought about mentally reaching out to Luke, but then she decided to try using some of the skills he had taught her. As she looked down and began to search for tracks and broken limbs, another idea came to mind, and she stopped and shook her head.

"Maybe I should track the sun first and use that as a guide to know where to look," she said thoughtfully.

Not long after, Alissia stepped out of the woodland, feeling proud and confident. She knew she would have truly been lost in the woods a year ago, yet she could now track her way back. If she had been desperate, she could have also foraged for food.

As she neared the cabin, Mia ran up from behind and leapt onto the porch, causing Alissia to jump and cry out in surprise. The furball began to growl, and Alissia scowled back at her.

"Really?" she chided.

The door opened and Luke stepped onto the porch. "What's happening out here? I almost fell into the fire while trying to warm myself." Glancing down at Mia, he closed the door before turning to Alissia with raised brows.

She shrugged and looked at Mia, confused by her growling.

"Well, what'd you do to get her angry?" Luke asked. "And where were you? Until I felt your fear, I thought you were somewhere in the cabin, since I didn't see you outside or in the barn."

"How long have y'all been back?" she asked, still eyeing Mia.

"Not long. I had just started warming my hands."

Alissia stepped closer to Mia and stared into her eyes. "Are you angry, because I left?"

The creature's growling intensified, but she nodded.

"Look!" Alissia exclaimed, holding out her hand. "Another guardian visited me. That can't be a bad thing, can it?"

Her expression turned troubled, and she added thoughtfully, "Well, technically, it could be a bad thing, since the Medicians said they only come when needed."

Luke rushed down the steps and grabbed her hand for a closer inspection. "What does it do?"

She shrugged and looked at Mia. No longer growling, the tiny furball stared curiously at Alissia's hand.

"Let's show Salvatore," he said, before pulling her toward the steps.

As soon as they entered the cabin, Luke announced, "Another guardian bit Alissia."

Everyone surrounded her in the sitting room, and as Luke passed her hand to Salvatore, he revealed, "I didn't feel anything when it happened."

"Nothing at all?" she asked, surprised. "Did you not feel the overwhelming happiness I felt before the stinging pain?"

"I didn't feel anything," he asserted, locking eyes with Alissia.

"Same spot as the other one," Salvatore noted, holding up her hand. "What do you think it'll do?"

Alissia pulled her confused gaze from Luke's and shrugged. "I don't know. I tried to ask questions, but it wouldn't talk to me—unless you count laughing as talking."

Salvatore let go of her hand, and as she removed the other glove, she said, "I don't want to experiment with it until it fully heals." After tucking, the glove into her back pocket, she held out her hands to compare them.

Her new puncture wound throbbed, with the skin around it already turning blue. Just like her right hand, the wound was located on the meaty section between her thumb and pointer finger. She predicted eight blue lines would soon grow from the puncture mark, creating an eight-pointed star.

"Well, now it'll look like I have matching tattoos." Alissia left the circle and plopped onto the couch, looking confused.

"I thought you and Luke shared each other's pain," Duff replied. He took a seat on one of the beanbags, and Lita sat down on the floor in front of him.

"We do, and that's what makes this more confusing," Luke responded. As he went to sit next to Alissia, Mia hopped onto the sofa, forcing her way between them. He seemed to barely notice as he looked at Alissia and said, "Tell us what happened."

She nodded as Salvatore sat down in the oversized chair, and Santo plopped onto the other beanbag. After describing the morning encounter, she told about the one from the previous year. Then she reminded everyone what she had learned from the Medicians on the island, ending with, "They believe these guardians only make themselves known when the Medicians are in danger, and it's extremely rare. Now I'm a bit worried something's going to happen."

"We just need to be more cautious when we're near Pallen and the mountains," Salvatore replied. "I'll look over our papers again tonight to make sure nothing's out of place. I've already sent a message for some traders to meet me in the village with additional goods." To Luke, he added, "And we need to make sure our story doesn't have a weakness."

Luke nodded thoughtfully, and Alissia imagined his mind already at work, searching for danger.

*****

As predicted, an eight-pointed star soon began to appear on Alissia's hand. Although she wanted to wait a week before experimenting, she only lasted a few days without using her abilities.

Luke always added more wood to the fire when he woke early before hunting, but on the days he decided not to go, the job went to the person most bothered by the cold. On one such day, Alissia's shivering roused her, and she reluctantly crawled from her bedding. With eyes barely open, she stared at the stack of wood and frowned. She shook her head, not wanting to rekindle the fire, and stumbled over to the nearest heat stone.

Nothing unusual happened as she charged all the heat stones in the room, and while visiting the bathroom, she charged a glow stone as well. Her curiosity stirred as she finished in the bathroom, and while walking back to her bedding, she stopped by the wall and began to heal a group of bella flowers. Her new mark instantly began to glow beneath her skin, and she could feel the extra power coming from it. Intrigued, she sent a burst of healing into the plant and grinned when the bella flowers opened to their fullest, while new growth shot out from the roots.

By the time the others woke, fresh, glowing flowers covered the walls of the cabin, and the potted plants overflowed. Excited to show them her enhanced ability, Alissia led them into the bathroom, where she began to heal the purifying plant.

The flower firmed, and the red streaks along its white petals grew brighter before Luke grabbed her hand and pulled it away. Pointing to the thick roots, he explained they did not want an oversized purifying plant to take over the pool.

Everyone seemed confused as to why the guardians would increase her ability with plants, as they all agreed it did not seem like something she would need in a life-threatening situation. This helped to ease Alissia's worries, but as time passed, she noticed Luke's lessons becoming more frequent, leading the others to call her his little apprentice.

The two of them spent countless hours in training, and although Luke still called them self-defense lessons, he now spent most of his time showing her how to attack. She knew many ways to kill a person with one strike, and she could easily find and harvest toxins from various plants and animals in the area.

She especially enjoyed the few occasions Luke persuaded Duff and Santo into attacking her at the same time. She would burst into laughter when they conceded, and it usually ended with them in pain.

As soon as the weather began to warm, they loaded fresh supplies and trading goods onto the carriages and resumed their journey early one morning. They traveled for about three weeks before visiting a small village situated along the mountains, where Alissia and Mia remained hidden in one of the secret compartments as the others rushed to buy needed supplies.

The guards thoroughly searched the carriages and reviewed everyone's identification papers before allowing access to the mountain trails, and although Alissia spent most of her day in a cramped compartment, she laughed and threw herself into Luke's arms when he finally opened the hatch.

"We did it!" she exclaimed. "We're here."

Luke closed the compartment before covering it with the rug and tossing the two beanbags on it, and after she sat down, he handed her two flasks—one warm and one cold.

"Why two?" she asked, looking confused.

"They had a fresh batch of gya juice, the first pickings of the season, and Lita bought a barrel of it." He set a small bundle and mug down beside Mia in the corner, where she scratched at a pile of blankets in her usual way of trying to arrange them. "The other one is the local chet, made from mountain pines. You may find it a bit bitter."

"Well, we'll have to stop soon if I drink them both."

Luke set a sackcloth bundle by her feet and sat down in the other beanbag. "Salvatore knows you've been stuck in the carriage all day, and he plans to stop once we get a comfortable distance between us and the checkpoint."

Alissia took a sip of the juice and grimaced. "Wow, that's sweet."

He chuckled. "I didn't think you'd like it."

She set the flask down and picked up the bundle, surprised to find it still warm. Pulling back the sackcloth revealed a smaller bundle, along with a spoon and covered, clay pot. She lifted the lid and peered in. "This looks yummy."

"It's some kind of vegetable casserole. There's bread and a pastry in there as well."

She moaned softly, savoring the tasty blend of spices in the thick, creamy sauce.

Luke waited until she had taken a few bites before asking, "How long do you think it will be before they come for you?"

Alissia shrugged. "I don't know. I just know they're in these mountains somewhere, and they know we're here. I've been feeling their presence every night lately."

Turning to Mia, he asked, "Think they'll come?"

The tiny furball nodded before ripping a piece of meat from a bone, causing Alissia to look away in disgust.

"Do you think we'll find Fang?" she asked softly, to Luke.

"I hope so."

A comfortable silence fell between them, and Alissia began to wonder what it would be like to meet the ones who saved her. Although she desperately wanted to believe they would accept her, she often thought of the ancients on the island. They were divided because of her, and she could not help but think it would be the same with the Medicians in the mountains.

Looking at Luke, she smiled to herself. No matter what they thought of her, she still had him.

As they traveled deeper into the mountains, Alissia felt troubled by the amount of patrols they passed. She imagined the Medicians not happy about the extra people in their territory, and she wondered how a human civil war would affect them.

After a week had passed without hearing anything, she began to worry they would not reach out to her. The last time she had traveled through the mountains, they filled her nightly dreams with visions of tunnels and mountainous terrain. Surprised by their silence, she appreciated Salvatore and the others for not asking questions.

Mia disappeared often, which was normal for her. Because she had taken a different route to Pallen from the mountains, Alissia believed her tiny protector possibly did not know her way back home.

While unhooking one of the horses from a carriage one evening, Alissia froze at the sound of a long, dismal howl from somewhere in the distance. One by one, other wolves began to add their voices, creating a beautiful, yet eerie, harmony.

As soon as she reached out with her mind to connect with them, the howls ended abruptly, instantly filling the air with silence.

A grin spread to Alissia's face, as she could feel them racing toward her.

"Is this your wolf?" Lita asked, pulling her sword from the driver's seat of a carriage.

"You know you won't need that," Alissia asserted, giving a warning look.

"We may need to put the dogs in one of the carriages," Luke said.

Salvatore nodded without taking his gaze from the mountainside. He stood between his two dogs, both alert and ready. The setting sun silhouetted the three figures as they stared ahead.

"I'll calm them and the horses," Alissia replied, just as some of the wolves began to let out small cries while heading toward them. She turned around and placed her hand on the fidgeting horse next to her and closed her eyes, focusing on the horses around her.

Shortly thereafter, Duff interrupted, "Uh, Alissia?"

She opened her eyes and patted the horse. "Much better," she soothed, before turning around.

Fang yipped in excitement, drawing her eyes to him. Unlike the other wolves walking and sitting about the edge of the woodland, he circled and pawed the air.

Massive and fierce, with thick, grey and black fur, he looked exactly as she remembered. She took a few steps before he bounded toward her, and she stopped to brace herself, fearing he would tackle her.

Fang circled a few times, rubbing his body against hers, before he stood on his hind feet and placed his front paws over her shoulders.

Struggling against his heavy weight, Alissia shut her eyes and laughed with her mouth closed as he repeatedly licked her face and neck. When she tumbled to her knees, he continued to cover her face with slobber, and she waited a while before calling out, "Okay! Okay! You've loved on me. Fang, you're drowning me!"

She gave a quick, mental command telling him to sit, and after wiping her sleeve across her face a few times, she opened her eyes and smiled.

"My turn. Let me love on you." Alissia stood and wrapped her arms around Fang's neck, rubbing her fingers through his fur. "I've missed you, too. I didn't know if I'd ever see you again, and I hated having to send you away."

She stepped in front of him and chuckled when he licked her face. "I see you have a new family now. Let's see what else is new with you."

Alissia placed her hands on each side of Fang's face and closed her eyes, letting his excitement flood through her consciousness. His latest memories began to play through her mind, and she felt his consuming desire to find her. She saw visions of tunnels and mountainous terrain, and then she found herself staring into the face of a middle-aged, female Medician.

"Find Alissia. She's come back to you, Fang. Bring her home."

Alissia pulled her hand away, breaking the bond. "Did they send you? You're to take me to them?"

He stood and walked to the edge of the clearing, where he stopped and looked back over his shoulder. One of the other wolves disappeared into the woodland, while the others watched Alissia, as if waiting for her lead.

"We can't leave tonight," she mentally replied. *"It's almost dark. Let me prepare so that we can leave in the morning. Come back for me then."*

Fang stared at her for a moment before walking into the woodland, and the remaining wolves followed.

"They sent him to find me," Alissia announced. Looking around, she thought she noticed relief on some of their faces. She grinned, remembering how formidable a pack of wolves actually were—especially the massive ones in this reality.

"I'll go with you and Luke, while the others continue on to Allure," Salvatore replied.

Alissia glanced at Lita, aware this could be their last night together. She quickly pushed the thought aside and turned toward the horses. "Then we should hurry and prepare camp so we can get to bed. I think we've got a lot of backpacking to do."

Everyone finished their chores in silence, and as they ate by the fire, Salvatore looked over at his children and said, "We need to review the map to make sure you know which trails to follow. And don't forget to stay on the paths. You mustn't go into the woodland."

"We know, Father," Lita replied. "You've continuously reminded us about the attacking wild animals, and we've heard the stories and warnings."

"It's the Medicians' way of protecting themselves," Alissia reminded them. She set aside her bowl of uneaten beans, hoping Luke could not feel her stressed stomach. Glancing his way, she found him eating much slower than usual.

"Where are y'all going in Allure?" she asked, turning to Santo.

"We plan to stop by Langley's ranch to check on them," he answered. "Then we'll do a bit of trading in town until Father returns."

Alissia nodded and turned her gaze to the fire. She wanted to tell them how much she would miss them, and it seemed like the perfect opportunity to do so. She even knew the exact words to speak. However, she remained silent, unable to give a voice to her feelings, and the moment soon passed as Salvatore continued giving instructions to his children.

After a while, she grabbed her bowl and stood before bending down to retrieve her drink. "I guess I need to finish packing."

"Don't worry about your wardrobe trunk," Salvatore responded. "I'll talk to the Medicians to see if we can get it to you from Allure. I believe Grady said the tunnel he found you in wasn't too far off the trails." Alissia nodded, and he added, "Just take the necessities."

"Goodnight," Lita said.

"Get plenty of rest," Luke instructed. A grin spread to his face. "We leave at dawn for a day of backpacking, and we'll probably be trekking uphill."

She frowned, glancing at the mountainside. "And I suppose you're eager for another day of torture. Oops, I mean adventure."

"Always!" he exclaimed, giving a playful wink.

Chapter 8

"*I* made something for the two of you," Lita said, her breath fogging the air.

Alissia shivered and tugged on her cap, patting it tight over her ears. She held out her gloved hands to accept the cloth-wrapped gift, while Luke lifted his glow stone for a better view in the dim, early morning light.

After untying the knot on top, Alissia pulled back the cloth to reveal a round, container with elaborate carriages carved out of the wood.

"You made this?" Luke asked, sounding surprised and impressed.

Lita pulled away the cloth, nodding.

"Oh, wow!" Alissia breathed, rotating the piece of art in her hands. "I had no idea you had this much talent. Is this what you started whittling back on the boat?"

Lita nodded. "The wood's from our island. It's the best there is—smooth and will last a lifetime." She began to rub her gloved fingers along the inside. "To help keep it heat resistant, Santo sanded it with ground goula beans, and I rubbed onyar oil into it. You can put a large candle in it, but I plan to have a glass bowl made for it when I get to Allure. That way you can burn oil in it, and the shadows on the wall will look like the carriages are moving."

She took it from Alissia's hands and pointed at a driver in one of the carriages. "This is Luke, and here's Father. See Luke's hair bun?" She grinned at him and added, "I know you'll probably cut your hair once you're settled, but this way you'll always remember how uninhibited you were with us."

To Alissia, she asked, "Can you find yourself or Mia?"

Alissia stared briefly at the carriage. Then she laughed and pointed to the back of the wagon, where a tiny face with sunglasses peeped out from the slightly lifted covering. Mia's furry head peered upside down from beneath.

While rotating the container, Lita pointed out each person sitting in the front of the carriages before she stopped at the only one with a cage. "Although Shade and my cousins weren't with us the entire time, I thought you'd want me to include them, so I put them all in Shade's carriage. I even included Devon."

She handed it back to Alissia and shrugged. "I didn't think you'd want me to include Selona, so I left her out."

"Good idea," Alissia agreed.

Lita chuckled. Looking at the cloth in her hands, she began to fold it. "I . . . uh . . . now you have something to show your children, when you tell them about your adventures."

Alissia felt Luke's emotions mixing with hers as he lowered the glow stone, and she instinctively smiled, concealing her sudden awkwardness. "Thank you. It's the best gift I've ever received."

"Same here," Luke added. He stepped toward Lita and pulled her in for a hug. "We'll miss you."

Lita nodded, her arms down by her sides. "I'll miss you, too." When Luke released her, she turned to Alissia. "Want me to put it with your wardrobe trunk?"

"Yeah," Alissia answered, giving back the container. "Are you sure I'll be able to get it?"

"I think we'll be able to deliver it to the tunnels near Allure," Salvatore responded. "We're also setting up their trade, so there shouldn't be a problem getting it to you."

Mia scampered up Santo's body and gave him a quick peck on the cheek. Then she threw herself onto Duff, causing him to jump in surprise. After a quick kiss, she turned to Lita and held out her arms.

Everyone laughed as Lita passed the cloth and container to Santo and pulled the tiny creature into her arms. After a quick snuggle, Mia jumped to the ground and scurried toward Fang. She stopped about a foot away from the massive wolf and turned to stare at Alissia.

"Well, I believe she's ready to get back home," Alissia replied.

After accepting hugs from Duff and Santo, she turned to Salvatore. "Don't forget to keep one of the orbs the king gave me, so we can still talk to each other. I'll try to get some jades after we meet the Medicians."

"I won't," he responded.

He tugged the straps of her backpack, and once he finished tightening them, Alissia turned to face her three friends. She smiled, looking into each of their eyes for the last time. Switching to the modern language, she promised, "I'll never forget y'all, and I'm sorry I've been so cranky these past few months. I've just been a bit stressed."

Without waiting for a response, she quickly turned toward Fang and started walking. "Bye, y'all."

"Stay out of trouble!" Santo called out.

"Always!" she responded, not looking back. With a fresh sense of purpose, she followed Fang into the woodland.

Hours later, Alissia stood between Luke and Salvatore, all three of them staring at an overgrowth of dark green ivy along the mountainside.

"There's no way around it," Luke replied, frowning.

Alissia shrugged. "We've hiked around similar plants. The forest was full of stuff like this."

"Not with this much growth," he stated. "Or this exact variety. There'll be heavy consequences walking through there."

"Except for a minor rash, it shouldn't bother me too much," Salvatore replied.

"And I heal quickly, so it probably won't bother me, either," Alissia added. She looked at Luke, expecting a response, and noticed his jaw twitch. He remained silent, still staring ahead at the poisonous chink.

"How bad can it be?" she asked.

He turned and met her gaze. "I'm allergic to plants in the eupholia family, which only grow along rocks or in high altitudes." Motioning to Fang, he told her to instruct the wolves to find a different route.

Alissia looked to the left and right, doubting there would be a way around the dense foliage. She met Fang's gaze as he and the other wolves stood in the midst of the ivy, waiting patiently for the three of them to follow.

"Can you find a different way around these plants?" she mentally asked, pointing to the ivy in front of her. *"They're toxic to humans."* Glancing at the seven other wolves, she reached out to them with her question.

Alissia received a variety of responses, from barking to remaining completely still. However, none of the wolves left the ivy to begin a new route.

"I got nothing," she said, turning to Luke. Seeing his frustration, she let out a sigh. "But I might be able to fix it."

"How?" Salvatore asked.

She squatted and placed her left hand on the ground. No longer wearing her cap and gloves, the earth felt cool against her skin.

"How is there this much growth when we just had winter?" she asked.

"Chink is a hearty plant," Salvatore answered, "and it'll survive most temperatures. We're lucky we're not coming through here in a few months, when it will be as tall as you."

Alissia located a thick string of ivy and began to focus on it, causing her new eight-pointed star to glow. Unlike how she usually poured vitality into the roots of plants, she guided energy into the exact strands she wanted to grow. Those strands thickened and slithered along the ground, pushing down any vegetation in their way.

Although it took a lot of concentration at first to choose the strands and route they would take, Alissia grew faster at guiding the ivy once a path began to form.

She continued to work with the plants until Luke warned her to take a break, and after a quick lunch, she walked to the end of the narrow path—careful not to let her body or clothing touch the chink. She began again, lengthening the trail, and after a while, she noticed the overgrowth thinning, with the terrain turning rough with stone.

"You need to rest," Luke instructed, as she walked toward the end of her latest trail.

"I'm almost done."

"You're pushing yourself, and I can feel it."

"Yeah, but there's only a little bit left." Alissia squatted and placed her palm on the ivy at her feet. After selecting which strands she would use, she forced a great surge of energy from her body and watched as the ivy shot across the ground.

With a satisfied grin, she stood, only to have Luke catch her from behind.

"I'm struggling here, Alissia."

She fought against her light-headed feeling and straightened. "I'm fine," she said, walking along the fresh path.

"That's not how I'm feeling right now," he complained.

She scowled, annoyed with their bond, and focused on the wall of stone in front of her. As soon as she reached it, she turned around and sat down. Leaning back against the stone, she tried to appear natural.

Salvatore bent down beside her. "Let's get this off you." He began to unbuckle the straps of her backpack.

"I'm really fine," Alissia slurred. She tried to wave her hand through the air, only to have it fall into her lap. She felt warm and queasy.

"Don't touch her hand," Luke mumbled.

She turned to find him sitting beside her. She thought he looked weak with his eyes closed and head resting against the stone.

"She touched the chink and is contagious," he added.

Alissia wanted to tell Luke he was overreacting, but her mouth refused to open. Her eyes closed, and darkness consumed her.

*****

"You need some water."

Salvatore held a waterskin in front of Alissia's face, and she blinked in confusion. Then her eyes filled with dread, and she turned to look at Luke.

"This could have easily been avoided," he grumbled, setting his flask down beside him.

She turned back to Salvatore and gulped down some water as he held the waterskin to her mouth. After wiping her arm across her chin, she huffed, "I got you through the chink, didn't I?"

"Yes, but look where we are now."

"We're taking a water break."

"You call this a water break?"

Alissia scowled back at Luke. "You know, you should be thanking me right now for getting you through the chink." Holding up her hand, she threatened, "If you want some chink, I can easily give you some."

"I should go roll around in it, just so you'll feel the effects," he countered.

Before she could respond, Salvatore took ahold of her wrist and said, "How about we wash your hands? Think you can stand?"

She gave Luke a dirty look before smiling up at Salvatore. "I'm fine. I can stand."

"Let me help," he insisted, pulling her to her feet.

After washing her hands, Alissia began to dry them on her shirt. "It doesn't look like the ivy's growing along the rocks," she observed, looking around.

"I glimpsed an ibexan while you were working on the chink," Salvatore responded. "They travel in herds, and I believe this is their feeding area." He pointed to a group of stones near a ledge and added, "That's probably the path they use to get down here, and that's why the overgrowth ends abruptly."

"Aren't they like goats?" she asked, remembering a picture she had seen in a book.

A faint smile appeared on Salvatore's face. "They do resemble a goat somewhat."

Hearing Luke's laughter, Alissia frowned and crossed her arms. "What?"

He stood before answering, "I wouldn't want to confuse an ibexan with a goat. They're extremely territorial and aggressive, and the males grow as tall as you—without even including their horns! Salvatore and I would have a lot to worry about if it were just the two of us."

Salvatore nodded. "Especially since these mountains have been untouched by humans for so many years. Although there's plenty of predators in the area, I expect the herd to be quite large without anyone thinning it."

The sound of heavy rustling drew their attention, and all three of them turned toward the path Alissia created. She squinted, straining to catch a glimpse of the animal rooting around in the overgrowth.

A clump of ivy suddenly flung out of the moving brush, and Luke stepped aside as it landed nearby on the ground.

"You're doing a wonderful job of covering our trail," he called out. "But could you try to watch where you throw the chink?"

"It's Mia?" Alissia asked.

Luke looked back over his shoulder and nodded. As he turned back around, another clump of chink flew through the air, only landing about a foot away.

He snatched his pack and flask from the ground. "I'm surrounded by pixets," he grumbled, walking toward the wolves.

Alissia chuckled and grabbed her pack. "Keep up the good work, Mia!" she cheered, walking past the path.

They continued backpacking until it began to get dark, and after their meal, they fell asleep beneath the stars, exhausted from a day of trekking uphill.

The mountainous terrain proved more difficult the following day. Although the wolves led them along a tolerable route, it often involved tight spaces between rocks and along narrow ledges. At one point, Salvatore went to place his hand in a crevice, and Mia shot past him to grab a small, venomous viper before it bit him. The tiny pixet's teeth ripped the snake apart as she devoured it.

Alissia reached out with her mind to locate other snakes, and the amount of wildlife hidden around them surprised her. She warned the others to keep their hands to themselves and to watch where they grabbed for support.

They traveled hard for five days, not knowing when their journey would end, and although Luke carried a tarp, Alissia worried they would have to endure a storm on the mountainside. Sleeping in layers of clothing helped with the nightly drops in temperatures, and Mia proved herself a lifesaver with gathering water.

Luke and Salvatore appreciated the rare opportunity of getting close to a pack of wolves, while the leader seemed to enjoy Luke's company.

When they finally reached the other side of the mountain, they all stopped and stared at the valley below. After a moment of silence, Salvatore placed his hand on Alissia's shoulder and gave it a light squeeze. "It's beautiful."

She nodded, her eyes never leaving the valley. "It's so big. And green."

From her other side, Luke pointed to one of the distant waterfalls. "More than one fresh water supply. Lush vegetation. They have everything they need down there."

Alissia nodded. "I imagined them living in tunnels, but it's more like paradise. Can you see any houses?"

Luke shook his head. "No, it's too far away, and with their sensitive eyes, I'm guessing they live beneath the trees."

"Or in them," Alissia replied, remembering the tree houses on the island. "How long do you think it will take us to get down there?"

"Should be faster going down," Luke answered.

"They probably have trails along this side of the mountain," Salvatore surmised. "I expect they do mining."

"True." Alissia turned around and stepped toward the wolves. "Shall we continue or take a lunch break?"

"Lunch!" Salvatore and Luke answered simultaneously.

After a quick picnic, they resumed their journey with a renewed sense of anticipation, and they continued until Luke and Salvatore could barely see in the evening light.

Once they cleared the rockiest terrain and they began to see more vegetation, their trek became much easier. Their steps felt lighter, and their pace quickened.

By afternoon, they found themselves surrounded by foliage, and after so many days of conserving their use of water, they grew eager to find a stream. They wanted to question Mia about it, but the tiny creature disappeared soon after they entered the woodland.

Alissia sensed the wolves' excitement shortly before they began to run, and when she and the others caught up with them, two young Medician men stood in their midst. They smiled and waved as soon as they saw Alissia's group, and the wolves disappeared into the woodland.

Wearing dark glasses and loose brimmed hats, they carried backpacks on their small, thin frames, and unlike the Medicians on the island, who dressed in bright, shimmery clothing, they wore neutral colors with boots.

"We've been waiting for you," one of them said, stepping forward.

As Alissia stopped in front of him, she thought their facial features looked similar to young men in their late teens or early twenties, which meant they could be over a hundred years old.

"Welcome, Sister. My name's Eaton, and this is Meyer, our cousin. We're here to lead you home."

She smiled, somewhat taken aback. "Thank you. This is Salvatore and—"

"Luke," Eaton finished. He gave a bow. "We welcome you, my future brother." Turning to Salvatore, he added, "And it's an honor to meet a trusted protector of our distant relatives. Shall we continue?"

Alissia nodded and started walking beside him. "How much farther?"

"We should be home tomorrow evening. It's only a short hike to our camp, and tomorrow we'll ride through the provinces to get to the other side of the valley. We live in the capital."

"Is that where I was found?"

Eaton nodded. "It is. Mother and father found you in one of the caves they worked." With a grin, he added, "You're now my sister, Alissia."

She hoped her smile concealed her sudden awkwardness, and it took a moment before she asked, "Why did they decide to save me?"

"I'll let them answer that. But I can tell you they don't regret it. Even the ancients are impressed with your honor and bravery. No one expected you'd find our lost kin, and you've put your own life in danger more than once to keep us a secret." He paused before emphasizing, "It's an honor to have you as my sister, and our parents are very proud of you."

Alissia glanced over her shoulder at Luke, walking beside Meyer, and he smiled. *"They're welcoming you and don't see you as a mistake,"* he said mentally.

Her emotions began to swell within her, and she stared ahead, wishing she could have a moment alone.

"From our view atop the mountain, this valley appears self-sustaining," Luke remarked.

Alissia smiled slightly, grateful for the change in subject.

"Yes, we're very blessed," Meyer responded. "Our ancestors thought of everything when they developed the area."

Eaton nodded. "Although we're limited to this valley, there's great variation in the terrain. Our ancestors brought in numerous plants and animals, and they designed each area differently." He turned to Alissia. "I believe you're going to love it here."

She smiled. "How does the bond work between me and . . . uh . . . the ones who changed me?"

"You don't need to feel uncomfortable on what to call them," Eaton assured. "Their names are Hoyle and Farrah, caretakers of Bertly Caves on the outskirts of Fandue, the capital province. They have two sons—my younger brother, Gil, and me. Although we consider you as one of our own, we don't expect you to feel the same about us so soon."

He nudged his sunglasses up his small nose and added, "My parents speak great things about you. When you're within range, they're able to visit your subconscious."

"Is that dangerous for them?" Alissia asked. "The Medicians on the island said it could kill them, especially when they talked to me."

"It is, but they've been extremely careful by harnessing power from some of our ancestors' jades. That's how they've been able to reach you so often and at such a great distance."

"How exactly does that work?" she asked, stepping over a root sticking out from the ground. Seeing the vegetation thickening ahead, she stopped to let Eaton pass before continuing.

"The way they explained it is that they enter your subconscious while you're sleeping," Eaton responded. "Together, they weave through the echoes of your thoughts from that day. However, certain powerful memories stay in your subconscious even longer, and they can get to those for many days, or even weeks, after they happen. And if they visit during a nightmare, they see it clearly."

Alissia cringed as she considered how many night terrors had woken her since entering this reality. "Are your parents in trouble with the ancients for saving me?"

"They were at first, but you've proven yourself. The ancients have accepted you, and they've dropped the charges against my parents."

Eaton stepped to the side and smiled up at Alissia as she began to walk beside him. "All is well, and now you're home."

"You even found a zeer among your own people," Meyer added from behind, "and you reunited us with our distant kin."

Eaton nodded. "You're blessed. Even the guardians have come to you—not once, but twice. No one can deny your acceptance now. You're one of us."

Alissia chuckled, shaking her head. "I don't know if I'd call this past year a blessing."

"Ah, but without seeing the darkness," Eaton replied, "you could never appreciate the blessings. Life is a mix of both, and although you've suffered greatly over the past year, you've gained some true blessings."

He added enthusiastically, "And now that you're home, you'll see how blessed you truly are. Your journey's over! You can marry your love and one day have that son you've dreamt of."

Blood rushed to Alissia's face, and she smiled weakly.

"A son?" Luke mentally asked.

"Zip it! It must have been in a dream I had while sleeping. Possibly a nightmare."

Ignoring the sound of his laughter in her head, she turned her attention back to Eaton. "So, what do you do for a living here?"

"I help with Bertly Caves."

"Doing what?"

"Upkeep and maintaining the proper balance between the animal and plant life." Staring ahead, Eaton smiled and added, "You'll see."

"I heard your people are protectors of our kin," Meyer said, from behind. "How does that work?"

"Our ancestors oversaw the relocation of your relatives," Salvatore explained. "By selling enough jade, they were able to purchase the island and take control of it under the pretense of a mining company. The continued sale of jade, along with exotic animals trained by the Medicians, have proven quite lucrative, and we're able to afford extra protection for the island."

"So, it's a beneficial relationship for your people, along with our relatives?" Eaton asked.

"Oh, definitely!" Salvatore responded. He went on to explain how the humans lived on the clear side of the island, while massive cliffs and rocks surrounded and protected the Medicians' shores.

Alissia enjoyed not having to share in the conversation, as it allowed her to withdraw to her thoughts. Eaton's words of acceptance encouraged her greatly, and she needed to remind herself not to get too excited or start expecting a perfect future. From her experience, expectations almost always led to pain, and they needed to be kept to a minimum.

The conversation remained light and informative as they continued through the woodland, and after a few hours, they stepped onto a beautifully landscaped trail. Eaton stopped and pointed to the right of them, where the path ended at a cave entrance. Carved into the shape of a large mushroom and surrounded by colorful flowers, its whimsical appearance intrigued Alissia, and she immediately envisioned gnomes and fairies living there.

"That leads to an underground mushroom farm," he replied.

"It's a farm?" she asked, expecting more.

Eaton nodded as he set his pack on the ground. "We have one like it on our side of the valley that you can visit later. For now, we need to continue on to Galda."

He took his flask from his pack, and Alissia turned to look at the path she assumed they would follow. The leaves of the trees planted along each side of the trail produced a stunning, bright blue canopy, which matched the color of the tiny flowers bordering the grassy trail. Strands of pink bella flowers wound abundantly around each tree, adding sparkling light along the shady path.

"You need to drink some water," Luke instructed.

She accepted his flask and took a few sips before handing it back to him. "It all looks like something from a fairytale."

"You say that a lot." He chuckled when she elbowed his side.

"Things just don't look like this where I come from."

"What's that word you love to use?" Luke asked, cocking his head in thought. "Advanced technology. That's it. All that advanced technology requires destroying everything else."

"Well, we never had glowing flowers and rocks in the first place," she retorted.

"I doubt we'll pass anyone," Eaton said, walking by. Luke took Alissia by the hand, and they started beside him along the path.

"They're having a festival tonight in one of the nearby villages, and it should have started by now," Meyer explained. He and Salvatore walked behind the others, although the trail was wide enough for all of them.

"It shouldn't take long for us to get to Galda," Eaton replied.

Alissia smiled slightly, enjoying Luke's touch and the floral scent drifting in the air. Like everywhere else in her new reality, a variety of birds and small critters flitted about the trees. She looked around, appreciating the vibrant colors around her.

"Think we'll be able to hear any of the music?" Meyer asked.

"I don't know," Eaton answered. "How far is Menca from Galda?"

"It's about—"

"Aah, Mia!" Alissia cried, as the tiny furball leapt from a tree and landed on the ground in front of her. Salvatore bumped into Alissia's pack as she jumped backward.

"Why? Why does she always do that?" Alissia fussed. She scowled at Mia, bothered by the tiny creature's look of indifference.

Eaton and Meyer chuckled.

"My parents told me she's been a bit naughty," Eaton replied. "Although you may think that's a bad quality, it's actually one of the reasons she was chosen for you."

"She's got spunk!" Meyer exclaimed.

"More like an evil streak," Alissia muttered.

"Well, now I see why they'd choose her for you," Luke said. "You two really do have a lot in common."

Alissia responded with a dirty look and walked away. Hearing his laughter, she huffed, "I'm done with you, and you can hold Salvatore's hand tonight."

About an hour later, they stopped at a cave entrance. Like the other one, it appeared inviting, with colorful flowers thriving around it. Bright green algae and bella ivy covered the exterior rock, while ancient stairs made of stone led downward. Two small carriages parked nearby finished off the picturesque setting. However, a sign posted outside read, *"Closed!"*

"This is Galda," Eaton said. "We'll stay here for the night." He started toward the stairs, and the others followed. "Meyer and I've been staying here while waiting for your arrival. The caretakers arranged for us to be the only ones here."

The stairs led to a soft, grassy bank near a large, clear pool of water. An opening in the rock above acted as a skylight, allowing plants to thrive from within. The bella flowers growing along the walls escaped through the opening, with a thick mass of their roots falling into the water at two opposite ends of the pool.

The cave looked like a vacation, camping spot to Alissia, furnished with woven, hanging hammocks throughout. Rope ladders hung down from the highest ones, and intricately carved statues made from glow and heat stones adorned each camping area.

After leading them to a group of five hammocks with pillows and bedding, Eaton removed his backpack and turned to Alissia and the others. "Want to take a swim while we prepare dinner? You'll find the water warm and inviting." He motioned to one of the packs in his gear. "And we brought each of you fresh clothing."

"Sounds great," Alissia answered.

Eaton pulled three parcels from the pack and passed them to Alissia, Luke, and Salvatore. "I'll show you where you can find privacy."

He led them to one of the grouping of bella roots hanging down into the water. Behind the thick wall of glowing ivy, small changing rooms made from bamboo-like material lined the walls, leaving enough space between the rooms and ivy for a passageway.

Alissia gave Luke a private grin when Eaton showed them one of the two bathrooms among the row of changing rooms. Although quite charming and surprisingly modern, with a sink artistically carved from stone, she knew Luke would have to adjust to the size of the Medicians' things. Even though she never really regretted being petite, she now considered her size a tremendous blessing.

In the privacy of one of the changing rooms, she found a towel and an assortment of clothing in the parcel she received from Eaton. She recognized the shimmery material of some of the clothing as the same from the island, where the Medicians explained how it came from veolla bugs.

Her dark blue bathing suit consisted of a tank top and small, shimmery shorts with a drawstring. After pulling her hair from its braid, she grabbed the towel and stepped out of the room.

Luke stood at the entrance of the wall of ivy. Seeing that his bathing suit matched the style of the one he wore in Pallen—a mini skirt concealing a bikini bottom—she wondered if the Medician men wore the same style or if it had been made to match her memory.

His eyes immediately went to her hair, and she lifted her finger in warning. "Don't even think about it, Mountain Man. Once you pull your hair from its bun, you're going to look beastly too." Walking past him, she added, "And at least I don't have a forest growing on my face."

The sparkle of the bella flowers intensified in the setting sun, turning the open cave into a magical place. Alissia and Luke stopped at the edge of the pool and watched Salvatore swimming beneath the surface. His movements caused the water around him to momentarily glow in a blue color, and she asked Luke about it.

"I believe it has something to do with the algae in the water, and it's a method of defense. I've never seen it myself, but I've read about it."

He dipped his toes into the water and swirled it around, causing it to glow.

"That is *so* cool! Is it harmful?"

"Not from what I read," he responded.

Without warning, Luke picked up Alissia and ran into the water, dunking them both before letting her go.

"You're lucky the water feels good, and I need some major washing," she said, after coming up for air. Moving her hand through the water, she watched the sparkly, blue glow. Then she used her feet against Luke's chest to shove off in a swim.

After days of backpacking on the mountainside, she relished her first swim of the year, and by the time she pulled herself onto a large rock, her heart pounded rapidly within her chest.

Wringing the water from her hair, she watched as Luke swam toward her. With the sun gone for the night, the blue glow shined much brighter than before, and as she looked around, she noticed small ripples of glowing water in various places around the pool.

Luke grabbed her feet and gave them a playful tug before he emerged from the water and plopped down beside her. He began to shake his head vigorously, and she turned away and held up her hands as his loosened hair sprayed her.

Once he stopped, she gave an unimpressed look. "Really?"

He laughed and kissed her cheek before lying back against the rock, placing his arm beneath his head.

"Mmm, that feels good," she said, as his fingertips moved along her back. Her stomach grumbled from the scent of spices drifting in the air, and she looked to find Eaton and Meyer cooking on a group of heat stones built into the wall of the cave. "I guess they don't need a fire to cook with, since they can control the temperatures of the heat stones."

"It does help," Luke responded.

Looking up at the stars, Alissia noticed movement along the bella ivy near the opening, and she turned to look back over her shoulder. "Why is Mia climbing out of the cave?"

She watched as Luke opened his eyes and began to stare up at the opening. Then she turned back around.

"She probably thinks she's finding the perfect hiding place to watch us from," he mumbled. "Secretly, she can fly."

"That would explain a lot," Alissia responded. Looking around, she said, "This place is amazing. Even the caves are decorated and carved."

"I'm guessing there's a lot of talent in this valley."

Alissia frowned, from both confusion and the feel of Luke's fingers leaving her back. "What do you mean?"

"I've occasionally wondered what it would be like to live over three hundred years. Have you not thought about how much you could learn and how much experience you could gain during all that time?"

"Not really. I haven't really let myself think too much about the future, and when I do, it often ends in a horrible death."

Luke chuckled. "Ah, there's that happy spirit."

"Just keeping it real. We can't all live in a dream world."

Mia let out a loud screech, and Alissia looked up in time to see her dive from the cave's opening.

"She's crazy," Alissia breathed, as the tiny furball plunged into the center of the pool, creating a spectacular scene of glowing, blue ripples, which spread along the water.

When Mia's head popped up where she landed, Alissia laughed, and her stomach growled. "I'm going to get dressed," she said, before hopping into the water.

In the small changing room, she selected one of two outfits from the parcel and put on the shimmery, moss green pants, quickly tying the drawstring before slipping the matching top over her head.

She picked up one of her new boots—similar to moccasins—and paused to run her fingers along the material. Then she put them on and slid her daggers into the built-in sheaths. After tying the laces, she checked the fitting to find them slightly too big in the toes. They worked, however, and the folded material along the top concealed the contours of her daggers.

Staring down at the knives she usually wore attached to her belt and upper leg, Alissia chewed on her bottom lip as she pondered whether it would be rude to wear them around the Medicians. In the end, she gave a shrug and mumbled, "Well, they gave me boots with sheaths in them, so I guess it's no big deal."

Once finished with the belt and thigh sheath, she let out a sigh and frowned. "I guess there's nothing to hide. They know everything."

She wrapped a shimmery, brown shawl over her shoulder and fiddled a bit with the hat attached to her shirt before deciding the shawl went over it. Holding up the greatest gift in the bag, she smiled and ran her fingers along the hand-carved, wooden clip, which looked exactly like Mia.

The bag even contained fresh oils for her body and hair, and she left the changing room feeling refreshed and confident, grateful she would not be meeting the Medicians looking like a vagrant.

Both dressed in new clothing, Luke and Salvatore stood near a statue in their camping area, and Alissia joined them in admiring the intriguing piece of art. It glowed in a variety of colors, and since the others in the cave seemed much dimmer, she knew Eaton and Meyer must have charged it—for its warmth, as well as its beauty.

"It resembles a plant, but it also looks like underwater coral," Salvatore replied thoughtfully.

"I can see that," Alissia agreed, "but it reminds me of a slug. See the little horns." She looked to Luke to get his opinion, and her heart fluttered when she saw his piercing gaze eyeing the full-length of her body.

His eyes locked with hers, just as Eaton took the wet bathing suit from her hand. "You look beautiful. Mother will be so happy when she sees you."

"Did she make my clothes?" Alissia asked, trying not to appear flustered.

Eaton nodded, passing her suit to Meyer. "But Father made the clip. She wanted to give you a distinct look of a human warrior with our clothing." To Luke, he said, "She wanted the same for you but had a difficult time deciding on your size. She finally decided to use a stretchy material and make your shirt oversized, and I brought more than one pair of sandals for your feet."

"Thank you," Luke responded. "That's very considerate, and everything fits well."

Eaton reached up and turned Alissia's shawl to where the clip rested on her shoulder. Then he stepped back and smiled. "She wants you to feel confident."

"I can't wait to meet her," Alissia replied.

He motioned to a group of mats arranged on the ground nearby. "You must be famished."

"Definitely!" Alissia scanned the cave as she and the others sat down. "Where did Mia go?"

"She's probably hunting," Meyer answered, giving her a plate of food.

"Oh, wow! This looks good." Alissia took a bite of the warm flatbread and grinned. "Mmm, I've missed real food."

Eaton chuckled as he handed Luke a drink. "Mother planned our meals and gave us strict instructions not to feed you anything similar to the travel food you've been eating."

"She didn't have to do that," Alissia responded, feeling somewhat guilty. She also felt uncomfortable at how they seemed to know every little detail about her.

"No worries," he replied, setting a drink down beside her. "She enjoys cooking, and it makes her happy."

Meyer nodded as he sat down on a mat holding his own plate of food. "Mia's favorite prey happens to be abundant in this valley, and I imagine she's missed it."

"How does that work?" Alissia asked. She swallowed her bite of food and added, "I thought we were friends to the animals, and they would be protected here." Glancing at Luke and Salvatore, she found them both devouring their food.

Meyer shook his head. "Our ancestors brought a variety of creatures into the valley, and many of them work alongside our people. In fact, I don't know how we'd live without them—especially the tree dwellers."

Noticing Alissia's confusion, he explained, "Many of our people choose to live in tree houses, which require a lot of bridges and plumbing structures to be built high off the ground. The tree creatures are better climbers, and they help to build and maintain those structures."

Eaton nodded, sitting next to Meyer. "It's a maze up there."

"The animals in our service," Meyer continued, "wear collars to let other animals know they're not to be considered prey. However, we can't do that with all the animals. There's just not enough room in the valley to sustain all of them, and an overpopulation of certain animals would wreak havoc on the environment."

"It's not the natural way of life," Eaton replied. "They already live longer with our help, and if we didn't allow them to go along with their natural urges, the valley would be overpopulated and bare of resources."

"We couldn't keep up with the loss of vegetation needed to sustain massive herds," Meyer added.

"Makes sense," Salvatore said, lifting his drink to his mouth.

Meyer gave a half shrug. "Most of the animals serving in populated areas don't hunt, because they're surrounded by other service animals. They'd have to enter the woodland to find prey, and many of them just don't do it."

"Where does Fang live, and how did he get here?" Alissia asked, before filling her mouth with another bite.

"When Father realized you sent Fang toward the mountains," Eaton responded, "he sent letters to all the provinces on that side of the valley. The people in that area located a pack of wolves living near them, and they sent the pack out to search for him. When Fang returned with the pack, they sent word to us, and Meyer and I traveled to meet him so we could bring him home."

"Now he can live with you," Meyer added, "or he can return to the mountains with the pack. No decisions have to be made right now, and he knows where to find them if he wants to stay with you for a bit."

After dinner, Eaton served a soothing, herbal chet. The warm, relaxing drink, along with the beauty of the cave, lulled Alissia into a comfortable silence. When she crawled into a hammock shortly thereafter, peace filled her soul, and she said a silent prayer of gratitude as she pulled the blanket over her.

Fighting against the night creatures singing her spirit to sleep, she struggled to stay awake, her gaze fixed on the twinkling bella flowers at the skylight.

"I love you, Pixet," Luke's voice whispered into her consciousness.

Alissia's mouth curled slightly, just as she succumbed to her body's exhaustion.

Chapter 9

*T*he sound of laughter and the smell of food pulled Alissia from her slumber, and she joined the others standing around the glowing statue.

While eating breakfast, two creatures entered the cave. Resembling large, grey mice and about three feet tall, they walked on their pudgy hind legs. They stopped near Alissia, both staring back at her with large, round eyes.

"They're curious of you," Meyer replied, setting a pack down beside a group of others.

Furry, pink ears twitched on top of a round face with a black, protruding nose. The other creature's long, skinny fingers reached up to scratch at one of his rounded ears.

Remembering a book she read, Alissia asked, "They're umbals, aren't they?"

"We call them scotters," Meyer answered.

"But humans call them umbals," Luke replied, passing his empty bowl to Eaton. "They're usually very skittish and rarely seen."

Eaton chuckled. "I've never known any animal to be skittish."

"I called them here to help carry our equipment to the wagon," Meyer explained.

The creatures walked over to the pile of gear, and they each picked up a pack and headed toward the stairs.

"Well, that's convenient," Luke commented, lifting a bottle of cleanser to his mouth.

"I think you're going to like it here," Eaton responded, giving a half-grin.

Shortly thereafter, everyone put on their backpacks and climbed the stairs to find four miniature horses waiting outside the cave. Eaton and Meyer bonded with the other two creatures, pouring energy into them, before sending them on their way, and as they turned their attention to the horses' manure bags, Fang ran out of the woodland, nearly knocking Alissia to the ground.

"I know. I missed you, too," she cooed, running her hands through his fur. She played with him a bit before watching him run back into the woodland.

"Well, I guess he's off to his friends," she remarked, turning back to the others.

"Ready?" Eaton asked, hopping into one of the carriages. He flipped the backrest around on the front bench and looked back at them with a grin. "Now we can ride facing each other."

Alissia smiled, staring at the two adorable little horses, and Luke took her hand and led her to the carriage, where they sat down on the bench seat facing the road. Mia hopped in and climbed into Alissia's lap, as Eaton sat down across from them.

"I suddenly feel tall," Alissia said mentally.

"You? How do you think I feel?"

Their carriage lurched forward, taking the lead, with Meyer and Salvatore's following. Traveling along a scenic path, surrounded by dense woodland, Alissia's gaze followed the sound of the many birds singing and flitting about the trees.

"I want to apologize for any curious stares you'll receive today while traveling," Eaton replied.

"Will they fear us?" Luke asked.

"Some, but not everyone." Eaton smiled encouragingly. "The ancients appointed a representative to visit each of the provinces. He explained the situation and told Alissia's story, and he answered the people's questions."

"Everyone knows about me?" she asked, surprised.

He nodded. "The ancients rarely declare meetings for our people, and everyone usually attends when they transpire. The representative reported that fear seemed to be the first response, but when he told of how you've constantly put your own life at risk to protect us, most of them left the meeting chatting about your bravery." Locking eyes with her, he added, "You'll be accepted here. Most people consider you and Luke heroes."

"Do they know about the other creatures and Medicians on the island?" she asked.

He shook his head. "No, they only know of your interactions with humans. The ancients are keeping everything else private until they decide what to do. They only know what Mother and Father have told them, which is only what you know. They need to read the letters you bring."

"Did your parents tell the ancients about what happened at the bog?" Alissia asked.

"They did. They don't know all the details, so you'll need to explain everything when you meet the ancients."

"They need to know how horrible those creatures are," Alissia stressed. She began to talk about what happened at the bog, emphasizing the cruelty of the tattooed beings. Eaton asked many questions, while listening intently, but as they entered a village, her voice drifted beneath an intricate network of hanging bridges.

"Is it similar for our kin?" Eaton asked.

"Somewhat," she answered, staring upward. "The trees on the island are tropical. These are much different—fuller."

"The houses are built from stained wood here also," Luke added. "You see a lot of thatch on the island."

Alissia nodded, looking at Eaton. "These seem more sophisticated, and they look like they would last longer."

She smiled, trying to hide her sudden unease. Still early morning, many Medicians sat outside on their small porches, relaxing on rockers, swings, hammocks, and hanging pods lined with pillows. A variety of animals, ranging from large, menacing wildcats to tiny finger monkeys, roamed freely and fearlessly about.

Some Medicians ran inside, only to burst back out, bringing more excited spectators with them.

"You're a hero to them," Eaton replied, smiling. He looked upward and waved before turning back. "Does the attention make you feel uncomfortable?"

"A little," Alissia answered.

He leaned closer, taking one of their hands in each of his. "You have a home in this valley and don't have to worry about hiding or fearing for your lives anymore," he said firmly. "I've always wanted a sister, and now I have another brother as well."

Releasing his grip on their hands, he leaned back in his seat and added confidently, "You're going to love it here."

Luke put his arm around Alissia, and she smiled. "Thank you, Eaton. Alissia and I are both honored to be accepted into your family, and we're eager to meet the others."

Eaton asked about her former reality, and as she described the life she once knew, he stared with wide eyes and shook his head often in disbelief. She eventually began to smile and wave when they rode through a village. Her anxiety of everyone's stares lessened, allowing her to notice the impressive gardens and common areas beneath the tree houses.

On the outskirts of each village, rare patches of sunlight nourished vegetable gardens. The Medicians' powers enhanced the plant life in the valley, creating enchanting beauty all around. Abundant shade from the tall trees appeared to be the only constant, as the floral colors and themes greatly varied.

They stopped for lunch along the side of the road, in a fragrant tunnel made from long strands of bright pink bella flowers hanging down from trees. Matching wild flowers growing along the forest floor mixed with the ivy climbing up the trees, and countless butterflies, in a deep shade of blue, fluttered about.

The homes outside the villages intrigued Alissia the most. Along with stone cottages and log cabins, barely visible amid enormous trees and dense greenery, she occasionally spied doors built into the bottoms of large trees. She began to seek them out for fun and soon discovered doors and windows hidden along the slopes of the land.

She often saw woven nests and pods—too small to be a Medician's home—in the trees, and when she pointed one out to Eaton, he explained they were children's playhouses. Young ones spent much time in them, frequently camping with their friends.

He stated the Medicians loved nature, and the mountains and valley provided numerous resources. He named stone, aged wood, geodes, clay, and farmed bamboo as some of the items available. He reminded Alissia and Luke that his people lived over three hundred years, giving them plenty of time to become greatly skilled in their passions.

Grinning proudly, he said that even if one of their dwellings looked simple on the outside, beauty filled the inside. Turning to Luke, he replied, "We're eager to help you design your home, and you may get overwhelmed by all the choices." To Alissia, he said, "You'll find my parents' house similar to what they saw in your subconscious, as they wanted you to feel comfortable."

"They didn't change their home because of me, did they?" she asked.

"We don't want Luke and Salvatore sleeping outside," Eaton answered, chuckling. He shook his head. "I can't say anything more, as it would spoil it for Mother. She'll certainly want to show you everything as soon as we arrive."

He asked about the Medicians on the island, and the conversation eventually led to the glowing creatures found in the forest. Engrossed in describing the glowing, underground world, Alissia failed to notice her surroundings as the sky darkened.

The horses stopped unexpectedly, and Eaton grinned as he swiftly hopped to the ground. "Welcome home, Luke and Alissia."

She and Luke stood, both scanning their surroundings. With her night vision, she clearly saw a log cabin, much bigger than all the others she had seen in the valley. A mix of wooden swings and rockers lined the porch.

Built at the base of a mountain, large trees surrounded the lone cabin. Glowing bella flowers, in a variety of colors, grew along the lower portion of the evergreens. The sound of flowing water from a nearby stream and tiny glow bugs twinkling in the night sky added to the splendor of the place.

"Not what you expected?"

She looked down at Eaton and shook her head. "It's bigger and—"

"You're finally here!" a shrill, female voice interrupted.

Alissia turned to find three Medicians now standing on the porch.

Luke put his hand on her shoulder and gave it a squeeze as the only woman of the three rushed down the stairs. With open arms, she said, "Come give me a hug, child. I've been waiting for this moment for a long time."

Alissia stepped from the carriage and bent down to share in the embrace. When the small woman pulled away, the man threw his arms around Alissia's waist. As soon as he let go, Mia jumped into his arms, and he laughed.

"Yes, you did perfect, my little friend," he replied, scratching the top of Mia's head. "You brought her home and kept her safe."

"Let's go inside," the woman said, dropping her arms from Luke's neck. She took his and Alissia's hands and began to walk toward the house.

The man motioned for Salvatore to join him, and as he turned toward the cabin, he said to Eaton and Meyer, "You boys take care of everything out here. I'll send Gil out in a moment."

Gil, who greatly resembled his mother, rushed to stay ahead. He opened the front door and continued to hold it as everyone passed. Luke and Salvatore easily fit through the entrance, and Alissia guessed the first floor of the cabin to be around nine feet tall, leaving three feet of extra space above Luke's head.

The smell of a hot meal welcomed them, and with an open floor plan, Alissia noticed a short table arranged next to a taller one in the dining area. Cushioned sofas and chairs circled an oversized ottoman in the sitting area, with one sofa noticeably larger than the others.

The many blankets, baskets, rugs, pillows, and fresh flowers created a cozy ambiance, along with the soft lighting produced by the combination of glow stones, bella flowers, and candles. Polished stone and geode statues adorned tall bookcases lined with books, and all the handcrafted kitchen cabinets and other wooden furnishings looked like works of art.

The woman led them into the sitting room, where Alissia, Luke, and Salvatore sat down on the larger sofa. As the three Medicians took a seat on the oversized ottoman, Mia hopped into Alissia's lap.

"I'm Farrah, and this is Hoyle," the woman replied, motioning. "And this is our youngest son, Gil."

Gil smiled, somewhat shyly, and Alissia mentally tried to guess his age. With the size of his body matching his father's, she assumed the Medicians considered him a teenager, which meant he could be around fifty years old.

Although their thin bodies resembled young children, the creases on Hoyle and Farrah's face looked similar to people in their fifties. Hoyle's fuchsia and somewhat curly, shoulder-length hair showed more pale streaks than Farrah's long, lilac hair, pulled atop her head.

"I'm sure you already know," Alissia responded, "but this is Luke and our friend, Salvatore."

Farrah smiled at Luke. "You had us worried there for a while, but you turned out to be a blessing." She turned to Salvatore. "Thank you for coming to their aid and bringing them to us."

He nodded. "It's been a pleasure and an honor." Glancing at Luke and Alissia, he added, "I consider them both my own."

Alissia pointed at the ceiling. "It's much bigger than I expected."

"It's new," Farrah responded, looking around. "We knew we'd have to build something to accommodate your size, but we didn't imagine anything like this."

"The ancients thought it best to create a place large enough for them to come to you," Hoyle explained. "And with the possibility of future trading, they predicted we could be hosting humans here in the future." Looking at Salvatore, he added, "We're assuming it would be your people doing the actual traveling."

Salvatore shrugged. "I haven't been told anything. My final instructions were to get Alissia and Luke here and return to the island."

The sight of three furry, little balls scurrying out of a basket near the wall caught Alissia's attention.

"They're beanies," Farrah replied. She lowered her hands and waited until a solid white one came within reach before picking it up. The other two—one white and one grey—rushed to her feet and began to scrape her ankles with their pink, padded paws.

Hoyle laughed as he bent down and scooped them up. "Mischievous little things, but they keep the floor free of crumbs and dust." He set them down on the ottoman, and the white one immediately pounced on top of the grey one. "There are more of them around here somewhere, but they know to stay clear of your feet. Don't worry about stepping on them."

Alissia grinned, staring into the black, glassy eyes of the white one in Farrah's hands. With its tiny paws turned inward, it looked completely round, about the size of a ball found in a toddler's basketball set. A tiny, pink nose sat above tiny, pink lips.

"Oh, my goodness. They're so cute," Alissia gushed. "I've never seen anything like them. Are they different, like Mia?"

Farrah shook her head and began to rub her fingers through the creature's thick fur. "They're regular animals, although quite helpless when it comes to predators. Even though they know they'll be safe on our porch or in the yard, you won't see them going outside."

"How do you keep their fur so clean—especially the white ones?" Salvatore asked.

Alissia nodded, wondering the same. She recalled how much dirt collected in the mane of the black lion that had traveled with Salvatore when they first met.

Farrah chuckled. "They're a bit obsessed with their own cleanliness, and I sometimes wonder if they shun the outdoors because of the grass and dirt instead of the predators."

"True," Hoyle agreed, amused. "They love water, but they're horrible swimmers and avoid our bathing pools. That's why you'll find a shallow area of water in the corner of our bathing room, and you'll often see them gathered there."

Turning to his son, he said, "You need to help your brother."

Gil nodded and smiled at Alissia and the others before making his way to the door.

"We're near the cave we found Alissia," Hoyle replied, "and if the ancients decide to begin trading, accommodations will need to be built near here to hold meetings between the human traders and the ancients. For now, our home is big enough to hold such gatherings."

"The ancients will be here in the morning," Farrah added. "They're eager to meet all of you and learn about the trade proposal."

"Are they angry with you?" Alissia asked. "About me?"

The two Medicians glanced at each other before Farrah shook her head. "They were. What we did has never been done since our ancestors entered the valley, and our people thrive here. The last thing we want is for the humans to learn of our existence."

"It puts us all at risk," Hoyle added.

Alissia nodded in understanding.

"I'm sure you can easily imagine how angry everyone was at first," Hoyle continued. "We put our people in great danger, just by saving your life, and when you were taken away, we could do nothing but watch."

"You planned to bring me here, didn't you?"

Farrah nodded, dabbing the corner of her eye. "We were working near the cave when we felt an explosion of power, so we ran to see what happened. Blood was everywhere, and we found you barely alive."

"Many of your bones were broken or crushed," Hoyle added, taking hold of Farrah's hand. "We weren't even sure we could save you."

"I believe you would have died within minutes," Farrah said, her voice cracking.

Surprised and somewhat uncomfortable by the rise in their emotions, Alissia asked, "Why did you decide to save me?"

The woman smiled, staring into Alissia's eyes. "The moment we connected with you, neither one of us questioned what needed to be done. You were broken—both mentally and physically." Shaking her head, she added, "We'd never felt such pain before."

"At first, we only put our hands on you to find out what happened," Hoyle explained, "but your body still surged with power—which helped to save you. The connection instantly revealed everything about you." Looking hard into Alissia's eyes, he replied, "You were worth saving."

Alissia recalled how she had experienced Luke's most intense memories while saving his life, and she assumed the same thing happened to Hoyle and Farrah when they connected with her. Without a doubt, they would have experienced her darkest memories—those of her childhood.

"I . . . uh . . . thank you," she stammered, aware of everyone looking at her.

The door opened, and the boys began to set the camping gear inside.

"Let me show you all where to wash up for dinner," Farrah said. She set the beany on the floor and stood before taking Alissia's hand.

Except for the bathing pool, the bathroom contained two of each plumbing fixture, sized to accommodate both humans and Medicians. Fresh flowers, geodes, glow stones, baskets, and bella flowers decorated the room, along with polished stone, bamboo, and wood for practical purposes. A bathing pool built into the floor contained a pink purifying flower, while in a corner, fresh water trickled from a small fountain of shallow water. Two grey beanies rested in a small hammock near a heat stone, drying their fur.

Farrah seemed eager to show off her new cabin. Built to accommodate gatherings with the ancients and humans, the rooms were much taller and wider than other homes in the valley.

Unexpected Beginning

The upstairs contained Hoyle and Farrah's small bedroom, along with their two sons. Unlike the downstairs, the furniture and bedding did not look new, and the space was a bit cramped for Salvatore and Luke. Not needing sunlight to charge their glow stones, the ceiling consisted of wooden beams instead of the tinted, clear material mostly used in human dwellings.

A dresser with a mirror and two single beds furnished Luke's temporary room downstairs, and Farrah explained it would be used as a guestroom if the ancients decided to allow Salvatore's people to enter the valley for trading.

When they got to the last unknown room downstairs, she turned around with an excited grin. Eyeing Alissia, she placed her hand on the doorknob. "We got our ideas for this room from what Hoyle and I saw in your consciousness. Our entire family got involved—mine and Hoyle's sisters, brothers, mothers, and fathers all contributed to this room. Even our children helped in some way."

She opened the door and stepped inside, revealing a large canopy bed with deep brown and olive toned bedding and pillows, made from the shimmery material of the veolla bugs. Beige bella flowers winding up the posts covered the sheer curtain atop the bed, adding contrast to the rich tones, along with the sheer curtains covering the only window and hanging down from each side of the bed. On one side, the curtains were pulled back and held in place with tassels, and all the shimmery material adorning the room sparkled in the soft lighting.

Farrah opened the armoire at the end of the bed to show new clothes hanging in a variety of shimmery colors. "We tried to make everything a little big, so we can hem them to fit you." Closing the cabinet, she explained, "Customarily, during your long engagement, you and the women in your and Luke's families would sew all your bedding and other home décor, while the men would help Luke to build your house and furniture."

Glancing at Hoyle, she paused before stammering, "We . . . uh . . . thought you probably don't need to wait a year before your zeer ceremony—especially since the bond has already started. That's why we've already begun preparing things."

She held up her hands, assuring, "Oh, but there's plenty more to do, and our family's eager to help you prepare your new home. I don't know how humans do their zeer ceremonies, but I hope you don't mind that we went ahead and started on the preparations."

Alissia smiled, shaking her head. She avoided looking at Luke, hoping to hide the surprise and excitement she felt at the mention of a quick wedding.

Farrah lifted her fingers to the bed's sheer curtain. "From what I saw in your consciousness, you love the glowing flowers in this reality and our sparkly material, and we decided to use dark colors for the bedding, since Luke seems to be drawn to them."

Turning to him, she dropped her hand to her side. "We glimpsed one of Alissia's thoughts on the clothing you bought her. They all seemed to be dark."

Farrah suddenly appeared nervous, as her eyes went from Luke to Alissia. "Well, what do you think?"

Alissia fought to hide the overwhelming emotions swelling within her. The talk of being accepted into a large family and preparing her and Luke's home before their wedding sent her thoughts into a frenzy. Add the beautiful new bedroom suite she would be sharing with Luke, and she could barely breathe.

Luke seemed to be battling with his own emotions, as they seeped into Alissia and increased her confusion at how to react.

She tried to tell herself something would happen to mess things up, and she should not let herself believe in the perfect life, as she would only be setting herself up for a fall her heart could never recover.

Standing behind her, Salvatore chuckled as he grabbed her and Luke's shoulders and gave them a squeeze. "I believe they're both in shock." He added more seriously, "I don't think they expected such a warm welcome, and this is much more than they imagined."

"Thank you," Luke said, sounding sincere.

Alissia nodded. "Yes, thank you for everything. It's definitely more than I ever imagined." Trying not to sound too emotional, she smiled and added, "I wasn't sure how we would be accepted here."

Hoyle smiled and put his hand on his wife's shoulder as she wiped at the tears in her eyes. "We're just glad you made it home. I know things have been rough this past year, but you overcame all the obstacles and threats that came your way. We've continuously seen your persistence and loyalty, and your consciousness shouted your determination to keep us a secret, even at the risk of your own life."

He looked to Luke. "And the same goes for you. Although we've not visited your consciousness, we've seen the same determination and loyalty in you through Alissia's eyes. The two of you have endured struggles for our people's sake, and now that you're finally here, we want you to know none of it was in vain."

"However," Eaton began, from where he and the other two boys stood at the doorway, "you might find it a bit boring here compared to the lifestyle you're both accustomed to."

Having everyone's attention, he looked at his mother and grinned. "We're hungry, and I know you prepared one of your special meals."

Meyer and Gil nodded eagerly in agreement, their expressions imploring Farrah to let them eat.

She laughed, urging everyone toward the dining area, where a large, mouthwatering meal awaited.

Chapter *10*

*A*lissia rolled over and stared up at the bella flowers canopying her bed. After a while, she turned and began to watch the window curtains dancing in the breeze. A shady, morning light entered the room, along with a cacophony of chirping from the birds outside. Noticing a distinct, squeaking sound, matching that of a dog's chew toy, she smiled and wondered what type of bird made the noise.

She did not have the feeling of being watched through the night, as Farrah and Hoyle promised they would never do it again. With her safely in the valley, they no longer needed to enter her nightly visions, which required extra power from jades.

Rolling over, she found herself alone in the bed, and she smiled as she imagined Mia on a morning hunt—carefree and happy in her homeland.

At the sound of laughter outside her door, Alissia considered leaving her new, cozy bed, but the thought suddenly filled her with dread.

Her brows crinkled, and she let out a sigh, while rolling onto her back. Staring up at the glowing flowers, she whispered knowingly, "It's too good to be true. Something's going to happen."

The mental conversation she and Luke shared as they drifted to sleep played through her mind. They had both seemed unlike themselves, talking about their picture-perfect future in the valley.

Alissia considered herself a realist, and her reality never included this much happiness. Allowing herself to believe in what Farrah and Luke described would only set her up for an unsuspecting fall.

At some point, the Medicians would turn on her. They may consider her a hero at the moment, but once they truly got to know her, they'd see her as cold and uncaring.

Her father's laughter filled her head, along with the image of his bloody face. *"You're just like me, Alissia."*

Visions of the two men she dragged behind horses flashed through her mind. Then she saw Ian's body after she bludgeoned him repeatedly with a knife. Blood. So much blood. She may look petite and innocent on the outside, but she knew her true self—capable of immense cruelty.

Closing her eyes, she whispered, "I'm worse than my father."

Someone knocked lightly on the door, and without waiting for a response, Luke entered and closed the door before stepping to the side of her bed.

Seeing the strained look on his face, Alissia immediately regretted letting her thoughts get out of control. She could tell he had felt her mood, and she wondered if he had seen her memories as well.

"I don't think you're supposed to be in here," she said, trying to sound playful.

Luke gestured for her to slide over before he sat down. "I told them you weren't feeling well, and it would be best if I talked to you for a bit."

"Yeah, but it's probably out of place to be alone in my bedroom before we're married. I bet Farrah and Hoyle aren't comfortable with it."

Her bothered tone surprised her, and she instinctively smiled. However, knowing he could see through her façade irked her even more. Glancing at the window, she wished Mia would bound into the room, like she often did when Alissia and Luke spent time alone.

He frowned and let out a sigh. "Do you realize you sometimes go through more emotions within a matter of minutes than I usually experience in a whole month?"

"Well, I guess you're lucky I don't have my menstrual cycle anymore," Alissia quipped. "Then we'd really have some fun."

Chuckling, Luke took her hand and laced his fingers through hers before setting them in his lap. "Are you finished with letting your past control you today?"

Alissia nodded, noticing his freshly groomed face. Her gaze went to his tan line, no longer hidden behind a mass of wild, dark hair.

"Do I need to remind you that none of those thoughts are true?" he asked.

Distracted by the pleasant scent of entamen, Alissia felt a small sense of accomplishment at recognizing an ingredient in his bath products, which she assumed Farrah made. It reminded her of how much she had learned recently, as only a year ago, the wild plant—along with many other things—had been foreign to her.

Alissia frowned, her thoughts returning back to the conversation. "I would have had everything under control soon enough," she said haughtily.

Although her expression remained sour when he laughed, she wanted to rub her fingers along his jawline. His soft, thin lips appeared much more inviting without all the furry distraction, and she secretly enjoyed the look of his cocky grin.

Luke unexpectedly leaned down and pinned her hands at each side of her head, his weight pressing them into her pillow. Rubbing his cheek along hers, his fresh scent and smooth skin tantalized her senses. When he lifted his head and stared down at her, looking confident, she tried to appear unfazed.

As if accepting a challenge, he grinned and bent down to brush his lips across hers, sending shivers throughout her entire body. His mouth slowly traveled to her ear, where he whispered, "We've fought so hard to get here, Alissia. You have more important things to think about than your past."

His tongue teased her neck for a moment before he added, "If you have to worry about something, then it should be about what I plan to do with you on our wedding night."

Reality fell away as a clear vision took over Alissia's mind.

Standing beside the bed, white flowers crowned her head. She wore a thin, shimmery white gown—elegant, yet simple. Seeing herself through Luke's eyes, she noticed the beauty in her smile and the way her purple eyes glimmered in the soft lighting. She felt his longing, raging within him.

"You are mine, Alissia," his voice whispered into her thoughts.

Luke pulled away abruptly, ending the vision. He stepped to the door and put his hand on the handle. Turning back around, he winked. "Don't get too comfortable in our bed without me."

As soon as the door closed after him, Alissia threw the covers over her head and groaned, no longer haunted by her past.

Suddenly full of energy, she pulled the bedding aside and stood. Knowing she would be meeting the ancients, it took a while for her to select a dress from the armoire, and after putting it on, she looked in the mirror and frowned.

Alissia quickly pulled off the oversized dress and went back to the armoire. In the end, she found a pair of drawstring, brown pants and matched it with a tan poet's shirt. She put on the boots she wore the day before and checked her knives before tightening the laces.

"Now, what about y'all?" she mumbled thoughtfully, staring down at her hip and thigh knives on the floor.

After a while, she shrugged and placed them in one of the armoire's drawers, not wanting to risk offending the ancients. Although she still wore knives in her boots and beneath her shirt, she felt somewhat bare without all of them.

"Good morning," Farrah sang, as Alissia stepped out of her room. "Breakfast is ready."

Salvatore smiled and waved. Freshly groomed, he looked comfortable chopping vegetables from his seat at the table. Luke sat across from him, helping with the chore, and beneath the table, about a dozen beanies watched intently for stray pieces.

The kitchen buzzed with activity, with Gil and Eaton washing dishes and Hoyle arranging mugs on the counter. Near the front door, Meyer unloaded gear from the packs.

Alissia smiled and pointed at the bathroom before heading that way. When she came back out, Farrah motioned to a mug of herbal chet and a plate of food beside Luke on the table.

"There you go, dear. There's plenty of food."

"What can I do to help?" Alissia asked, sitting down.

The small woman smiled and shook her head. "Nothing today. Luke told us you're nervous about meeting the ancients."

"Really?" she mentally asked, looking at Luke.

He gave an innocent smile. *"What else should I have told them to get into your room? That your emotions slammed into me, just as I was about to take a bite of my hot breakfast? Maybe I should have told them you need my special touch to pull you out of bed."*

"You should take your time getting ready," Farrah suggested. "I put a basket of oils and creams I made for you in the bathroom. Maybe they'll help you to relax."

Salvatore cleared his throat. "You'll love this," he said, pointing to a brown, lumpy mush on her plate. It looked similar to a grits casserole containing unknown vegetables.

"It's a common breakfast food here in the valley," Farrah replied, grinning.

Alissia smiled, hoping to conceal her confusion. She had never seen Salvatore and Luke this polite and domesticated, not even on the ship. She took a bite of the mush and nodded. "It *is* good."

"I'll have to teach you how to make it," Farrah said, patting Alissia's back.

"Yes, please," Luke chimed in. He winked at Alissia. "I'll want it for breakfast every morning."

She narrowed her eyes at him as Farrah walked to the counter and began to roll out a ball of dough.

Alissia ate her breakfast in silence, smiling often from the fresh breeze and pleasant conversation filling the cabin. Once finished, she sought out the basket Farrah told her about and took a quick bath, pampering herself with the scented gifts.

When she returned to the kitchen, she asked for a knife to help Luke and Salvatore prepare a platter of sliced fruit. Shortly thereafter, Hoyle lined the counters with heat and cold stones, and Farrah began to organize the many covered dishes of food. Once finished, she looked around the kitchen and smiled.

"We're done! Let's go to the porch and sit."

"I'm going home," Meyer announced, opening the door. He picked up his pack and waved. "See you tomorrow." Stepping onto the porch, he turned back around. "You have a visitor waiting out here."

"Who is it today?" Farrah asked, bustling out the door.

Everyone casually followed to find her sitting in a rocking chair. Leaning down, her hand rested on the back of a wildcat lying at her feet. With sleek, brown and black fur, the animal's large paws seemed too big for her short, powerful body.

Hoyle chose a rocking chair next to his zeer and motioned to a human-sized porch swing across from him. Alissia sat down and quickly bent over to shake out her curls, now almost dry. She straightened and patted the empty spaces next to her, and Luke and Salvatore chuckled as they sat down beside her. Eaton and Gil took a seat at the top of the steps, where they watched Meyer walking along the path.

"She's pregnant," Farrah replied, removing her hand from the cat.

Hoyle nodded as he clasped his hands in his lap, setting the rocker in motion. "I doubt we'll get many visits from other animals this morning, with her on the porch." He grinned, adding, "She's small, but she's a fierce predator."

"Can she attack other animals in front of you?" Alissia asked.

"No," he answered, "but unless they're wearing a collar, they'll stay away while she's here. She'll only visit for a few hours, at the most, and unless she gets hurt, we won't see her again for a while."

"Are you still nervous?" Farrah inquired.

Alissia shook her head. "I'm fine."

"Well, there's nothing to be afraid of," Farrah replied. "The ancients only want to hear what you've been through. Hoyle and I only know portions of it ourselves."

Hoyle nodded. "Tomorrow you'll get to meet the rest of the family, and we'll celebrate your arrival with lots of food and music."

"Company's coming," Eaton announced.

"Right on time," Hoyle responded, watching the small cart traveling along the path.

The miniature horses stopped in front of the cabin, and two elderly men stepped down. They waved while offering a pleasant greeting, and Eaton and Gil began to unharness the horses.

Unlike the ancients on the island, they dressed in casual clothing instead of formal robes. They smiled as they introduced themselves, and then they took a seat in one of the smaller swings.

Mia bounded up the steps and leapt into Alissia's lap, causing everyone to laugh. Another carriage arrived, and the conversation remained casual as the ancients gradually filled the swings and rockers.

Alissia tucked a lock of hair behind her ear as a gentle breeze tickled her skin. The memory of sitting on her grandparents' porch as a young girl came to mind, bringing a smile to her face.

With childlike innocence and bare feet, she often shelled peas or shucked corn alongside a much older generation. Fresh air and laughter—along with cold watermelon and hot, boiled peanuts—created scarce memories of untainted happiness.

When the eleventh ancient arrived, he introduced himself like the others before. Then he took a seat in one of the small rocking chairs. With a long piece of sweet grass hanging from his mouth, he sat back and crossed his feet out in front of him.

After a while, Alissa began to wonder if an official meeting would ever begin. Everyone seemed content listening to Luke and Salvatore talk about the various lifestyles of humans, and although she enjoyed not having to speak, the lack of formality surprised her.

The conversation eventually drifted to Farrah's cooking, and everyone made their way into the cabin for a buffet lunch. Alissia smiled to herself when she saw Salvatore and Luke bending to get their food. They towered over everyone around them.

Farrah appeared at ease in her role as a host, and Gil and Eaton impressed Alissia when they got up to clear away the food without being asked. The two boys washed the dishes as their parents served mugs of herbal chet alongside dessert.

With full bellies, the guests gradually made their way into the sitting room. Farrah and Eaton walked around refilling mugs with fresh chet, while many of the ancients took turns in the bathroom.

Alissia sat between Salvatore and Luke on the larger sofa, with Mia in her lap. When the last ancient took his seat, everyone quieted, and their eyes turned to her.

"Most of us have overeaten," one of the ancients replied, "and we need to let our food settle. Why don't you tell us about this past year?"

"Take your time, and tell us everything you can remember," another one added. "Start from the moment you landed in the cave nearby. What happened? How did you get there?"

Alissia nodded, glancing around the room. The kind and relaxed expressions staring back at her eased her nerves, and she began to pet Mia absentmindedly as she thought back to the moment she picked up her diary.

Everyone listened intently as she talked, often asking questions. Luke, Salvatore, Farrah, and Hoyle occasionally added to what she said, and when she described her first encounter with one of the guardians, all the ancients wanted a closer look at the marks on her hands. She walked around the room so they could touch and examine them up close, while excited conversations filled the air.

Not wanting to miss anything, the ancients eventually called for a short bathroom break. Farrah gave her a glass of water, and once everyone settled back into their seats, Alissia continued.

When she finished, Salvatore retrieved the sealed letters and small boxes from the other great races. Although Alissia had already described the abuse she and Luke endured in the bog, she again stressed her distrust for Selona's people.

The ancients decided to wait until they were alone to open the items and said they would probably need to meet with Salvatore later that week. Two of them followed Alissia onto the porch, where she mentally reached out to the birds still in her care from the island. The two ancients bonded with the animals, relieving her of her duties.

Shortly thereafter, the ancients gathered on the porch to say their goodbyes. Many of them hugged Alissia, and they shook Luke and Salvatore's hands. They welcomed her and Luke into the valley and said they looked forward to attending the zeer ceremony.

Salvatore agreed to stay until after the ceremony, giving the ancients time to decide upon a trade plan. As soon as the last ancient rode away in his carriage, Hoyle and Farrah took a seat in a porch swing, and everyone else followed their lead and sat down.

Hoyle put his arm around Farrah, nudging their swing into motion. "That wasn't so bad, was it?"

Alissia smiled and shook her head. "A lot better than I expected."

"You really are accepted here, Alissia," Farrah said. She smiled at Luke. "You too."

He nodded and put his arm around Alissia.

"What do you two have planned for the future?" Hoyle asked. "Will you commit to staying in the valley? Obviously, we want to avoid more risks with humans and would love for you to stay." Looking at Luke, he added, "I understand our lifestyle is much different than what you're accustomed to. Are you willing to give up everything?"

"I won't be giving up anything." Luke looked at Alissia. "Everything I need is right here." Turning back to Hoyle, he added, "You chose to save Alissia's life, and you've welcomed us both as one of your own. I believe Alissia agrees that this is where we belong."

She nodded. "I'm tired of running and hiding."

Salvatore gently squeezed Alissia's knee. "Although I'm going to miss them, I think they'll both be happy here."

She smiled up at him as he set the swing into a slow pace.

Farrah clapped her hands together and grinned. "It's been a long time since I planned a zeer ceremony. We have a lot to do."

"And not much time," Hoyle added. He turned to Salvatore. "When are you hoping to leave?"

"I wish I could stay longer, but if I want to visit my nephews before going back to the island, I'll need to leave here in a month."

Hoyle nodded. "Farrah and I've already made arrangements with others in the family, and we think we can get everything done by then."

"What all needs to be done?" Alissia asked.

"Luke and the men need to build your home and prepare a garden," Farrah responded, "while we need to make everything else." She shared a knowing smile with Hoyle before adding, "Everyone in the family's eager to contribute, and you may decide you have too much help."

"We thought you'd want to live near the cave in which we found Alissia," Hoyle said. "That way you can meet with the traders when they enter the valley—if the ancients decide to take part in the trading plans."

"We would also like for you to live near us," Farrah added, "so we can help you adjust to your new lifestyle."

Hoyle nodded. "We have a few spots already picked out for the house." He looked at Luke. "We'll ride out to them so you can choose, and then we'll start building. We already have the supplies to get started. You just need to decide which style you want."

"And tomorrow you can choose the fabrics and color schemes," Farrah said, to Alissia. She grinned. "The women in our family are a bit overzealous, and I don't want you to feel pressured into anything you don't want."

Hoyle chuckled beside her.

"If you don't like something," Farrah continued, "just let me know. Don't worry about hurting anyone's feelings. This will be your ceremony and home, and I want it to be to your liking."

"I don't know about human women," Hoyle smirked, "but the women in this family enjoy planning celebrations. They also love to decorate, and they've been talking about food, color schemes, and patterns for months. They've been busy!"

"I think it helped to keep Mother from worrying," Eaton replied, sitting in one of the rockers. His eyes met Alissia's. "She always had faith you'd find your way back, even when the odds were greatly against you."

Farrah nodded, looking at Alissia. "I knew you'd persevere."

Alissia smiled, not knowing how to respond.

"Anyone else ready to eat?" Gil asked.

"I could eat now," Alissia answered, eager for a change in subject. She waited for Gil to stand before hopping to her feet. "I'll go wash my hands."

Chapter 11

*A*lissia studied her reflection in the mirror in the corner of her room. After trying on three different outfits, she finally found a casual dress that fit, along with a pair of flip-flops. She fluffed her curls with her hands and smiled, hoping to ease her nerves.

"You got this," she told herself. She let out a shaky breath and scowled. "You've survived everything else and made it this far. Surely, you can handle meeting people who already consider you part of their family."

Creases lined her forehead, and she pulled her lower lip between her teeth. "Oh, who am I kidding?"

Alissia made her way to the open curtain at the side of her bed and fell back into the soft bedding. She stared up at the canopy of bella flowers for a moment before closing her eyes.

"God, I can't do this," she prayed softly. "I can't open my heart up to this many people."

She opened her eyes and wiped at an escaping tear. Fearing her thoughts would reach Luke, she sat up and tried to force her melancholy mood away. She stood and closed her eyes, taking in a deep breath through her nose before exhaling through her mouth.

Opening her eyes, she forced a smile onto her face. "I got this." She squared her shoulders and opened the bedroom door.

"You look lovely," Farrah said, stirring the liquid in a pitcher. Alissia thought the pottery looked like something normally reserved for an art display, too beautiful for actual use.

"What can I do to help?" she asked, joining the older woman in the kitchen.

Farrah set the wooden spoon on the counter and smiled. "Everything's ready." She placed the pitcher on a cold stone. "Unlike yesterday, I don't have to prepare a lot of food. Everyone's bringing something, so I mainly focused on the drinks."

Pointing to a group of handcrafted decanters, she said, "I've already warned Salvatore and Luke not to drink from those. They're much too strong for humans, but they're safe for us."

She touched the design on one of the handles of the pitchers. "See how this one shows fruit?" Alissia nodded. "That means it's a cold, fruit blend." She pointed to a different pitcher. "The ones with the flowers contain herbal drinks. Some are hot, while some are cold. You can tell by which type of stone they're on."

Farrah placed her fingers on the cold stone beneath the last drink she prepared. When she pulled her hand back, she smiled. "That'll get it cool enough. Want to try one?"

"I wouldn't even know where to begin," Alissia answered, scanning the row of pitchers.

"Then I'll pour you one of my favorites." Farrah grabbed one of the few larger mugs and poured a small amount of an herbal drink into it. "See if you like this one, but don't burn your mouth."

Alissia accepted the drink and blew on it for a while before taking a small sip. She held it in her mouth for a moment, enjoying the smooth, earthy flavor. After swallowing, she nodded. "It's perfect."

Farrah took the mug and poured more.

"Where's everyone at?" Alissia asked, looking around. She accepted the drink, careful not to spill the hot liquid.

"Gil and Eaton are outside doing some chores, and Hoyle's showing Luke and Salvatore the land choices this morning. They'll need to start building this week, and while everyone's here today, the men will finish the planning."

While Farrah poured herself a drink in one of the smaller mugs, Alissia considered how to respond without sounding rude.

"Um . . . shouldn't I be there to help decide on the location?"

Farrah smiled and motioned for Alissia to follow her to the larger table. They sat down across from each other before she responded, "Luke thought you'd say that. He decided this morning he wanted to surprise you on the night of your ceremony. It was actually Hoyle's idea, since it's somewhat of a custom among our people, but Luke and Salvatore both seemed excited about it. They immediately began to discuss things you'd like."

Alissia frowned, wondering whether they made the decision before she joined them for breakfast or while she dressed.

A Medician woman carrying a covered dish walked through the open doorway. "The boys said we're the first to arrive."

She set the dish on a cooling stone and touched her fingers to the stone. A man walked in, carrying another covered dish, and three children followed him.

"Where do you want this?" he asked, strolling toward the woman.

She pointed to one of the heating stones before walking over to the table.

"Alissia, this is my younger sister, Corrah," Farrah said, "and that's her zeer, Dayne." Pointing to the older girls standing in the sitting room, she said, "It's very uncommon for our people to have twins, so Celia and Delia are a rare blessing." She grinned at the young boy now standing at his mother's side. "And this one's Micah."

Alissia smiled, hoping to conceal her confusion as she tried to guess the ages of the children. The boy appeared to be an elementary child, while his sisters looked like small tweens, and although still young, she could not help but wonder if they were older than her.

Micah took off his sunglasses, revealing bright, purple eyes, and held them out to his mother. Accepting them, she placed them on the table.

"Hoyle's showing the properties to Luke and Salvatore," Farrah replied, as Dayne sat down beside her. He smiled at Alissia, and Farrah continued, "I was just telling Alissia that it's not uncommon for her not to see her home until the night of the zeer ceremony."

"Unless you're a tree dweller," Corrah said, nodding. "They have their own ways."

"I don't think you'll be disappointed," Dayne stated confidently. "We know you're ready to settle down after all you've been through, and a lot of planning has already taken place." A mysterious smile spread to his face. "I know I've been working on my addition to the home for quite some time."

Alissia smiled, feeling awkward. "I hope you haven't gone through too much trouble."

"Oh, please don't consider any of this trouble," Corrah said, placing her hand on Alissia's shoulder. "The entire family has come together on this. It's both a pleasure and a blessing."

Everyone turned to the open door as an elderly woman bustled in. Carrying a covered dish, she wore her white hair atop her head in a loose bun.

"Where's that dear child?" she asked.

Corrah rushed over and took the load from her hands, and Farrah motioned to the smaller table, saying, "Come join us, Mammula. Where's Pappula?"

Shuffling toward them, the old woman swiped her hand through the air. "He's outside with the boys." Stopping in front of Alissia, she grinned. "There she is. Welcome to the family, child."

Alissia braced herself for the side hug. Not knowing what to do with her hands, she self-consciously began to pat the old woman's back.

"You're finally here," Mammula said. After a hearty squeeze, she pulled back and looked at Alissia, through her dark glasses. "I knew you'd get here. Our prayers are never in vain."

Alissia nodded, and Mammula sat down at the smaller table.

"This is Hoyle's mother," Farrah explained. She gave a questioning look to the elderly woman. "And I believe you're wearing one of the dresses she made."

Mammula grinned proudly and nodded. "It is." Glancing down, she added, "The shoes too."

Dayne placed his hand on Micah's shoulder. "Let's go see if Pappula needs any help outside."

The young boy nodded and picked up his glasses before running out the door, leaving his father behind. Everyone chuckled as Dayne followed at a leisurely pace.

"Mammula, would you like a drink?" Corrah asked, pouring herself something.

"No thanks."

The twin girls sat down across from Mammula, both watching Alissia with curious eyes.

"Shall we go ahead and measure Alissia before everyone gets here?" Corrah asked, walking toward the tables.

Mammula leaned closer to Alissia with an eager grin. "I brought fabric samples for you to look at, so we can discuss the dress for your zeer ceremony."

Farrah chuckled as she set her mug on the table. Looking at Alissia, she swallowed and said, "Everyone will probably bring you fabric samples today, and they're all going to want to be the one to design your dress."

"I blended a variety of tones, hoping to match your hair," Mammula revealed.

"What color is a zeer dress supposed to be?" Alissia asked.

"It's usually a deep shade of purple," Farrah answered, "to represent the zeer bond. As you already know, it's a process that ties the two of you together for a lifetime—and believed even into eternity."

She reached across the table and took Alissia's hand, her expression becoming serious. "Although you've already triggered the bond, you've not experienced its full power," she warned. "That only happens when the two of you become one. That's when you truly meld together."

Farrah lightly squeezed Alissia's hand before releasing her grip and leaning back in her seat.

Alissia nodded, feeling slightly uncomfortable. Hoping to change the subject, she smiled and said, "I think I have an idea of what Luke imagines the dress to look like. He kind of showed me in a vision."

"Ooh, now that's different," Corrah crooned.

Farrah stood abruptly and started toward the sitting room. "I can pull that image from you, and we can work from that."

"You need to stop using your power," Corrah warned, suddenly serious.

"It won't hurt anything," Farrah responded confidently. Stopping at a bookshelf, she lifted the lid from a small box and took something out. When she turned around, she grinned and held up a jade before heading back to the table.

"We'll hold the jade together," she said, looking at Alissia. She sat down and placed her hand in the middle of the table, with the jade resting in her palm.

Alissia looked to Corrah questioningly, not wanting to put Farrah in danger.

Although still frowning, Corrah nodded. "She'll be fine. It's nothing compared to what she's already done."

Alissia placed her hand on top of the jade.

"Close your eyes and think back to what you saw," Farrah instructed, gripping Alissia's hand.

They both closed their eyes, and Alissia took her mind to Luke's vision from the day before. She felt warmth from the jade as power surged into her body, and she suddenly felt Farrah's presence within her mind.

The strength from the jade helped to pull the memory in exact detail, and she again saw Luke's image of her standing by the bed. His longing filled her as he whispered, "You are mine, Alissia."

The vision ended, and Farrah released her grip and pulled her hand away, looking as flushed as Alissia felt. She cleared her throat before stammering, "Well . . . uh . . . I think we can give him the dress he craves." Shaking her head, she quickly corrected, "I mean imagines. He imagines."

She stood and walked into the sitting room. After putting the jade back into its container, she turned around and smiled. "Shall we start on the alterations? Alissia needs measuring."

Chapter 12

The house soon filled with conversation and laughter as relatives, distant and near, arrived to meet Alissia and her human protectors. When Luke returned, a group of women immediately surrounded him, and against cheerful protests from the men, they led the towering warrior into the dining area to get his measurements.

Alissia laughed from her seat at the table as she watched the tiny women scurrying around his body. Two of them stood on chairs to reach his head.

Being a gentleman, Luke quietly submitted to every command, lifting his arms and holding out each leg when told. He kept his composure during their poking and prodding, even when a few commented on his toned physique.

As soon as the women finished, some of the men rushed to Luke's side for a rescue mission. Cheering triumphantly, they led him outside to Hoyle's workshop at the side of the house, where they congregated beneath the pavilion for most of the day.

Hoping to overhear some of the details of her and Luke's future home, Alissia carried drinks out to Luke on two occasions, only to have the men go completely silent as soon as they noticed her. Grinning, they watched and listened as she attempted to probe information from Luke, and they playfully taunted her each time she walked away in defeat.

Alissia spent most of the day in the sitting room with the women, laughing often at their lively conversations. She felt at ease in their presence, and with all the women, young and old, working on her and Luke's alterations, they finished the chore quickly.

Wanting to make Salvatore an outfit for the zeer ceremony, Farrah called him inside, and when he entered the house, the women immediately quieted and began to watch him. He answered a variety of questions regarding humans while Farrah and Corrah took his measurements, and he seemed to enjoy all the women's curiosity, often exaggerating his responses to make them giggle.

When he walked out, the conversation immediately turned back to the excitement of the ceremony, as it seemed like every woman—even the young girls too old for outside play—wanted to contribute in some way. They all brought something for Alissia to look at, and in the end, they divided into small groups, with each committing to certain tasks.

Surrounded by artistic talent, Alissia began to feel inadequate at her lack of skills. The women kindly reminded her she had plenty of time to learn things, and they all offered to teach her their abilities.

Although they seemed eager to do the work, Alissia felt uncomfortable for being an inconvenience. Each time she expressed her concern, they adamantly told her she needed to spend the month learning how to live in the valley and not to worry about anything else.

Farrah practically pleaded with the women to let her make Alissia's ceremonial dress, reminding them it was her motherly right. The others reasoned she would not have enough time while helping Alissia transition into their culture. She eventually agreed to pass the honor to Corrah and their mother, causing both women to squeal in delight.

Unable to relate with their excitement, Alissia felt sorry for her future children. An image of her and Luke teaching their young daughter how to throw knives entered her mind, and she chuckled to herself. If anyone ever expected a ceremonial dress from her, at least she could easily pass the job to someone else.

That thought led her to wonder how her children would differ from others in the valley, and she made a mental note to ask about it later. She then realized she had barely seen any Medician children at the gathering. Although they occasionally snuck into the kitchen to pilfer food, they mostly played outside, and everyone seemed content to let the animals watch over them. The tiny beanies also stayed out of sight.

The women finalized the ceremony and home décor plans shortly before the sky began to darken. Then they made their way into the kitchen and helped themselves to the large buffet of food. Even though everyone gorged for lunch, the serving dishes still contained more than enough for dinner.

As the women began to take turns washing dishes, the men and children drifted into the kitchen. After they made their plates and sat down, the women worked together to combine the leftovers and clean the empty serving containers.

Most of the men spoke words of gratitude when they added their dirty dishes to the pile on the counter. Then they went to the decanters and funneled the strong liquid into pouches hanging from their belts. A few ignored warnings from their zeers about how they needed some sleep that night, and more than one whistled or hummed as they strolled out the door.

Shortly after the last one walked out, a single instrument, similar to a harmonica, began to play a slow melody. The women chuckled, sharing a knowing look, and their cleaning became rushed.

After a while, an instrument sounding like a fiddle joined in, and the tune repeated at a faster rate. The song continued to repeat, growing livelier and adding an additional instrument each time around.

Eventually, a full band played at an impressive pace, and when a man's cackle added to the song, laughter erupted in the kitchen. An elderly woman sitting on a couch in the living room called out, "You're running out of time!"

With all the chores finished, except for a small pile of dishes, all eyes went to the women at the sinks, and the frantic workers responded by shrieking in unison.

Alissia stood between the tables holding a wet rag. Laughing, she watched the high-spirited women. Many of them now danced to the music. Yelping and shouting, their tiny feet stomped along the floor in synchronized steps. They grabbed partners and twirled each other around, their feet constantly in motion.

Mammula stood from her seat on the sofa and began to shuffle her feet. Although Farrah's mother remained seated, she laughed, nodding to the music.

By the time the last dish went into the soapy water, a variety of yelping, whooping, and other wild sounds enhanced the lively tune.

Farrah snatched the rag from Alissia's hand and tossed it on the counter. "Tonight, we celebrate!" she yelled, her voice competing with the loud music and shouting. She grabbed Alissia's hand and led her toward the back door. "We kept this part of the house a surprise."

With her hand on the knob, she looked back over her shoulder at all the women standing behind Alissia. "Are we ready?"

Loud screams erupted, and the women began to stomp their feet, clogging in rhythm to the music. When the door opened, the band immediately switched to a lively, new song, with the men singing along.

Farrah shot out the door, dragging Alissia with her, and they entered a clearing surrounded by trees, with glowing, white bella flowers coiled around them. Their vines strung overhead from tree to tree, giving light to a bright blue, floral ground covering.

Alissia stumbled, but quickly regained her footing. As the women began to sing a verse, her eyes darted around the clearing, and the men soon began to sing again. Realizing her situation, she froze, and Farrah looked back at her. Locking eyes, Alissia shook her head, silently pleading.

"Come!" Farrah responded. Laughing, she turned back around and continued forward.

Alissia began to stomp in desperation, and shouts and laughter erupted around her. Watching Farrah's feet, she hoped to find a pattern in the movements as the women formed a dancing circle. Although she understood the song consisted of the men asking questions and the women answering, she could not focus on her feet and the words at the same time.

A sweet aroma arose from the tiny flowers beneath their feet, and Alissia soon gave up trying to match her steps with the others. Free to move in her own chaotic way, she glanced around the circle and grinned. Farrah laughed and released her hand.

She gazed out to the edge of the clearing and spotted Luke and Salvatore standing near the band. The music stopped abruptly, and she bumped into Farrah. When the women began to sing in unison, she bolted toward Luke.

"Not a word!" Alissia warned. Slamming against him, she locked her arms around his waist and rested the side of her face against his chest. She closed her eyes, hoping to calm her breathing.

"You've got skills," Luke teased, wrapping his arms around her.

"Care to teach us some of your moves?" Salvatore added.

The band began a new tune, and Alissia tightened her grip.

"Wasn't that fun?" Farrah called out from behind.

Alissia opened her eyes and looked over her shoulder to see Farrah stopping in front of them. "I'm done!" she exclaimed, shaking her head adamantly. She grabbed the back of Luke's shirt, locking her body to his.

Farrah laughed and shook her head. "Maybe for now, but this celebration's for you, Alissia." She paused as she watched Hoyle walking toward them. When he stepped beside her, she turned back to Alissia and grinned. "We celebrate your arrival, along with your birthday!"

"My birthday?"

Luke's body shook with laughter, and she looked up at him. "Tomorrow's your birthday," he answered loudly, his voice competing with the music.

"But we never even celebrated your birthday." Alissia frowned. "That's not fair. I don't even know when your birthday is."

"You don't even know what day your own birthday is," he replied, shrugging.

"Tonight we celebrate with dancing!" Hoyle announced. "Before the work begins."

"That's right," Farrah replied. "We have much to do before the zeer ceremony, so be sure to dance and have fun." To Salvatore, she added, "It's an honor to have you as a guest among our people, as we never imagined entertaining humans in this valley, much less having one in our home. You've proven yourself highly worthy, and we thank you."

Salvatore gave a nod and smiled. "Thank you for welcoming me into your home." He glanced at Luke and Alissia. "And thank you for giving me peace in knowing these two will be taken care of when I leave."

Alissia released her hold on Luke, and he took her by the hand as she moved to stand next to him. Smiling up at Salvatore, she pushed back the pain she felt at the thought of him leaving.

Salvatore turned to Hoyle. "I'd like to get a closer look at those instruments."

"Ah, yes! Let's see if there's something you can try." Hoyle motioned for Salvatore to follow as he started toward the band.

After watching the two of them walk away, Farrah turned back around. "Take a break. You'll have plenty of opportunities to dance tonight." She grinned and turned to the clearing, where both men and women now danced in a circle. Stomping in time with the music, she made her way toward them.

Luke leaned toward Alissia's ear. "Let's sit down."

"Definitely!" she agreed.

He led her away from the band, to a hammock on the opposite side of the clearing, and grabbed the folded blanket in it before sitting down. With a wink, he said, "This one's ours for the night."

"For the night?" she asked, plopping down beside him.

He arranged the blanket over their legs and began to rock the hammock. "I was told this thing's going to last most of the night. Everyone tied their own hammocks shortly after the house was built, and they brought their own bedding with them today."

Alissia eyed the dancers. She loved how their clothing shimmered beneath the canopy of bella flowers. Shaking her head, she responded, "There's no way they can go all night—not at the rate they're going."

Luke laughed and took her hand, setting it on the blanket. "This isn't a small thing for them. They've been planning and looking forward to this for a long time."

"How long do you think they can last dancing like that? I mean, look at them."

"That depends on how much energy drink they use."

"Energy drink?" Alissia turned to Luke in confusion.

He nodded. "It doesn't affect their mental state that much, but they only drink it on special occasions." He looked thoughtful for a moment before explaining, "Although it lowers their desire to work, it gives them much more energy, which means it'll keep them singing and dancing for a while. Then they'll sleep and feel sluggish for most of tomorrow."

"It doesn't get them drunk?"

"From what I understand, no." He turned to watch the dancers. "Hoyle said dancing's a big thing here, and they often hold gatherings in the community spaces, beneath the tree dwellers." Turning back to Alissia, he smiled. "It's nothing like this, though. The people go home, and the party ends much earlier. However, they sip on the energy drinks, and many of them participate in dance competitions."

"How come I didn't know any of this?"

Luke grinned. "You've been around them all day. What did you talk about?"

"We planned the inside of the house and the zeer ceremony."

"Really?" he taunted, raising his brows. "How can you plan a house you know nothing about?"

She frowned and pulled her hand from his. "I'm not happy with you about that."

He laughed, and her frown deepened. "Ah, there's that look," he teased.

"Why do you enjoy making me mad?"

Luke's expression fell unexpectedly, and he stared out at the dancers for a moment before turning back to meet Alissia's gaze.

"I haven't been able to give you anything. I've had to stand by and watch others dance with you and buy you gifts, yet our time together has mostly been a struggle."

He let out a sigh and took her hand, threading his fingers between hers. "On our wedding night, I want to be able to surprise you with so many things, Alissia." Pleading with his eyes, he added, "Let me do this one thing. I promise I'll make you happy."

She lifted his hand and gave it a kiss before responding, "You have no idea how much you already make me happy. I never needed gifts or fancy things to fall in love with you."

Luke pulled his hand from hers and put his arm around her, drawing her close. "In one month, you'll completely be mine, and I'll spend the rest of my life making up for all that we missed out on."

Alissia rolled onto her side and placed her hand on Luke's chest. She closed her eyes and smiled. "We're sleeping together tonight?"

He chuckled, placing his hand over hers. "In their eyes, we're already somewhat married. I believe our situation confuses them."

She lifted her head so that he could see her frown. "Yeah, I hear we're stuck with each other for life."

A grin lit up his face, and she smiled, wishing she could fast forward to their wedding night.

"Do you think you're going to like it here?" she asked.

He gave her hand a light squeeze and nodded, his expression turning thoughtful. "I do. I believe we both will."

His gaze traveled to the dancers, and she glanced over at them. Still going strong, they laughed and called out random yelps and howls.

"We both don't know much about family," he said, "but I believe they'll teach us. They seem genuine. They seem happy."

Luke's longing for a family suddenly filled Alissia. Orphaned as a baby, he never had a mother or father, and everyone she met that day already considered them both part of their family.

Consumed by her own fears of how destructive families could be, she had not even considered Luke's feelings or desires, and deep down, he ached for the one thing he never had.

"What do you think about the men you met today?" she asked.

He looked back at her and smiled. "They're extremely skilled craftsmen. I've spent the day listening to their ideas and designs, and you'd be amazed at all they can accomplish—especially in only a month."

"Are they all going to help you build?"

He nodded. "Most of them have already made things for us to use, and I was told that everyone here will add something, even the older children."

"Will the house be finished in a month?"

"I believe so. The plans are complete, and everyone knows their job." He gave her hair a tug with his free hand and added, "You're not going to see much of me and Salvatore after tonight, and knowing you, we'll already be working by the time you wake each morning."

Alissia gave Luke a dirty look. "You never know. I could get up before you and have breakfast ready."

Laughing heartily, he shook his head. "That'll never happen."

"All right, you two. It's time for some fun," Farrah called out, leading a group of dancers toward them.

The group of Medicians surrounded the hammock, and one of them snatched the blanket away. They grabbed Luke and Alissia's hands, pulling them to their feet. Like two adults mobbed at an elementary school, the tiny creatures tugged and pushed them into the clearing.

Hoyle grabbed Alissia's hand, and everyone began to group into pairs. As they formed a circle, she laughed when she spotted Salvatore attempting an escape from Corrah. Determined, the tiny woman shook her head, pulling him back to her side.

The band began to play, and shouting and whooping filled the air. Hoyle squeezed Alissia's hand and yelled, "Ready?" Without waiting for an answer, he started skipping along to the music.

"Spin!" he called out, just before urging her into an awkward twirl. Leading her around the circle, he forewarned her of each move. Instead of clogging, the dancers pranced around, spinning and going under one another's arms.

Alissia laughed while bending down to clear Hoyle's raised arm. He passed her to someone else, and she struggled to keep up. Although a great dancer, her new partner failed to call out the movements.

After going through two more partners, she and Salvatore stumbled into each other. As they looked around in confusion, another couple bumped into them, and he quickly grabbed Alissia's hand. The two of them began to wildly skip and twirl about in a dance of their own.

No longer focused on trying to learn the proper moves, she giggled and shouted out random hoots and howls. With locked arms, they skipped around in a circle, and Alissia hollered, "Yeeeehaaaaawww!!"

Salvatore stopped abruptly, and her enthusiasm ended with, "Oomph! Ow!" Pulling away from his chest, she smiled guiltily at the two Medicians staring up at them. Not wanting to disrupt the moving circle, she quickly grabbed the hand of her new partner and stepped forward.

"Lead on, my little dancer!"

Alissia eventually found herself in front of Luke. He took her by the hand, and not surprisingly, he began to lead her through the proper movements.

Responding to her rolling eyes, he gave a smug grin and winked. "It's easy." Her frown deepened, and he laughed while lifting their hands. As she passed under them, he said, "If you watch closely, you'll see there's a pattern."

"I *have* been watching closely!"

"You and Salvatore should teach me some moves," he teased, nudging her into a spin.

Once back at his side, she grinned mischievously. "You couldn't keep up with us. Some things are just too wild and free."

Luke's expression turned roguish. Knowing that look often meant trouble for her, Alissia's eyes narrowed, and she lifted her chin defiantly.

In one swift move, he pulled her into his arms, with her back against his torso and their hands at her ribcage. Never missing a step, he continued to guide her along the moving circle.

His free hand drew her hair away from her neck, and he bent down to her ear. "Oh, I look forward to seeing just how wild you can be, my little pixet."

With that, he pulled her into a spin that ended in front of her new partner.

Chapter 13

*A*lissia slowly lifted her head from Luke's chest, careful not to wake him. She glanced around the clearing and smiled at the exhausted dancers, still sleeping in their hammocks. The sound of birds flitting about in the trees replaced the music from the night before, and she guessed it to be late morning.

Hearing faint voices, she looked to the house with squinted eyes and saw a few women in the kitchen. When she turned her attention to Luke, she smiled, basking in the rare occasion of waking before him. He looked so peaceful, so different from the hardened assassin she grew to love.

In that moment, she promised to spend the rest of her life trying to make him happy. The phrase he often used with her came to mind, and she told herself that not only was she his, but he was hers. For the rest of their lives, he was hers.

The usual lock of hair fell over his forehead, and she stared at it, trying to imagine what he would soon look like with purple hair. She would miss those dark eyes and hair. All of her best memories—the heated ones—included his black eyes boring into hers. Fiery and passionate, would he lose that look?

After a while, she began to crave the herbal drink she had tasted the day before, and she frowned, knowing Luke would most likely wake upon the slightest movement.

When she looked down at her legs, she smiled faintly at the sight of Mia asleep in his lap. Slowly and carefully, she lifted the blanket from her body and began to sit up.

Luke's arm slid around Alissia's waist, and his muscles tightened, locking her in place. When she turned to look at him, she found his eyes still closed.

"Shhh," she whispered at his ear. "Almost everyone's asleep, and you should rest up before you start building a house. I'm going to see if I can help in the kitchen."

She kissed him on the temple, and his grip loosened, allowing her to slowly pull away.

"*I love you,*" he mentally whispered.

She stood and looked down at him. His eyes remained closed as she gently pulled the blanket up around him.

"*I love you, too,*" she mentally responded. One corner of his mouth turned up slightly, and she rewarded him with a light kiss to the side of his mouth.

Once inside, Alissia closed the door and said good morning to the children and senior men and women preparing food in the kitchen. After a quick visit to the bathroom, she asked what she could do to help, and Farrah's mother gave her a hot drink and led her to a large mixing bowl on the counter.

"I can teach you how to prepare one of our common breakfast foods," she said, lifting the lid of a container. "Are you familiar with pagos?"

Alissia looked down at the black specks and shook her head. "It looks similar to something we call grits in my old reality, but I've only seen white or yellow ones. They're ground from corn."

The woman chuckled and set the lid on the counter. Patting Alissia's back, she said, "You've much to learn before your ceremony."

Eager to start her lessons, Alissia smiled and picked up a nearby, wooden spoon. "I'm ready."

Although many still slumbered in their hammocks, the morning workers seemed to enjoy their tasks. Children and a variety of animals often strolled through the open front door, carrying baskets of fresh herbs, fruits, and vegetables. After the women washed the ingredients, they placed them on the table for the men to chop, grate, or peel.

Salvatore had entered the house shortly after Alissia, and he now sat at the large table helping the men. With the smell of hot food drifting outside, groggy Medicians eventually began to trickle in.

After rolling out a ball of dough—made with the black specks—Alissia placed it on a cooking stone and grabbed a spatula.

"Don't forget to sprinkle some grated zenga rind on it for extra flavor," Farrah's mother instructed.

Alissia nodded and took a pinch of the fresh ingredient from a small, nearby bowl. As she sprinkled it on the bubbling cake, a warm sensation came over her, and she looked around to find Luke standing unnoticed in a corner of the kitchen.

Freshly bathed, he leaned against the wall with his arms crossed, watching Alissia intently. When she met his gaze, heat rose to her face as his emotions of pride and love seeped into her.

She quickly looked down at the patty on the cooking stone and started lifting the edges, hoping to appear busy. She felt herself swallow as she tucked her hair behind her ear.

"Oh, dear," Mammula said, taking the spatula from Alissia's hand. "Your unfinished bond's going to drive you both mad before the ceremony."

Alissia watched as Luke took a seat across from Salvatore. Then she turned her attention to the woman in front of her. Shrugging, she responded lightly, "We've been fine for months now."

The old woman smiled up at Alissia, shaking her head. "You two have been distracted with travel and thoughts of survival." She set the spatula on the counter and took Alissia's hand in both of hers. "Child, the zeer bond is much more powerful than feelings. It's the purest bond created. Our young are taught to hold it sacred, yet to fear it."

Mammula squeezed Alissia's hand, emphasizing, "It has the power to bring great joy, but it also has the power to destroy."

She paused, letting her words sink in. "We've never heard of a partial bond, as our people live by strict rules when it comes to the bonding process. Once it's complete, it should be much stronger, especially in the beginning. That's why we believe in the two of you retreating after the ceremony. Your combined emotions could easily overwhelm you."

Releasing Alissia's hand, the old woman smiled. "I imagine the pull will become stronger now that the two of you can focus on each other."

"I don't know," Alissia responded. "I heard we're barely even going to see each other until the night of the ceremony."

"That's right," Farrah replied, stepping next to Mammula. "You both have a lot to do." She frowned, looking exhausted. "I need a morning tonic. What herbs have been brewed?"

Alissia smiled to herself as Mammula led Farrah to the row of beverages arranged along a counter. Picking up the spatula, she glanced around the room and chuckled at the sight of worn-out faces.

She wondered what time the party finally ended, as she had fallen asleep while watching a dance contest from her and Luke's hammock. Feeling safe and secure in his arms, she drifted into a deep slumber, her exhaustion overpowering the loud music and laughter filling the air.

After eating a large brunch, Alissia took a seat on the big sofa and noticed how everyone cleaned their own dishes and did something to help before preparing to leave. On their way out, they all walked over and wished her a happy birthday, while many of them gave her a hug. The men told Luke and Salvatore they would see them in the morning.

When the last visitor stepped out the door, Alissia joined Hoyle in the kitchen. "Anything need to be done?" she asked, looking around. With so many guests and the lack of paper plates and plastic utensils, she found it hard to believe the kitchen could be so clean.

Leaning against the counter with a mug in his hands, he smiled and shook his head. "I think we need to recover from last night."

Alissia glanced up at Luke when he put his arm around her shoulders. "Where's Farrah?" she asked, turning back to Hoyle.

"She's in the back yard. Probably still working on the finland."

"What's finland?" she questioned.

Hoyle set his drink aside and pulled his body from the counter. "Now's a good time to see what you can do with plants."

They found Farrah on her hands and knees in the middle of the clearing, with Eaton and Gil both sprawled out nearby.

"Everyone's gone," Hoyle announced, strolling toward them.

Farrah sat on her bottom and rubbed her hands together. "I know. They all helped out here before they left." She smiled up at Alissia. "Want to help?"

"What do you want me to do?"

Farrah patted the ground in front of her. "We weren't very nice to the finland last night, so it needs a bit of nurturing."

"The flowers?" Alissia asked, sitting down.

Farrah nodded. "A beautiful, hardy ground covering that thrives in the shade." She frowned, eyeing the faint, circular path in the clearing. "However, we abused it a bit last night."

Turning to Alissia, she smiled. "Everyone put a little energy into it before they left, and under normal circumstances, I'd just continue to work with it over the next few days. It'll return to normal, but I'm curious to see what you can do."

Alissia placed her palm on the ground and closed her eyes. Her body instantly responded to her thoughts, and she felt heat flowing into the ground from her hand. Her latest scar tingled.

After a while, Farrah touched Alissia's shoulder and exclaimed, "That's enough!"

Alissia opened her eyes and looked around to find the ground covered in the tiny, blue flowers. Like a thick carpet, no gaps could be seen.

Farrah pointed at a patch of the tiny flowers growing along the bottom of a nearby tree. "You've been gifted with so much power, Alissia." Shaking her head, she added, "You didn't just heal the flowers. You added new growth."

"What's the difference?" Alissia asked, setting her hand in her lap.

"A lot!" Gil exclaimed. No longer sprawled out and looking half asleep, he and his brother now sat watching her.

Hoyle sat down beside her. "Our people easily heal plants, and they thrive just by being around us. We spend a lot of time and energy planting and maintaining the vegetation in this valley. Although we can make our squashes grow at a much faster rate than the natural timing, we can't bring a seed to full fruition within minutes."

He picked up Alissia's hand and rubbed his thumb over her mark, inspecting it. "I'm wondering if you have enough power to actually give full growth to a squash seed."

"What about the other one?" she asked, holding out her right hand.

He let go of her hand and shook his head. "Luke wouldn't be alive without it."

Alissia frowned, dropping both hands in her lap. "Why did they give me these powers? I don't understand."

"We knew you were special the moment we saw you in the caves!" Farrah proclaimed. "And the guardians know it as well."

"I just don't know why they gave me the last gift," Alissia replied. With a shrug, she added, "Unless Luke's the special one, and they wanted to prevent him from getting a bad rash. However, the forest was covered in poisonous growth, and they should have given it to me last fall."

"Yes, but most of the vegetation was growing dormant in time for winter," Salvatore said, from behind. "Your gift would be needed most in spring."

"You call that dormant?" she asked wryly, looking over her shoulder. "Even with a do-rag, my hair and clothes constantly snagged on all the thorns and brush we trampled through."

Luke chuckled. "It would have been much worse in late spring."

"Well, I'm just glad we're done with that. And don't expect me to ever go camping or backpacking again. I'm over it!" A mischievous smile spread to Alissia's face before she added, "I think the guardians gave me this gift to help with all the farming we'll have to do. It's going to take a lot of prepping to feed my little vegetarian homesteader."

She grinned up at Luke, "I know how much you love your veggies."

Chapter 14

Alissia barely saw Luke and Salvatore over the next two weeks. She and Farrah woke before daylight each day to prepare breakfast and pack a lunch for the men, and although not a morning person, she looked forward to seeing Luke before he left each day.

She enjoyed learning new recipes and having Luke's breakfast waiting on the table. Always the first man to enter the kitchen, his eyes went straight to Alissia. The way he looked at her in those moments sent shivers throughout her body.

To help with her nerves, she learned to sit next to him while eating breakfast. If she sat across from him, she continuously caught him watching her.

The men came home each evening dirty and exhausted. Unlike the early morning hours, conversation and laughter filled the air, and Luke seemed more relaxed and playful than his usual self.

Farrah explained no one would visit Luke and Alissia during the first few months after their zeer ceremony, maybe even longer. Their time alone would help with the bonding process. Like the Medicians on the island, a couple usually retreated for a year after their ceremony.

Alissia needed to learn how to survive in the valley so she could teach Luke all she knew, and Farrah's lessons kept her busy. Thanks to her powerful ability to grow vegetation, she quickly learned how to plant and grow a garden. She learned which animals helped the most with harvesting food, along with which ones helped with chores around the house.

Most of her lessons consisted of preparing food. Alissia spent an entire day learning how to dry, crush, and mix herbs to drink or use with certain foods. They prepared small containers, which she kept hidden from Luke, and Farrah promised to put them, along with her other gifts, in their home without Luke's knowledge.

She learned how to pull oil from nuts and seeds, and she made butters, jams, and breads. With Farrah's extensive supply of essential oils and mineral rock powders, she looked forward to learning how to make bath and cleaning items as well.

Each night Alissia fell into her bed exhausted. Holding Mia to her chest, she drifted to sleep with a smile on her face. Visions of Luke and dancing Medicians replaced her haunting nightmares.

Alissia woke early one morning to the promise of a day off with Farrah. After the men left, the two women quickly prepared dinner and put it away. They harnessed a small buggy onto two miniature horses and stepped inside, and Mia hopped into Alissia's lap.

"I usually walk," Farrah said, as the buggy began to move.

"Are you going to tell me where we're going?" Alissia questioned, holding her hand out to the side. She enjoyed the feel of the breeze on her skin.

"I thought you'd like to see where we're planning to have your ceremony."

"And where would that be?" Alissia asked, trying to conceal her excitement.

"We thought Bertly Caves would be fitting, since we found you near them."

Alissia pulled her hand from the breeze and set it next to Mia. She squinted behind her dark glasses, trying to get a better glimpse of a group of animals walking ahead of them. As they drew closer, she recognized them as the mouse creatures that often helped the Medicians.

After they turned onto a different path, Farrah said, "You should look at me now."

Alissia stared at Farrah for a moment, her face twisted in confusion. Then a smile spread to her face. Hearing the sound of hammering and men's voices, she could not resist the urge to look toward the noise.

Farrah chuckled. "You won't see anything but trees. Turn back around."

"We should see if they need anything," Alissia urged, straining to see past the trees.

"They don't."

"So this means I won't be living in a cave," Alissia said thoughtfully. She turned to Farrah and grinned. "Or a tree house."

"It could still be a tree house," Farrah responded. She shrugged. "It could also be a cave. We have ways."

Cocking her head, Alissia listened intently to the distant sounds of construction. She thought she heard Salvatore's voice.

"You'll see soon enough," Farrah replied, "and I know you're going to love it."

"You know about it?"

"Of course!" Farrah leaned closer, emphasizing, "You could *never* imagine what it's going to look like."

"That's just cruel," Alissia complained.

Farrah laughed heartily, and Alissia shook her head.

They soon stopped in a small clearing in front of a cave entrance. After they unhitched the horses, Farrah grabbed the backpack holding their lunch and began to put it on.

"What do you think about this area for the celebration?"

Alissia nodded, gazing around the clearing. "It's perfect."

Motioning upward, Farrah said, "Imagine orbs of bella flowers hanging from the trees." She pointed to the right of the cave entrance. "And the band will go there."

"Plenty of room for dancing," Alissia muttered.

"Exactly!" Farrah started toward the entrance. "Let me show you where the ceremony will be."

Alissia followed Farrah into the cave, where blue bella flowers grew along the walls, lighting their way. After a brief walk, they stepped into a large cavern, and Alissia froze, instantly transfixed by her luminous surroundings.

Glowing, green moss carpeted the ground, and in the center, moss-covered, stone steps led to a large glow stone, cut into the shape of a round platform. A lustrous, blue tree grew directly behind the stage area, while radiant, pale blue mushrooms—at least seven feet tall—lined the walls and dotted the cavern. Overhead, tiny specks of light, in a variety of colors, flew near the ceiling, providing a shimmery light show.

Farrah took Alissia by the hand and began to lead her toward the platform. "That's where you and Luke will say your vows to each other. What do you think?"

"It's beyond what I imagined," Alissia responded, staring up at the glowing mushroom they walked under. It reminded her of the underground world in the forest.

Farrah veered to the right of the platform. "Let me show you the source of the lighting. Remember what Ian showed you?"

Alissia nodded, cringing at the thought of her last date with Ian. Behind the platform, she found a pool of water near the glowing tree, where a Medician man and woman stood from one of the small benches positioned around the pool.

"We were waiting for you," the woman replied, giving a nervous smile.

"Alissia, this is Royce and Kayla," Farrah said, stopping in front of the couple. "They're some of the caretakers of these caves, and they're helping with your ceremony."

"It's a pleasure to finally meet you," Royce replied, clasping his hands in front of his body. "We've heard so much. Do you have any questions about the cavern? Is it suitable for the ceremony?"

"Oh, yes," Alissia answered, nodding. "It's beautiful."

"The tree's the source of the luminous plants and animals," Farrah explained, pointing to the pool.

Alissia turned toward the willow-like tree. Just like the one Ian had showed her, its roots drifted into the pool of water, where a few glowing fish swam near the surface. Full of life, she spotted salamanders and other tiny creatures scurrying about in a variety of bright, glowing colors. Seeing a cluster of tiny frogs, she quickly turned back to Farrah and smiled, determined not to let the memories of Ian ruin her wedding.

"Shall we show her where the meal will take place?" Farrah asked.

"Yes, definitely," Royce answered, before stepping past them.

"Everything's ready," Kayla said, walking beside Farrah. "Corrah stopped by yesterday to look around, and she got a few more ideas."

"I won't be involved in the preparations," Farrah replied. "I'm trusting my sister with things. Should I be worried?"

Kayla chuckled, shaking her head. "She has a lot of help."

As they passed one of the large mushrooms, Alissia drew close and reached out to touch the stalk with her fingers. With its brilliant glow, she somewhat expected warmth to come from it and was surprised to find that it felt cool and fleshy, yet firm.

Rushing to catch up with the others, she recalled Ian's explanation of how the tree produced a certain algae in the water. Although toxic to many animals, it caused others to glow, and she wondered if the mushrooms and moss got their light from the water or if they naturally grew that way.

They entered a large cave, with white bella flowers covering the walls and a floor of glowing, green moss. Four chandeliers—made from tree roots and covered in bella flowers—hung over two long, oversized tables, and Alissia wondered how the tiny Medicians managed to haul the massive tables into the cave.

Royce explained their rare beauty came from having been cut from a great tree. After cutting out two long pieces of wood, the skilled carpenters smoothed and stained them, keeping their edges naturally shaped. They placed the thick pieces of wood on top of stained tree stumps, creating exquisite pieces of art.

The many small chairs surrounding the tables matched the fine craftsmanship—each piece carved from matching wood, leaving their natural imperfections.

"Your table hasn't arrived yet," Royce said, pointing to a corner.

"Is there a possibility of a delay?" Farrah asked, looking worried.

He gave a reassuring smile and shook his head. "No, it should be here in plenty of time."

"If not, we could probably sit at these," Alissia assured.

Farrah frowned, shaking her head. "You could, but Luke and Salvatore wouldn't be comfortable. We've got a taller table being built."

"And it'll be here in time," Kayla replied. "All is going as planned."

Although Farrah nodded, her smile seemed weak, and Alissia felt a bit guilty for not caring much about the details of her own wedding. She could easily see herself getting married in a pair of traveling clothes in the back of a carriage, if needed. The thought of a formal wedding never really appealed to her. She just looked forward to it finally being over.

After thanking the caretakers for their time, Alissia and Farrah followed a tunnel into the mountains. Leaving the bella flowers and maintained areas behind, they relied upon their ability to see in the dark while hiking through the damp and eerie tunnels.

Every creature they passed looked strange and menacing, but Farrah found something nice to say about each one. Alissia learned that nearly every plant and animal provided a natural resource to the Medicians or helped the ecosystem in some way.

"It's the perfect season to walk through here," Farrah said.

"Really? There are different seasons in tunnels?" Alissia winced at the sarcasm in her voice, but the sound of clicking from somewhere ahead distracted her.

Farrah chuckled. "Of course! Why would things be different down here?"

"I'm surprised anything even lives down here, and I'm starting to worry about what's making all that noise up ahead. Something tells me it's not a group of furry little bunnies—or anything cute and furry."

"I was wondering when you'd ask about that. You do remember that you have no reason to fear animals, right?"

Alissia stopped walking, and Farrah took her hand and pulled her forward. "This is one of the reasons why Hoyle and I were this far in the tunnels the day we found you."

"What reason?" Alissia asked, her voice full of distrust.

"Well, you're about to find out."

Farrah turned at an opening on the right and continued to pull Alissia forward. The eerie clicking grew stronger, but Alissia pushed her unease aside. When they turned another corner, she froze, refusing to take another step.

"What's wrong?" Luke mentally asked. *"Where are you?"*

Even her thoughts froze.

"Alissia, why are you sending me visions of spiders? You're a Medician. They can't hurt you."

"Don't even go there!" she mentally snapped. *"I'm in a cave with thousands of spiders—maybe even millions. They're all over the place, with tons of web sacks hanging from the ceiling. And each of them are bigger than your entire head. Get out of my mind!"*

"You're the one who called me."

She turned to Farrah. "This isn't normal."

Farrah chuckled. "I warned Hoyle to make sure Luke wasn't doing anything dangerous before we entered this area. We both thought this might be a bit overwhelming."

"Overwhelming? I don't even think we have spiders this big in my other reality. This is wrong in so many ways."

Watching the spiders moving along the walls, she cringed and took a step back. They had a tough, shiny exoskeleton, with long, thin legs.

"I brought a glow stone, if you want a better look," Farrah offered.

"I'm good. I don't need to see them in color. Why are we here?"

"This is near where we found you, and—"

"Well, if we have to walk past them, I'm good!" Shaking her head, Alissia added, "I don't need to see where you found me. I'm good."

"We don't have to walk through there." Farrah started back down the tunnel, and Alissia eagerly followed. "It's their nesting season. You only saw the females."

"And where are the males?" Alissia asked, glancing behind her.

"Dead. The females feed on the males after mating. They need the energy to travel to the nesting cave, where they spend their final days enclosing their eggs in the sacs you saw hanging from the ceiling."

"Nice little creatures," Alissia muttered, starting to feel at ease.

"To be fair, they spend their last breaths guarding their eggs, and then the babies will feast on their bodies once they hatch."

"Does that mean all those babies are going to leave the cave after they eat?" Alissia envisioned a mass exodus of spiders filling the tunnels. "I don't think I want a house near the mountains. Even if I'm a friend to the animals, it's still just creepy."

Farrah shook her head, laughing. "They don't venture outside. And, yes, they'll leave the nesting cave and search for their own place in the tunnels. The cycle will repeat again."

Pointing into the air for emphasis, she added, "And that's a good thing!"

"Why is that a good thing? You don't eat animals, so I'm not picturing a hunting frenzy."

"No, but they help to balance the population of other creatures in the tunnels. We also collect all the empty egg sacs to make a strong adhesive."

Farrah smiled at Alissia. "And if it weren't for them, we probably wouldn't have been around to save you that day. Although the egg sacs had already been gathered, Hoyle and I made a random decision to inspect the nesting cave while checking the tunnels."

She added mysteriously, "There are other creatures in the area we monitor as well."

"Yeah, well I'm thinking mine and Luke's future careers are not going to be in the tunnels. I'll stick with plants and furry animals."

Farrah laughed, and they continued on. After a while, her expression turned somber, and she stopped and looked around.

"This is it. Hoyle and I suddenly felt an explosion of energy, and we ran through the tunnels searching for it. This is where we found you."

She began to take off her backpack. "Want the glow stone I brought?"

Alissia nodded before accepting the stone. Looking around, she found nothing special about the place—just a damp and dimly lit tunnel, with no evidence of her life-changing event.

Farrah pointed to the ground. "You were here, and we rushed over to find you barely breathing." She looked up at Alissia. "We knelt down beside you, but we didn't think we could save you. It's only because your body still surged with power."

Turning, she looked ahead and stared into the distance. "Then we heard the footsteps. We were terrified and didn't know what to do."

Seeing tears in Farrah's eyes, Alissia's body tensed, and she turned away. She held up the glow stone, hoping to appear interested in her surroundings.

"What's wrong?"

Alissia cringed at the sound of Luke's voice in her head, hating that she let her emotions rise up enough for him to feel. *"We're in the tunnel where they found me, and Farrah's starting to cry."*

"Hug her."

She felt herself swallow as she turned back around.

"Put your arms around the woman and hug her, Alissia. It's a normal response."

When Farrah met her gaze, Alissia forced a smile onto her face. Too late to pretend she had not see the tears, she walked the short distance between them and bent over to wrap her arms around the tiny woman.

"Are you hugging her?"

Alissia frowned, feeling completely awkward. *"Yes!"*

"It would help if you said something nice as well."

Her frown grew into a scowl. *"What am I supposed to say?"*

"I don't know. It's your conversation, not mine. Just do something. You're making me feel uncomfortable."

Alissia broke the hug and straightened. She tucked a strand of hair behind her ear and smiled, looking into Farrah's eyes. "Thank you so much for saving my life. I'd be dead without you."

Farrah smiled and wiped at her eyes. "You and Luke are family. You do know that, don't you?"

Alissia nodded. "You and Hoyle have given us much more than we ever imagined."

"How's it going?" Luke questioned.

"This is hard enough without you in my head," she mentally responded.

Farrah turned and motioned to one of the walls. "Do you want to look around some more?"

"No." Alissia shook her head and smiled. "There's nothing for me here, but thank you for letting me see it."

Chapter 15

"How nervous are you?" Corrah asked.

Alissia feverishly began to wave the fan in front of her face, her eyes wide.

"They feel each other's emotions," Mammula replied. She frowned, shaking her head. "That's why we don't bond before the zeer ceremony. They're both going to faint and fall down the stairs to land on top of us. It's a good thing we don't die easily."

"Mammula!" Farrah stepped in front of the old woman and caught Alissia's moving hand. "Take a deep breath. Remember? This is what you've been waiting for."

Alissia nodded.

"Think about tonight!" Farrah's mother yelled, from her seat on the sofa.

Alissia pulled her hand from Farrah's, and the fanning began again.

"That's it!" Farrah grabbed Alissia's other hand and pulled her toward the bathroom. She glanced over her shoulder. "We need some privacy."

After Alissia stumbled into the bathroom, Farrah closed and locked the door. "Come!" she ordered, pulling Alissia to the standing mirror.

Staring at their reflection, Farrah said, "I know this isn't the dress Luke imagined you in, but they made you a gown just like it. It's already at the house with your other belongings."

Alissia nodded.

"Now, tell me what you see," Farrah urged softly. "Do you like it?"

Taking in the shimmery makeup around her eyes, Alissia turned her face side to side. She leaned closer and squinted, impressed with the detail in the floral design painted along her forehead.

"It brings out the glow in your eyes," Farrah noted. "And they'll be glowing a *lot* later tonight."

"Are these bella flowers?" Alissia asked, eyeing her floral headdress. "They're so tiny. How are they glowing without water?"

"They're not fully grown." Farrah pointed to the back of Alissia's head. "There's a small capsule of water built into it, and it'll keep them glowing until morning."

"Everything shimmers. Even my hair."

Farrah nodded. "I know you said you're accustomed to white dresses for the ceremony, but there's a reason for all these purple hues."

She pointed to the bottom of the dress, where layers of silky, thin fabric in a variety of rich, purple tones hung down. Embellished with handcrafted flowers, a thick ribbon at Alissia's waist separated those loose layers from a fitted, deep purple and one-shoulder top.

"These colors represent the surge between the two of you." Farrah met Alissia's gaze in the mirror and smiled. "Under normal circumstances, you'd both have purple blood, and during the bonding process, a massive surge of power would happen between the two of you."

"Is that why my veins glowed and my temperature rose when I tried to kiss Luke?"

"Yes. Your body's eager to finish the bond, and it won't take much for that to happen."

Alissia turned around to look at Farrah. "What exactly *is* going to happen?"

"Well, I don't know much about human intimacy, but the first time—or rather, the first few times—Medicians are together, we not only connect physically, but we also connect mentally. You've already started the mental link, so I don't fully know what'll happen tonight."

She smiled and put her hand on Alissia's arm. "I do know the two of you have been through a lot, and tonight marks a new beginning for both of you."

A mysterious grin spread to her face, and she added, "You need to know how to work this dress." Tapping the floral ribbon at Alissia's waist, she said, "If you give a quick tug on the tie in the back, this'll fall away, turning the dress into a gown." She lifted her hand to the back of her own shoulder. "See if you can feel the tie back there."

Alissia felt along the soft material at her shoulder and nodded. "I feel something."

"Well, after the belt has been removed, it only takes a tug on that tie at your shoulder for the entire gown to fall away."

Farrah stepped back and smiled, taking in Alissia's appearance. "We customarily wear our zeer gowns again during our peaks of fertility, so this shouldn't be the only time you wear it."

Seeing Alissia's confusion, Farrah explained, "I don't know how your body was affected in that area during your transition, but

Medician women aren't as fertile as humans. For that reason, our ovulation times are somewhat special for us."

She paused thoughtfully before continuing, "When a bonded female goes through a fertile peak, she and her zeer take a break from their duties for a mini retreat. They devote their time to each other, and during those special occasions, the female sleeps in her zeer gown. It's a tradition."

"So that's why I haven't had a menstrual cycle since my change?"

Farrah nodded. "That makes sense."

"How will I know when I'm fertile?"

"Oh, you'll know," Farrah assured. "But let's not worry about that just yet." She turned Alissia back to the mirror. "Look how beautiful you are."

Alissia smiled at her reflection as she moved her head from side to side, admiring the subtle braiding mixed into her long, curly hair. "I look like a wingless fairy. What glasses am I going to wear?"

"The trail's highly shaded, and you won't need any."

Alissia held out her foot and looked down at her soft slipper. Decorated with smaller versions of the flowers along her belt, the shoe looked like a piece of art. It matched perfectly with her arm cuffs. Starting at her middle fingers, handcrafted vines with small, purple flowers wrapped around her arms, stopping below her elbows.

"It's beautiful," she said, setting her foot down.

"You mean *you're* beautiful. And tonight's going to be perfect. You have no worries."

"I feel his anticipation," Alissia confided. She placed her hands over her stomach, as if that would help to calm her nerves.

Farrah chuckled. "Yes, I'm sure you do. Mammula was right about the extra stress you're going to feel from the unfinished bond. I suggest you focus on your breathing as you go through the ceremony." She lifted her finger, stressing, "Or you can remind yourself this is the last night you'll see Salvatore. That could balance things out."

Alissia frowned slightly and nodded, dropping her hands from her waist. "I'm going to miss him."

"I know, dear."

"We're still doing the ceremony like I wanted, right?"

Farrah nodded. "He'll walk you down the aisle." She glanced at the door. "Are you ready?"

Alissia stared at her reflection for a moment before turning around. "Let's do this!"

She followed Farrah back into the dining room, and Corrah gave her a matching, shimmery cloak with a hood. Although lightweight and thin, the extra covering over her head and shoulders helped with her nerves.

Mammula handed her a stunning bouquet made with black and purple flowers. Then the women stood before Alissia for a final assessment. As they admired her beauty and praised the dress, a rush of emotions suddenly came over her.

She quickly looked down at the bouquet in her hands and fixed a smile onto her face. Looking back up, she said a short prayer of gratitude for the women in the room. Somehow, they made her feel like part of their family.

Satisfied with her appearance, the women ushered her out of the house, where a line of small carriages awaited. Salvatore, the lone person waiting outside, instantly stood from a nearby rocking chair.

Alissia stopped and smiled, taking comfort in his presence. The look on his face nearly brought a tear from her eye, and she blinked it away.

He rushed over and grabbed her hand. Taking in her appearance, he beamed his approval. "You're like a rare goya flower that grows in the harshest environs, only to bloom into one of the most beautiful plants in the world." Looking firmly into her eyes, he added, "It's your time to blossom, Alissia, and to share this moment with you, will always remain one of my greatest honors in life."

He held out his arm, and she accepted. Then he led her down the steps and toward the last carriage in the short line. Careful not to crush the many flowers decorating the ceremonial carriage, he helped her into her seat.

"Are you ready for this?" he asked, taking a seat beside her.

"I've been ready!"

Salvatore slipped his arm into hers and took hold of her hand. He lifted her arm cuff to his nose and smiled before dropping their hands onto his leg.

"You smell delightful."

"I should. Farrah's had me rubbing oil into my skin and hair for days." Alissia grinned, eyeing his loose, shimmery black shirt. "You look nice."

Their carriage began to move, and her heart fluttered in anticipation as she watched the small procession of excited women.

"You're going to be happy here," Salvatore replied.

Alissia nodded and looked down at their hands. Lines creased her forehead as she struggled for the right words. Without looking up, she said, "Thank you for walking me down the aisle today. It means a lot."

Lifting her chin, he looked into her eyes. "It means a lot for me, too, Alissia. This past year I've come to know you as my own daughter." He smiled. "You fit perfectly into my life—just as wild and stubborn as Lita and her mother."

His hand left her chin, and he stated confidently, "You chose the right man. I'm happy knowing Luke will always be by your side." Turning his gaze forward, he grinned and added, "I believe he's strong enough to handle you."

She laughed, and his expression turned serious as he looked back at her. "I told Luke the same thing. He needs you too, Alissia. You're the first woman to ever catch his interest, and I believe you're the first person he's ever let into his heart. You two belong together."

Salvatore motioned toward the carriages in front of them. "And you have a loving family in this valley." Dropping his hand in his lap, he said, "When I think of you and Luke, I'll always picture the two of you completely happy. That doesn't mean life will always be perfect, but I believe the two of you will have everything you'll need to get through things—especially each other."

Alissia felt her eyes moisten, and she smiled slightly. "I'll always miss you."

"None of that tonight," he replied, shaking his head. "I'm going back to the island—where I belong—and I imagine Lita, Duff, Santo, and I will often stare up at the stars thinking of you and Luke. You'll never be forgotten, but we'll always smile when thinking of you." He gave her hand a squeeze, "And I want you to promise the same. Always smile when you think of us."

She nodded. "We'll stay in touch with the globes. When are you leaving?"

"Tomorrow morning, but I plan to come back to the cave entrance within a few days to drop off your belongings. Hoyle and his sons have agreed to pick them up for you."

Alissia's face twisted in thought as she stared at their hands for a moment. Giving a sigh, she looked back up. "I guess I don't plan to leave the valley again. It's just too dangerous, and I know the Medicians don't want me too."

"And I agree."

"Can you do me a favor?" she asked hesitantly.

"Of course. Anything."

"Can you let Anika, Langley, and Grady know that I'm happy? I'll never forget them, and I wish them the best."

Salvatore smiled and squeezed her hand. "I will."

"Oh, and could you send me a note with my belongings to let me know if they made it back safely and how they're doing?"

He nodded as the carriage stopped in front of the cave. A small band of stringed instruments set up near the entrance began to play, and Alissia looked up to admire the large spheres hanging from the branches. Made with white bella flowers, the orbs sparkled in the evening shade.

"Ready?" Farrah asked, opening the door to the carriage. Mia and Fang stood behind her.

Salvatore stepped down, and Alissia accepted his help from the carriage.

"Hoyle's already inside to support Luke, so I'll walk alone." Farrah pointed to the small line of women forming at the entrance. "You and Salvatore will enter last, and you'll need to wait until the music changes before you begin." She put her hand on Alissia's arm and smiled. "Any questions?"

Alissia shook her head.

Farrah started toward the line, and Salvatore hooked his arm into Alissia's. He led her to the back of the procession, directly behind Fang and Mia.

"Are you all right?" he asked, reaching out to steady her.

Alissia blinked back a wave of emotions and nodded. "I think Luke just realized we're here." She closed her eyes and inhaled deeply before letting out a shaky breath. Looking up at Salvatore, she smiled.

"Since we're traditionally not supposed to see each other the week before the wedding, we decided not to mentally talk to each other today." Alissia gave a half shrug. "At least keep one day mysterious. Although, it's not fair that he got to sleep in our house and bed last night, while I still don't know anything about the house."

She added smugly, "This way he doesn't know anything about me or my dress today."

Salvatore chuckled and shook his head. Patting her hand at his arm, he said, "I promise you'll love the house."

Alissia's heartbeat quickened when she turned to see Farrah disappearing into the cave. Her grip tightened on her bouquet as Fang and Mia began to walk.

"I used to compare these things to funerals," she muttered.

"Really? I would have never guessed you to be so cynical," Salvatore teased.

The band paused briefly, and a new tune began to play.

Chapter *16*

*A*lissia's body trembled while walking through the tunnel of glowing bella flowers. Inhaling deeply, she squared her shoulders, and as she slowly exhaled through her mouth, she lifted her chin, forcing her emotions from her face.

Her grip tightened on her bouquet when she spotted Luke's intense gaze. Standing at the bottom of the steps to the platform, Fang and Mia sat at his feet, both watching her intently.

Unlike the rugged, Latin warrior that often came to mind when she thought of Luke, his traditional ceremonial clothing reminded Alissia of a South Asian groom. In a deep shade of purple, matching the shimmery top of her dress, his embroidered loafers and loose, long-sleeved shirt appeared soft and delicate, along with his black, relaxed pants.

Salvatore stopped in front of Luke and pulled Alissia's hand from his arm. He kissed it before holding it out, and a rush of heat filled her veins when Luke took her hand. Looking down, she focused on her feet as he led her up the stairs, where they stopped in front of an ancient dressed in a purple robe.

The elderly man smiled and cleared his throat before loudly announcing, "A zeer bond is a powerful gift from our Creator. It unites two, so they become one. When one feels joy, the other does as well, and when one feels pain, so shall the other.

"This bond carries throughout a lifetime, and it passes into death. The two of you shall always remain linked, and no one—or anything—of this world can break it. It is a powerful bond, having the strength to bring joy, but also the strength to cause pain—and even death."

He paused, glancing between Luke and Alissia, as if to let his words sink in. "It will take time to learn how to live as one, but keeping the Creator at the center of your relationship will help to guide you on your journey.

"Luke, you've chosen Alissia as your zeer, and you're committing to a life of love and service to her. What do you have to say at this time?"

Luke pulled a ring from a front pocket of his shirt and turned to Alissia. Lifting her hand between them, he held out the ring.

"I never imagined I would ever find love," he began, his voice strong and steady, "and I had long given up on such thoughts. I first noticed your beauty at the Eldership ball, and when I finally met you face-to-face, you surprised me with a painful kick—determined to save yourself."

He paused, and Alissia smiled at the sound of mild laughter coming from below.

Luke's mouth twitched, but he continued, "From that very moment, you threw my mind and emotions into a whirlwind, causing foreign feelings to rise within me. Even at your lowest, I see strength in you I've not seen in others. Your loyalty's true and rare, and it's something I never imagined I could find and depend on in a person."

His voice cracked on the last word, and he used his hand with the ring to quickly dab at the corner of his eye. As a tear threatened to escape, Alissia wondered how she could get to it, with both of her hands taken. When she glanced down at her bouquet, Luke chuckled and lifted his hand to her cheek.

"You've given me the hope I never had," he said, swiping the wetness from her face, "and you've given me a love I never knew existed." Pulling his hand back, he grinned. "You also drive me mad quite often, and I look forward to taming you."

Alissia laughed, shaking her head.

Luke glanced down at the ring in his palm. "Following tradition, I crafted our rings myself." In response to her raised brows, he nodded before continuing, "The three interwoven bands represent our zeer bond. With our Creator at the center of our bond, we'll never stray from what's truly important."

Lifting her hand, he placed the ring on the tip of her finger and gazed into her eyes. "I will always love you, Alissia. Like this ring, we're bound together. Through life—and into eternity—I'll always be at your side."

He slipped the ring down her finger and gave her hand a squeeze. Leaning closer, he whispered, "You're mine."

Following his lead, she turned back to the ancient. He smiled and said loudly, "Alissia, you've chosen Luke as your zeer, and you're committing to a life of love and service to him. What do you have to say at this time?"

She turned back to Luke, and he released her hand to retrieve another ring from his pocket. As he held it out, she gave the matching ring a quick inspection before taking it.

Looking up at Luke, warmth rushed up Alissia's neck. She felt herself swallow as she tried to remember the words she planned to say during this dreaded part of the ceremony. Seeing the corner of his mouth curl up in amusement, she met his gaze with determination.

"I remember you saying some people weren't meant for love," she began, forcing strength into her voice, "and those words sounded too familiar. Like you, I never imagined I could ever give all of myself to someone, and I only hoped to find a man I could share a portion of my heart with one day."

Her smile faltered, but she quickly regained her composure. "I tried to fight it—to fight you—but you wouldn't let me push you away." He shook his head, and her voice cracked as she continued, "You've given me something I never believed I could have—something I gave up on long ago."

Alissia looked at the bouquet she held, and the ancient must have noticed her confusion. Lifting his hands, he whispered, "I'll hold it for you."

She smiled and passed the flowers to him before taking Luke's hand. Placing the ring on the tip of his finger, she looked into his eyes.

"For the rest of our lives—and into eternity—I am yours, and you are mine," she vowed firmly. She felt his emotions swelling within her, and when his lips began to tremble, she smiled and squeezed his hand. "I love you, Luke Harrison, and I always will."

As soon as she slipped the ring over his finger, he pushed the hood of her cloak from her head. Loud cheers instantly rang out, filling the cavern with noise. Luke pulled her into his arms and kissed her lightly on the lips.

"There'll be more of that tonight," he whispered. He quickly pulled away and turned toward their guests before grabbing her hand and lifting it into the air.

Alissia laughed at the sound of Fang's howling, and she looked down to find Mia jumping around at the bottom of the steps.

Following tradition, Luke removed her cloak to reveal his prized zeer to the guests. He tossed it to Farrah before turning around to thank the ancient for his part in their ceremony. Then he swiftly picked up Alissia and carried her down the stairs. Setting her down in front of Salvatore, he wrapped his arms around her from behind.

"You're married!" Salvatore announced, his voice competing with the band and shouting around them.

Alissia laughed. "I am!" She lifted her hand. "And he made our rings!"

"I know. I was there."

"Did you help?"

Salvatore shook his head and leaned closer so that she could hear him better. "That's against tradition. He had to make them himself."

The sound of a horn filled the cavern, and everyone quieted and turned to face a woman standing on the platform. Alissia recognized her as the caretaker named Kayla. She waited for the horn to stop before saying loudly, "Thank you." Her eyes went to Luke and Alissia. "I would like to congratulate the two of you on your special occasion, as well as welcome you to the valley. We have a lot planned, and I know everyone's eager for the celebration." Scanning the crowd, she asked, "Shall we begin?"

"Come this way," Farrah directed, taking Alissia's hand. She and Hoyle led the new couple and Salvatore to the entrance of the dining room.

"We stand here, so the guests can congratulate you on their way in," she explained, positioning Luke by the door.

"Do I go in?" Salvatore asked.

Farrah shook her head. "No, we stand next to them as parents." She positioned him beside Alissia, and Hoyle stepped next to him before Farrah took her place at the beginning of the line.

Alissia tried not to appear awkward as she greeted each Medician entering the large dining area. It seemed as if everyone had helped in some way to build or decorate her new home, and they enjoyed giving mysterious hints to heighten her curiosity. The ancients and their zeers even contributed, and Luke and Salvatore seemed to remember everyone from their visits to the home.

Like a fine restaurant with soft lighting and a harpist playing in the background, the servers catered to the guests. The humans dined at the taller table in the corner, and each time Alissia caught someone looking her way, she smiled, knowing they had to be curious about humans.

Although she laughed and talked often during her meal, the soothing ambiance eventually calmed her, and after dessert, she sat back in her seat and looked around.

Surrounded by carefree conversation and laughter, Alissia suddenly felt like an outsider at her own party. The same still voice that often spoke to her as a child as she watched other children on the playground whispered into her thoughts, *You're not like them. You weren't made for happiness. Something will happen. It always does.*

The image of a young child seared into her memory came to mind. With haunting green eyes, bruised and swollen from crying, the ghost from her past whispered, *Never forget. Don't set yourself up for the pain.*

The tinkling sound of a bell pulled Alissia from her thoughts, and she instinctively glanced at Luke. Staring ahead, he appeared oblivious to her touch of melancholy, and she smiled in relief as she turned to Hoyle, now standing from his seat.

He set the bell on the table and picked up his drink. Turning to Luke and Alissia, he smiled and motioned to the Medicians around him.

"Everyone here knows the sacrifices the two of you made during your long journey. You could have easily given up or chosen to reveal our secrets, yet you never even considered that option. You never doubted our worth, and you repeatedly risked your own lives to protect ours."

Locking eyes with hers, he said, "Alissia, Farrah and I have never regretted saving you. Although we experienced great fear after you were taken, we never questioned the value of your life, and we continuously prayed for your safety."

He turned his gaze to Luke and smiled. "And, Luke, our Creator answered by sending you. Not only equipped with physical strength and special training, you're an honorable man. Honorable and worthy—just like Alissia."

Hoyle lifted his drink in the air. "Welcome to our valley, and welcome into our family. Your journey's over, and we welcome you both home."

Alissia took a sip of her warm drink and set it back on the table. Everyone clapped as Hoyle sat down, and when he looked her way, she mouthed, "Thank you."

He responded with a nod as Salvatore rose from his seat, and the room quieted again.

"I often have to remind myself that I've only known these two for about a year," Salvatore began. He motioned to Hoyle. "It's exactly like you said. I've watched them cope with their many struggles, and I've witnessed the choices they've made." Shaking his head, he said, "They never questioned putting your lives before their own. And, yes, they're both honorable and loyal."

His gaze went to Luke and Alissia as he said, "And they're so much more. My year with these two created enduring memories that I'll cherish for the rest of my life. Even through their struggles, they continuously gifted my heart with joy and laughter."

Salvatore smiled at Alissia, as she dabbed at her eye. "I'll never forget the fire in your heart, Alissia. Passionate in all you do and a bit rough around the edges, you can easily be a child of fury when needed."

Cocking his head, Salvatore's eyes never left hers. "But, you're also so much more. Cut and polished by the frictions you've endured in life, all the grit and ugliness forced away, you're now a true gem. When I look at you, I see a rare spectrum of beauty—not only in appearance, but also at the core of your being."

Alissia felt herself swallow as Luke set his hand in her lap and wrapped his fingers around hers. Aware of everyone watching her, she sat frozen in place.

"I've often told you that you remind me of Lita and her mother," Salvatore continued, "and I have no doubt I'm going to miss you with the intensity of a father." Leaning forward, he emphasized, "A *loving* father."

Alissia smiled up at Salvatore, grateful for the mild calmness flowing into her from Luke's hand. Her fear of losing control in front of everyone lessened.

"And, Luke," Salvatore said, turning his gaze, "after countless hours of traveling by your side, I will forever remember our private conversations, and I consider it a great honor to have earned the rare gift of your trust.

"When I look at you, I not only see a man of great strength and integrity, I also see a young boy who made a choice not to become jaded—with people or life. Without a father to help guide you through the struggles of your youth, you made many difficult choices on your own, and although I know the path you chose has never been easy, as it often weighs you down, I believe you've never strayed from your true purpose in life."

Alissia's eyes filled with moisture as Luke's emotions seeped into her. She pulled her hand from beneath his and placed it on top so that she could focus on soothing him.

"Since birth," Salvatore continued, "the flames of life have consumed you, and instead of leaving you charred and weak, those flames only made you stronger. Like gollian, the rarest and strongest form of steel to be made, the hands of our Creator crafted you. After removing all the impurities with the burning flames, He deposited the strongest and rarest minerals known to man, gifting you with the strength to endure the weight of this world—allowing you to suffer for others without yielding."

He lifted his drink, and Alissia picked up her chet with a trembling hand.

"I never asked either of you to think of me as a father, and that expectation has never been there. However, I can't control my feelings." Salvatore lifted his drink to each of them as he added, "Alissia, you will always be my beautiful gem. And, Luke, I'll always picture you riding at my side when I feel weak or threatened. My son. My daughter." He placed his hand over his heart. "You both live in my heart, and although I leave here tomorrow, you'll forever be a part of me."

Tears escaped both eyes as Alissia took a sip of her chet. The sound of clapping filled the air, and she set her drink on the table. Looking down, she grabbed her napkin and dabbed at her eyes with trembling hands, careful not to smear any paint.

She sniffed and looked up, patting her nose with the napkin. Seeing Salvatore watching her with a tender look on his face, she rolled her eyes and began to wipe away more tears.

"Time for dancing!" Farrah called out, rising to her feet.

Alissia laughed and nodded vigorously, thankful for the distraction.

Chapter 17

Once outside, Salvatore walked over to the silent band and picked up a small, stringed instrument. With a grin to Luke and Alissia, he lifted it to his chin and began to play a slow waltz.

"Shall we?"

Alissia accepted Luke's hand. "You knew?"

"Of course." He led her to the middle of the clearing before placing his hand on her back. As they began to move to the music, he closed his eyes and smiled. A wave of happiness flooded into Alissia. Staring up at him, she took pleasure in seeing his unguarded expression.

"We're going to hit someone," she gently teased.

Luke shook his head. "I can still lead you with my eyes closed. Besides, I think we're the only ones dancing."

"You think, but you don't know."

His eyes opened, and he stared at her for a moment. "You know, I've had to watch you dance in the arms of Grady and Ian—as they both claimed you for themselves. But tonight, in front of everyone, I get to hold you."

His mouth curled upward, and he added, "I'm dancing with *my* wife."

Heat filled Alissia's veins, and she dropped her gaze to his chest. When she looked back up, she found his eyes closed again. The smile on his face nearly brought her to tears. Knowing only struggles and pain since they first met, she could barely believe she would spend the rest of her life in his arms.

She smiled, and in that moment, she vowed she would do all she could to make her husband happy.

The corner of Luke's mouth twitched, and he opened his eyes. "Shall we leave now?"

Alissia glanced around the clearing, at the many faces staring their way. "But we're only on the first dance. Don't they expect more from us?"

"We're on the second song, and I really don't care what they expect from us at this moment."

She chuckled. "Then you can be the one to get us out of here— without offending anyone."

Luke stopped abruptly and winked. "Watch how it's done."

He spun around and pulled her toward the band area.

Salvatore waited until the two of them stopped in front of him before lowering his instrument. "Problem?"

Luke shook his head and glanced over his shoulder, at Hoyle and Farrah, currently walking toward them. He waited until they stopped beside him before explaining, "I wanted to show

Alissia the house before it gets dark. You know, let her see the outside area."

Salvatore raised his brows and grinned. *"Really?"*

"I'm dying to see it," Alissia replied, a bit too enthusiastically. She looked at Farrah. "What else do we need to do before leaving?"

Farrah motioned to the clearing behind her. "It's going to be beautiful out here after it gets dark, with all the spheres in the trees." She frowned, putting her hands on her hips. "And you haven't done your zeer dance."

Remembering her first dance in the valley, Alissia cringed. "I . . . uh . . . really don't want to get sweaty tonight." She lifted her arm and took a whiff of the floral cuff. "I mean, I smell like a flower."

Seeing Salvatore's amused expression, she added, "Luke should . . ." She shook her head and began again, "I want to continue to smell like a flower, not sweat."

Laughter erupted from Salvatore, and he walked behind her and Luke. Gripping both their shoulders, he said, "I believe they're done for the night. How about I say my goodbyes, and we let them leave?"

Farrah sighed. Dropping her hands from her hips, she pointed up at Salvatore. "This means you'll be dancing tonight," she said sternly. Turning around, she added over her shoulder, "I'll have them ready the carriage."

Hoyle watched Farrah as she walked away. Then he smiled up at Luke and Alissia. "You're not the first to leave a zeer ceremony early." Giving a shrug, he added, "You vowed. You greeted your guests. You ate, and you danced. You're now legally bonded."

Leaning closer, he winked at Alissia and grinned. "It would be a horrible thing if you lost your floral scent before getting home."

Without waiting for a response, Hoyle started after Farrah, and Alissia frowned, pulling her hand from Luke's.

He chuckled and gave a shrug. "I told you to let me handle it."

"She does smell nice," Salvatore noted. Leaning down, he sniffed Alissia's hair. "Is that sweet orion I smell?"

"Indigo," she mumbled, her frown deepening. "It grows on the mountain."

The band began to play a lively tune, and Alissia started toward the carriage, where Eaton and Gil stood waiting. Two miniature horses walked toward them.

Farrah and Hoyle met her at the carriage, and Salvatore and Luke stepped beside her.

"We have something for you," Farrah announced, holding out a small box with a bow on top. Looking between Luke and Alissia, she said solemnly, "It's time."

Alissia accepted the gift and untied the bow before passing the ribbon to Hoyle. Lifting the lid revealed two crystals hanging from cords. About an inch long, the clear, columned rods had dull, pointed ends. They looked identical.

Farrah reached beneath the top of her dress and pulled out a purple crystal. "I know you've heard about these, but it's time you receive your own."

"Jades," Alissia uttered, lifting one from the box. Luke picked up the other one and began to inspect it.

"Put them on and never take them off," Farrah instructed, dropping her crystal back in place. "They'll absorb your power over time and begin to change color." She took the box from Alissia and smiled. "And tonight there'll be a lot of power flowing between the two of you."

Alissia stared down at the powerless jade in her hand, confused by the Medicians' complete acceptance of her.

"Thank you," Luke said. He put on the necklace and dropped the crystal beneath his shirt. "You've given us more than we ever imagined."

Alissia nodded and slipped her head through the cord. She tucked the crystal beneath her dress and let it fall onto her chest.

"We should begin to gather everyone for their departure," Hoyle said. Farrah nodded, and he looked up at Salvatore. "How much time do you need?"

"Not long. Tonight's their night, and I don't want to take away from that."

Alissia began to regret the idea of leaving early, suddenly not wanting to part from Salvatore's side.

"We'll visit you after your zeer retreat," Farrah replied, wrapping her arms around Alissia's waist. She gave a squeeze before pulling away and smiled. "You're going to love your new home. It's fully stocked and has everything you need." Taking Alissia's hand, she added softly, "Enjoy tonight, child. Don't worry about anything."

Turning to Luke, Farrah waited for Hoyle to finish with him before switching places. Hoyle patted Alissia's back as he gave her a hug, and then he pulled away and smiled up at her.

"We'll see you again after your retreat. Enjoy. You've earned this rest." He took Farrah's hand, and they walked toward the clearing, now filled with dancers.

"You two deserve this zeer retreat," Salvatore replied. Alissia blinked back tears, and he shook his head. "None of that. Not tonight."

"Maybe we should stay longer," Alissia said, turning to Luke.

Salvatore put his fingers beneath her chin and lifted her face toward his. Staring down at her tenderly, he said, "This is the night you and Luke have been waiting for. We knew this moment would come, and we've made the most of our time together." He smiled, his face filling with emotion. "Please don't make me leave here thinking I ruined this night for the two of you."

Alissia wrapped her arms around him and squeezed. They held each other for a long moment as she struggled with what to say.

"It's never been this hard to say goodbye," she groaned.

"I feel the same," Salvatore replied softly. "But we still have the globes, and they gave me a few jades. That'll give us plenty of talking time. You'll even be able to see my face, and I'll get to see Luke after he changes."

Pulling away, Salvatore bent down and looked into her face. "I love you, Alissia." A tear escaped from his eye and streamed down his cheek. "Now promise me you'll forget about me tonight—and the next few days."

Alissia nodded, feeling her lips tremble. As he kissed her forehead, she whispered, "I love you, too."

"I know you do." He turned to Luke and pulled him in for a hug. "I'm happy for you, son."

Luke nodded, returning the embrace.

Salvatore pulled away and put his hand on Luke's shoulder, meeting his gaze. "Take care, and I'll talk to you on the globe soon."

He turned abruptly and started toward the clearing, where Hoyle and Farrah worked to gather everyone. Luke took Alissia's hand, and they both watched Salvatore for a moment.

"We'll talk to him again," Luke said, turning to her. His eyes gleamed with unshed tears. "Ready?"

She nodded, and he led her to the carriage, where Eaton and Gil stood waiting. Eaton held out her cloak, and she accepted it and put it on before stepping into the carriage. Luke sat down beside her, and they smiled and began to wave to the shouting guests gathering around.

Alissia easily spotted Salvatore standing alone beneath a tree. Her eyes locked with his, and he gave a nod and smiled. Just as her tears threatened to break free, a furry, little pixet landed in her lap, causing her to cry out in alarm.

"Mia!" she fussed, holding her hand to her heart. "Must you?"

The tiny creature sat down, staring up at her innocently.

"Oh, no, you don't! You're not going home with us tonight," Alissia asserted. "And you're not nannying us anymore, either."

"She only wants to say goodbye," Farrah yelled, from beside the carriage. Her voice competed with the laughter around them.

Luke began to scratch Mia vigorously behind the ear, and she closed her eyes, reveling in his touch.

"No more bites from you, little one." Leaning down, he taunted, "Alissia's finally *all* mine, and I can do whatever I want now."

With a smug grin, he pulled his hand away and sat back in his seat.

Mia opened her eyes and narrowed them his way. Her mouth curled up, revealing pointed teeth.

Alissia laughed while rubbing her hand through Mia's fur. "I'll see you soon," she promised, before passing the tiny creature to Farrah.

The carriage lurched forward, and Luke and Alissia waved. Locking eyes with Salvatore one last time, she kept sight of him until her head could turn no more.

As her gaze drifted to her lap, she closed her eyes and thought, *So this is how it feels to lose someone you love.*

Chapter 18

*L*uke picked up her hand and gave it a kiss before setting it on his leg. "I have something to show you at the house. I think it'll help."

"I'm sorry. It's our wedding night."

He shook his head. "You're forgetting that some of what you're feeling is from me. I miss him, too." His gaze drifted ahead, and he added softly, "I've never known anyone like him."

"He was special," Alissia agreed, before retreating back into her thoughts.

When the horses turned onto a side trail, Luke looked at her and grinned. "Ready to see your new home?"

"It's about time," she muttered, staring at the two-story log cabin. As they continued along the private trail, surrounded by massive trees, she noticed the cabin's stone accenting. She also envisioned her new Medician family filling the many rockers and swings lining the front porch.

"You haven't seen anything yet!" Luke exclaimed. He hopped from the carriage before it came to a stop. "Don't move while I unhitch the horses."

She nodded, taking in the fine craftsmanship of her new home.

Seconds later, Luke opened her side of the carriage and took her hand. "Ready?" Without waiting for an answer, he began to lead her toward the side of the house. "Although I know you can see in the dark, I can't, and I really do want to show you the outside before we lose our sunlight."

They stopped at a stone archway along the side of the cabin, and she peered inside to find a small, partially enclosed area with a wooden table in the center. The baskets, grass flooring, and lack of chairs gave the appearance of some kind of workroom.

"This is where we'll cut and sort our herbs and vegetables," Luke explained. Pointing, he said, "That wooden door leads to a small storage and drying room, while the curtain leads into the house. We don't have to worry about wild animals getting in—or burglars. The Medicians live openly out here."

He turned to Alissia and grinned. "And when we walk outside in the morning, we'll find the table full of freshly picked food."

She nodded, trying to conceal her amusement over his sudden enthusiasm, something rare coming from him. "We plant extra and employ certain animals," she replied. "It's one of the things Farrah taught me."

Luke turned back to the work area and pointed to a corner. "Oh, and I can build a distiller over there, if you decide you want to process your own oils later." He shrugged, "Or we can simply trade for them. It all depends on what you want to do out here. I can even build you an art room, if that's something you want to learn."

Alissia chuckled, shaking her head. "Definitely not art."

"Well, we have plenty of time to figure out how we want to contribute to the valley." He gave her a quick peck on the cheek and pointed to a nearby path that led into the trees.

"That goes to the garden, but we don't need to see it tonight. With all these trees, it gets dark out here early, and there are other things I want to show you."

Luke tugged Alissia along, and as soon as they entered the back yard, her eyes darted around the clearing. Seeing layers of curtains hanging along the back of the cabin, she squinted, hoping to glimpse more than the faint glow of white bella flowers on the opposite side.

"We didn't plant a ground covering," Luke said, as he continued leading her toward the thick woodland. "We wanted you to choose it for yourself. There's a supply of seeds and cuttings on the other side of the house, and we can go through them later."

"Oh, so I get to choose something," Alissia responded wryly.

Luke laughed. "With your exceptional ability with plants, everyone's expecting great things out here. They're also talking about how you can help with landscaping in the rest of the valley."

Stepping onto a path through the trees, he motioned upward. "We also need to plant bella flowers along this trail."

Alissia nodded. Hearing running water, she asked, "There's a creek back here?"

"It's the same one that flows by Hoyle and Farrah's house." Luke squeezed her hand and grinned. "Except, ours has a few additions."

"Like what?"

"You'll see."

The path soon ended, and they stopped near two benches on the grassy bank of the creek, where clear, flowing water moved along the rocks.

"Well?" he asked, grinning proudly.

Alissia shook her head, speechless, at the sight of an open hut built over the creek. Constructed on beams, high above the water, a large canvas hung beneath it, like a tightly woven circus net.

"Let me show you," Luke said, pulling her toward the stairs.

When they stopped on a small landing at the edge of the tarp, he put his arm around her waist. "Imagine a group of children playing and sleeping out here when we have gatherings."

She looked at him in disbelief, having a hard time imagining him as an eager host. "We're throwing parties now?"

He chuckled and let go of her waist. Turning to face her, he lifted her hand between them, where he held it with both of his. His expression turned somber, and he stared down at her for a moment.

"We've really only known trouble and chaos since we met," he began, "and neither of us have many great memories from our past." Pausing, he appeared to struggle with his words. "Today's the beginning of our new life together, where we get to make new memories—in a new place and with new people. We're even giving up our humanity, along with everything else we know."

He kissed her hand and smiled. "I promise to fill the rest of your life with happiness, and when we're old and frail, we'll both look back and cherish the life we lived together."

Alissia returned his smile and squeezed his hand. "I love you."

Luke turned back to the hanging canvas. "We need to continue with the tour, so we can get to the main part. There's some bedding upstairs, so our guests can sleep out here, too."

She nodded. Looking out at the massive tarp, she envisioned laughing Medician children rolling and running around before falling asleep. As she continued up the stairs, she imagined herself drifting to sleep in Luke's arms to the sound of flowing water.

Inside the rectangular hut, Luke dropped Alissia's hand and sat down in one of the swinging chairs clustered in the four corners. From there, he watched her expression as she eyed the many floor cushions and poofs lining the low, surrounding walls, leaving the center of the room empty.

Her gaze went to the thick curtains hanging down in each of the corners, with large chests arranged near them. The opposite end of the room contained a small bar with cooling and warming stones lining it, and she walked behind it to find a cooling box.

"Have you figured it out yet?" Luke asked, leaning back with his hands behind his head.

Alissia walked over to stand in front of him. "I see the bar, so we'll be entertaining here."

"And?"

"And what?"

He stood and strolled to the center of the room. Facing the breeze coming in from one of the long, open walls, his expression turned grave. He closed his eyes and lifted his hands above his head, positioning himself into the first warrior position.

Alissia laughed as he began to transition into the second position. "I see. I get it." With a playful scowl, she crossed her arms. "Luke, I do not make faces like that!"

He continued into the third warrior position, still mocking her expression, and she bounded over and reached out to knock him down. Without opening his eyes, he straightened and grabbed her hands, and she gasped as her back suddenly slammed into his chest.

Locked inside Luke's firm embrace, Alissia's skin tingled from the feel of pure muscle pressing against her body. A cool breeze caressed her face, filling her lungs with his spicy, woodsy scent. His warm breath at her ear drowned out the tranquil sound of water flowing outside, and she closed her eyes, melting into his body.

"No, not here," Luke said, backing away abruptly. "Not now. Let's finish this tour."

She turned around to see him running his hand through his hair. Looking at her, he shook his head before he spun around and pointed.

"The curtains close if we want to warm the place, and the chests are full of blankets for overnight guests." Grabbing her hand, he hurried toward the stairs. "Of course, you've seen the bar, and the ceiling's covered in bella flowers for lighting. Any questions?"

Alissia laughed as she hurried down the stairs after Luke. As they walked back to the path, he pointed out a small waterfall along the opposite bank. The water dropped into a partially enclosed area with large rocks, separating a pool of calm water from the moving creek.

"They made a swimming hole," he said, without stopping.

As they stepped onto the dark path through the woodland, she took the lead and asked, "How did everything get built so fast?"

"You'd be amazed how many people worked on this, Alissia. There were many times we had extra people and animals just sitting around watching, because there were too many of us. I've never heard of some of the animals that helped, and even the women came out to bring food. You should have seen them decorating the inside. There's a lot of amazing talent in this valley. They brought in some unique items."

The two of them continued in silence for a while before Luke added, "They all considered it an honor to contribute in some way, even the ancients and their zeers. It seemed to mean a lot to them."

Alissia smiled. Pulling him along, she baited, "Do you trust them?"

After a thoughtful pause, he answered, "I do."

Her eyes widened in surprise, but she said nothing.

As they stepped into the clearing, he said, "Oh, and you have new yoga students. They're already talking about it, and they promised to help you maintain and wash all the cushions and blankets back there."

"I haven't heard anything."

"Well, no one could mention it to you until you saw the place. They had to keep it a secret."

Alissia frowned. "Sounds like you got to meet everyone, while I was kept busy cooking and cleaning. What else did I miss?"

Luke chuckled, and they soon stopped near the curtains extending along the back, lower level of the house. "You didn't miss anything." Turning around, he motioned to the clearing, nearly dark from the setting sun. "Now, imagine this place decorated in bella flowers and the ground covering of your choice. Oh, and I plan to set up a moving target for your knife throwing."

She gave the clearing a quick glance before turning back around. "I want to see the house."

"Are you sure?" he teased.

She responded with a dirty look.

"All right, stand here while I pull the hangings back." He walked over to where the curtains met and turned around. "There's different areas back here."

Alissia nodded, fighting her urge to run past the curtains.

Luke pulled back one side of the curtains to reveal two long tables surrounded by chairs. Although beautifully handcrafted from wood, they were both sized for Medicians.

Seeing him watching her expectantly, she smiled, and he quickly tied the curtains in place before crossing to the other side to do the same.

"Um, how much entertaining are we planning to do?" she asked.

"Not as much as it looks like." He took her hand and pulled her into the outside dining area, where white bella flowers grew along the walls and ceiling. "But I'm guessing we'll be hosting more parties than attending, since I can't even stand up in their homes. I believe that's why they built the extra place on the water, or at least, why it's so big and accommodating."

Alissia turned around and put her arms around Luke's waist, grinning up at him. "You beast!"

His chest trembled with laughter as he put his arm around her and pointed to the table in the corner. "We still have our spot."

She nodded, pulling away. "Next."

"Let's see what's behind the other curtains," he said, walking into the clearing.

The next set of curtains revealed a cozy porch adorned with hanging chairs and hammocks, perfect for relaxing outside. Without delay, Luke led her into the cabin, and as he showed her each room, he pointed out unique features and artisan pieces.

Like Farrah and Hoyle's home, built large enough for gatherings, the sitting room contained plenty of sofas. Blankets and pillows made from Alissia's chosen colors and fabrics adorned the house, and although the closets and cupboards were fully stocked, a large pile of gifts waited for them in the corner of the sitting room.

Alissia laughed when she noticed a group of furry, little beanies shuffling along the floor, and Luke removed her cloak before opening the door to a bathroom abounding with flowers. Water flowed down a stone wall, landing in a pool, and he pointed out some of the detailed craftsmanship before leaving her to freshen up.

Upstairs, they stopped at a set of double doors, intricately carved into pieces of art, and her anticipation grew when Luke told her to close her eyes. Inside, she found a spacious veranda containing comfy poofs and lounge chairs, and after a quick look around, he pointed to the far wall, also covered in bella flowers.

"What?" Alissia asked, when he continued to point. "It's a wall."

Luke grinned as he took her hand and led her to the railing. "See anything different now?"

She stared, squinting. "It's still a wall."

"You're just not seeing it."

As he led her toward the wall, she noticed an opening at the railing. A second wall behind it, also covered in bella flowers, blended so well with the first one, she had confused the two of them for one wall.

Luke grabbed Alissia from behind, and she cried out in alarm. "Close your eyes," he instructed, holding her in his arms.

"Why?"

He grinned down at her. "You'll see. I promise you'll like it."

She closed her eyes and felt herself being carried a short distance before he placed her on something soft. When he pulled away, she opened her eyes to find herself on a spacious hanging bed.

Sprawling out on her back, she rubbed her hands over the soft, shimmery bedding. Then she propped herself up on her elbows and looked out at the stars beyond the railed opening.

Rolling over, Alissia found nightstands situated in the two corners. Both topped with books, one held a beautiful teapot on a small heat stone. A light breeze flew in from the railed opening, causing the white bella flowers growing along the three walls and ceiling to tremble.

"Well, what do you think?" Luke asked. He gave the bed a slight push, and it began to swing gently.

"This is heavenly," she answered.

"Did you notice our reading materials? They're basically homework."

Alissia pulled a shimmery pillow toward her, admiring its beauty. "Well, if any of them are from Farrah, they're about herbs, oils, and recipes." Holding up her finger, she added. "Oh, and gardening. There's always gardening."

Luke chuckled. "I've been told I don't know the proper uses for our natural resources."

"What? Killing or maiming isn't important here?"

"Apparently not."

She sat up and dangled her feet from the side. "Are you going to join me up here or not?"

"Not." He took her hand and pulled her to the floor. "I have one more thing to show you, and it's important."

Chapter *19*

"Slow down! My legs are shorter than yours."

"I promised I'd show you this tonight," Luke responded, decreasing his pace.

Inside, they stopped at a nearby door, and he motioned to another closed door opposite them. "That's an extra bedroom." He released her hand and gripped the handle in front of them. "The sunlight doesn't do it justice, so it's important you see this for the first time tonight."

Luke opened the door and stepped aside. "You first."

Walking into the softly lit room, Alissia immediately noticed a radiant display in the far, right corner, where white bella flowers heavily covered the walls and ceiling. Strands of the glowing ivy hung from above, shining light on an open book.

About three feet tall, the great book reclined on an elaborately carved pedestal, made from dark, stained wood. Glow stones built into the pedestal framed the book, adding soft, blue lighting around the prominent centerpiece.

She crossed the room and stopped in front of the pedestal, her gaze never leaving the two pictures displayed on the pages of the book. Forcing back tears, she smiled slightly when Luke put his arms around her from behind.

"I don't understand," she said softly. Reaching out, she touched her fingertips to Salvatore's face on the page. "I know there aren't any cameras in this reality, but it looks so real."

"They're drawings."

She pulled her hand away, shaking her head. "They look exactly like black and white photographs." Staring at Salvatore's laughing eyes, she whispered, "So real."

"The artist has the ability to remember things vividly, and that's how he remembers you and Salvatore dancing together."

Alissia smiled, remembering how she and Salvatore had laughed and shouted while trying to keep up with the dancing circle. The drawings captured that moment exactly as she remembered.

Searching for missing details, she found none. Astonishingly, the artist even noticed the creases around Salvatore's eyes, along with his tattoos and jewelry.

Luke flipped through the pages and stopped at an image of Farrah dragging Alissia into the clearing.

"Oh, my goodness," she laughed, seeing the look of terror on her face.

"I highly enjoy this one," he teased.

"You would." She began to flip through the pages. "Who did all this?"

"Zander. I don't think you'd remember him. He's quiet and reserved, and you've only seen him the night of the party, along with today's ceremony. Most of the pictures in this book are of the house being built."

She stopped at an image of Luke and Salvatore sitting on a log together. Gazing at something in front of them, they both appeared happy and hopeful. While they often laughed during the past year, the emotions depicted in their eyes seemed foreign to her. Captivated, she stared at the picture for a while.

"When Zander told me he planned to make this book, I told him you and I would want memories of Salvatore. He's also going to do another one with pictures of our zeer ceremony. He said it'll be in color."

Alissia began to flip through the pages again. "Who made the stand?"

"Mack. He's the boisterous old man who played in the band the night of the party."

"They were all lively," she responded.

"Most of them. Zander does a lot of these books in smaller versions, and Mack wanted to add something special to ours. He actually had most of the pedestal finished before we even arrived."

"Without even meeting us?" She turned around in his arms and looked up at him.

Luke nodded. "I told you everyone wanted to do something for us." Pulling away, he took her hand and turned around. "I don't think you noticed what else Zander did."

Alissia glanced around the room, noting the desk and stocked bookshelves. Then she pulled him toward a chaise lounger, where a large painting of Salvatore hung on the wall. Staring into his lifelike eyes, she felt her emotions rising.

"We'll talk to him again," Luke assured, giving her hand a squeeze. "We have the globes." She nodded, and his lips curled into a mischievous grin as he pulled her into his arms.

"You know, there's another room you haven't seen."

"Oh, *really*?" She placed her arms around his waist and smiled. "I don't think I've seen our bedroom. Whatever happened to my beautiful bed?"

He lifted his brows. "You mean *our* beautiful bed? There is a room we missed downstairs."

Luke led Alissia from the study, closing the door behind them, and as they strolled down the stairs in silence, her stomach grew tense.

Letting go of her hand, he opened the anticipated door and motioned her forward. "Welcome to our bedroom, Mrs. Harrison."

She smiled, trying to appear calm as she stepped past him. Looking around, she saw a door to the lower porch and another she assumed opened to a closet. Both sides of the bed's sheer curtains were pulled back, held in place with tassels, while the ones bordering the head and foot remained hanging.

One of her new yoga outfits hung on the wall near the head of the bed, while Luke's harem pants and loose shirt hung on the opposite side. As she wondered if he helped to decorate their bedroom, he snatched the sash from her waist, and she gasped and turned around.

"That was easy," Luke said, tossing it into a chair in the corner. With a roguish grin, he wrapped his arms around her waist. "Your zeer dress is now a nightgown, my little pixet."

"And what do you know about zeer dresses?" she asked, trying to sound calm as he pushed her hair away from her neck. She closed her eyes, both hands gripping the front of his shirt, when he began to kiss her bare shoulder.

"Hoyle informed me there are two simple steps," he breathed, at her ear. "First, turn the dress into a nightgown." Luke's fingers raked across her skin as he grasped the material at her shoulder. "And that leaves only one tie."

With his hands on her lower back, he shuffled her across the room.

"Wait!" Alissia exclaimed, when her legs bumped into the edge of the bed. She gently pushed against his chest. "I don't know when your eyes will change, and I want to look at them one last time." Her hand moved to his hair, and she added softly, "And this. I'm going to miss them both, your dark hair and eyes."

"You'll still have the paintings."

Alissia shook her head. "Not the same."

Luke's grip tightened around her waist, and she drew in a sharp breath. "I've waited a long time for this moment, Pixet. You have five seconds."

She nodded weakly, and his eyes never lefts hers as he slowly counted, "Five . . . Four . . . Three . . . Two." His brows lifted, and he leaned to her ear and whispered, "One."

Alissia yelped as she fell onto the bed, with Luke on top of her. Gripping her hands, he pressed them into the bedding, at each side of her head.

A trail burned into her skin as his lips slowly traveled along her neck and chest, just above the edge of her dress. Lifting his head, he murmured, "You do smell succulent."

He released her hands and took hold of the last tie of her gown. "You're finally mine, Alissia Harrison."

With glowing eyes, she lifted the back of his shirt, and her hands found flesh. Her veins surged with heat as she clung to him.

"All yours," she breathed.

Chapter 20

"I thought you were going to do yoga."

"Too comfortable," Alissia mumbled, not opening her eyes. She enjoyed the sound of Luke's heartbeat beneath her ear. Her hand left the hammock, and she began to fumble with the bottom of his shirt. With a smile, her fingers trailed up his abdomen, before finding a place to rest.

"You continue with that, and we'll start again," he warned.

She tried to shake her head. "Too tired. Definitely later."

"I should get up and go through a routine," he said thoughtfully.

"You're not moving," Alissia asserted. "Learn to relax and be still. It's early." She frowned when her head began to shake from his laughter.

"I think we have different opinions when it comes to what's considered early and late morning," Luke replied. "We've already eaten breakfast, and it'll soon be time for lunch."

Opening her eyes, she lifted her head to give him a dirty look.

"Oh, you're awake again." Luke grinned, and his arm resting above his head moved to wrap around her. "Shall we try again to see if my eyes will change? We haven't tried out the hammock yet."

Alissia groaned, rolling her eyes. "You're a beast."

"But I'm your beast, and you love it." He pulled her body on top of his, causing her hand to leave his shirt. "And I heard pixets love beasts."

Her brows lifted. *"Really?"*

"It's true. Legend says pixets are highly attracted to them. They're barely even able to keep their hands off them."

Alissia cocked her head, staring down at him.

"What?" Luke questioned.

Her lips curled up, and she combed her fingers through his unchanged, black hair. "I'm just not used to seeing you like this."

"Like what?"

"Happy and carefree. I'm used to seeing you brooding most of the time."

"And I can say the same for you," Luke responded. His expression turned serious, and he pushed her hair from her shoulder. "I meant every word of my vows, and I'm going to enjoy spending the rest of my life making you happy. I never imagined I'd ever feel this much love for anyone." He paused as a smile grew to his face. "You make me happy."

Alissia lowered her head and kissed the corner of his mouth. When he turned slightly and parted his lips, she chuckled and shook her head. "Uh, uh. It's my turn to torment you."

She began to graze her lips across his neck, but her body soon stiffened as something clattered inside the house. Her head shot up, and she looked to the open bedroom door.

Fully alert, Luke thrust her onto the hammock and sat up, just before a ball of fur burst from the room and sprang into the air, landing beside Alissia's feet.

"Mia!" Alissia sat up, glaring at the tiny creature. "We're married now and . . ." Her voice trailed off, as her expression switched to worry. Turning to Luke, she said, "I've never seen her breathing this hard."

"She's pushed herself running," he answered, never taking his eyes from Mia. When he reached out to pick her up, she quickly slapped his hand and shook her head, growling.

She hopped from the hammock and hobbled into the house, and Luke stood and pulled Alissia next to him. When they entered the bedroom, they found Mia pulling a backpack from beneath Luke's side of the bed.

His expression instantly turned fierce, scaring Alissia, and he rushed over and squatted in front of Mia.

"Is there danger?" he questioned, staring intently into her round eyes.

Mia nodded vigorously, while holding out the strap of his pack.

Luke snatched it from her tiny hand and set it on the bed. He barely glanced at Alissia when he commanded, "Get running shoes on and grab your pack from beneath your side of the bed." He opened the drawer of his nightstand and began to grab his knives.

Alissia ran to the closet and found a pair of fitted moccasin boots before pulling out a pair of socks from an armoire drawer. Adrenaline rushed through her, causing her hands to tremble as she sat on the floor putting on her boots.

As soon as she finished with the last tie, Luke pulled her up and helped her into her backpack.

"Your knives," he said, placing a crossbody sling bag over her shoulder. He quickly tightened the strap before picking up Mia and bounding toward the back door. "Let's go."

"Where are we going?" Alissia asked, staying close behind. Thunder sounded, and she looked up to see a dark cloud drawing near.

"I don't know. For now, we'll follow her gestures."

The wind grew strong as they cautiously made their way around the house and ran along the path. Stopping at the main trail, they peered left and right but saw no one.

Mia pointed toward the caves, and Luke told Alissia to run in front of him. She pulled the bag of jangling knives close to her body and darted up the path. Within seconds, she heard eerie laughter, and when she looked back over her shoulder, she let out a small yelp.

Fear and confusion slammed into her at the sight of a large warrior from the bog. Covered in tattoos depicting his internal organs and skeleton, he stood at a distance in the middle of the trail, pointing a rod their way.

Alissia turned her attention back to the trail in front of her and quickened her pace, but the sound of a high-pitched shriek from close behind caused her to look back again. As soon as she spotted Mia's smoking body on the ground, she stopped in horror.

"Into the woodland!" Luke commanded. His gaze went to her pack, and he began to slap at it. When he bent to pick up Mia, he yelled, "Now!"

Alissia ran behind a large, nearby tree and waited for him to stop beside her. "Is she dead?" she panted.

He kept his back to her, watching the warrior. "She's breathing. Fortunately, it hit her back, and she has a chance."

"What was that?"

"I don't know," he answered, turning around, "but I need you to hold Mia while I take care of him."

Alissia held up her hands and shook her head unwaveringly. "He'll kill you!"

Luke pressed Mia into her chest. "If you—"

The sound of vicious snarling erupted from the trail, and Luke spun around. Alissia stepped beside him and cringed, seeing Fang's pack tearing into the warrior on the ground. Although the large wolves blocked her view, she heard enough to know he would not survive.

"Run!" Luke commanded, as he stepped back on the trail. "They've given us more time."

"What about Hoyle and Farrah?" she asked, leaving the woodland.

"They were supposed to take Salvatore back this morning and should be in the tunnels."

A downpour began, and he yelled. "Now go!"

Alissia nodded and began to run, and she could soon hear Luke's steps splashing behind her. They passed Hoyle's carriage before entering the short tunnel of bella flowers, and when they reached the glowing cave, they saw Salvatore and Eaton rushing toward them, with Salvatore carrying Hoyle in his arms.

"The bog creatures are here!" Alissia yelled. She and Luke stopped near a glowing mushroom in the middle of the cavern, and she tried to calm her breathing.

"We know," Salvatore responded, stopping in front of them. "We were in the tunnels when Hoyle started screaming about it. Farrah's in town, and she's witnessing the attack."

"What's wrong with him now?" she asked, staring at Hoyle's trembling body. His head twitched as his eyes moved behind closed lids.

"Mother's calmer now, and she's no longer screaming in fear," Eaton replied. "I believe he's mentally with her, watching through her eyes."

"He can do that?" Luke asked.

Eaton nodded. "I've never seen it actually done, but a zeer bond reacts strongly to extreme fear. The connection becomes greater, and in a way, they become one."

"How did the creatures get here from the bog?" Alissia asked, squeezing the rain from her hair.

Salvatore frowned in annoyance. "I found out last night there was never a trading plan involving my people. It seems we delivered parts to finalize some portals their ancestors were working on."

"Portals?" Alissia dropped her hair, her heart suddenly pounding with fury. "What? Are they crazy? Did no one listen to my warnings about Gafeen and his people?" She turned to Eaton. "Did you know about this?"

He shook his head adamantly. "Not until last night. We didn't even know it was possible. The ancients didn't tell anyone—not even my parents."

"We can have this discussion later," Luke stated. "Mia needs medical attention, and we need to decide on a plan. What have you learned from Hoyle and Farrah?"

"When the attack began, Hoyle started screaming," Salvatore replied. "Some of the pixets and animals tried to defend the Medicians, and they were immediately killed."

"Are they killing the Medicians?" Luke asked.

"Not that I know of," Salvatore answered. "The screams were about the animals."

"They're bonded to their work animals," Alissia explained. "They'll feel the loss and pain if they're connected."

Eaton nodded. "We've never had anything like this happen."

"Do we know what they want?" Luke asked.

"Their biggest desire in trade is for the jades," Salvatore replied. "From what I learned last night, they would be getting those, so I don't see a reason why they would attack."

Luke held Mia out for everyone to see. "They've acquired new weapons, and I'm guessing they're powered by the jades. Can you wake Hoyle and see if we can get some answers? We need to know how many of them are here."

Salvatore placed Hoyle on the ground, and everyone squatted around him as Eaton attempted to wake his father. After a while, Hoyle opened his eyes and looked around in a daze. Seeing Alissia, he bolted into a sitting position and grabbed her arms.

"You must run! Gafeen's here, Alissia. Run!"

She shook her head, fighting against her emotions at the thought of Gafeen attacking the Medicians because of her. "I won't run," she said firmly.

Hoyle's grip tightened on her arms as he stared desperately into her eyes. His expression suddenly softened, and he lifted a hand to her face. Cupping her chin, he smiled and said tenderly, "You must go, child. There's too many to fight, and they promise not to hurt us if we do as they say."

Alissia wiped a tear away. Although she stared into Hoyle's face, she believed Farrah to be the one addressing her. "Luke and I can help."

"Yes, you can, but not today. The guardians believe in you, as do I, and I know you'll find a way." The grip tightened on her chin, and Hoyle's voice pleaded, "Gafeen's already looking for you. They're angry we saved you, and they're incensed with our relatives for supplying humans with jades."

Alissia's eyes widened, suddenly grasping the extent of the situation. "They attacked the island, too." She turned to Luke. "We need help. There's no way we can fix this on our own."

Hoyle screamed and pulled away, causing Alissia to lose her balance and fall onto her bottom. He shook his head, his expression grave. "They killed another pixet."

Eaton sighed, grimacing. "They're stubborn and highly protective, and since we can't control them, I foresee more of them getting themselves killed."

Luke stood and pulled Alissia up before turning to Salvatore. "Do you have someone waiting for you this morning?"

Salvatore stood and nodded.

"Then I suggest we take Mia to Langley. I believe he lives near this side of the mountain and will be able to get her some medical help."

"How bad is she?" Salvatore asked. Peering down at Mia, he winced, and Alissia leaned closer to get a better look.

A straight line from Mia's right shoulder trailed to her left buttock, exposing deep tissue. It resembled something done by a laser, not fire, and the soaked fur made her back look even gorier.

Alissia frowned up at Luke. "I thought you were holding her."

"I was," he replied firmly. "She jumped out of my arms to save you, and if I hadn't thrown a knife, things would have ended much worse."

Alissia dropped her gaze and glanced at the glowing mushroom.

"Do you and your father want to go with us?" Salvatore asked.

Eaton shook his head. "No, we could never leave."

"I didn't think so, but I thought I'd offer. Will you be able to get him to the carriage?"

Eaton nodded.

"We'll think of something," Luke promised, "and we'll be back. You do know that, don't you?"

"I know you won't forget us," Eaton responded, with a weak smile.

Alissia pulled Eaton into a hug. Although not one for emotional displays, she desperately wanted him to know she would be back. The idea of running away while leaving others in danger felt extremely wrong, and she frantically tried to think of a different solution.

Luke tugged on her backpack. "We need to go."

"I promise we'll be back," she vowed. As she straightened, she glanced at the pack of wolves near the entrance. "What about Fang?"

Luke's brows furrowed, and he ran his hand through his wet hair. "We may need him to deliver a message back to the valley once we leave. Have him and his pack follow us to the edge of the mountain, and they can remain there in case we need them."

Everyone rushed through their goodbyes before Luke, Alissia, and Salvatore began to follow the wolves through the maze of dark tunnels.

Worried for Mia, they ran at a steady pace, only stopping occasionally for Salvatore to lower his heart rate. Alissia's fear grew each time she glanced at her tiny protector, and she continuously prayed for healing.

When they finally stepped out into the sunlight, she vowed to spoil Mia for the rest of her days—if she survived.

Chapter *21*

The mountainside appeared untouched by the storm in the valley, and as soon as they reached the carriage, Salvatore explained the situation while helping Lita, Duff, and Santo to hastily put away the camping gear. Luke and Alissia hid in the secret compartment with Mia between them, and they were soon on their way.

Forced into stillness, Alissia's emotions surfaced, and she tightly closed her eyes and turned her face away from Luke. As her tears broke free, she struggled to keep her breathing steady and her body from trembling uncontrollably.

Although usually bothersome, the loud noise of the spinning wheels gave her some comfort, as she knew the sound helped to conceal her occasional sniffs. She could feel Luke's pain mixing with hers, but she dared not let him see her break.

When the carriage stopped for an inspection, Alissia kept the soldiers' dogs from revealing their location, and they soon resumed their short journey.

Shortly thereafter, they stopped again, and she gave a sigh of relief when she reached out with her mind. She mentally told Luke she recognized the animals from Langley's ranch, and they waited expectedly for the hatch to open.

Time passed slowly in the cramped compartment, and although she strained to hear her friends outside, she only heard her and Luke's breaths.

"Can you tell what's taking so long?" he mentally asked.

Alissia frowned as she attempted to blink away the sweat trickling into her eyes, but the pain continued. She considered rubbing them, but she knew her sticky hands would only add to the problem.

Closing her eyes, she sighed in frustration and mentally replied, *"I don't know what's taking so long, but we're going to die of heat if they don't let us out of here. Don't they remember the air vents don't work well when we're not moving? And how's Mia? Are you sure she's going to survive?"*

When he failed to respond, Alissia began to fumble with Mia's tiny arm in search of a pulse. Luke caught her hand and pulled it down, pinning it between them.

"She's alive, but I don't know if she'll live."

Alissia's body stiffened, and she fought against the tears rushing to break free. *"But you said you thought she'd make it."*

"And she could. I just can't promise she will."

"Do you think she will?"

Luke rotated her palm upward and threaded his fingers through hers. *"I truly don't know, and I don't want to give you any false hope. I had hoped her body would heal like the Medicians, but I believe she's weakening. She needs professional care, and she needed it back in the caves."*

Someone jumped into the carriage and began to roll up the rug, and Alissia cocked her head to listen. As soon as the hatch opened, she crawled out and sat down. After taking off her glasses, she pulled the top of her shirt up to dab at her eyes, and when a small towel landed in her lap, she picked it up and began to wipe the sweat from her face.

"We parked in the shade and hoped the screened ceiling would help to keep you cool," Lita said, "but we knew it would get hot down there."

"What took so long?" Alissia asked, accepting the flask Lita offered. Without waiting for an answer, she began to guzzle from it.

"Keep your voices down," Lita warned. "They're still leaving."

Alissia lowered the flask and went to pass it to Luke, but Lita had already given him one. She shrugged and splattered some of the cool water onto her face, before rubbing it over her neck and arms.

Lita frowned and plopped into one of the leather beanbags in the corner. "Anika's kitchen was full of women preserving berries, and although Father's already promised to haul everything to a different home, Langley's mother is suspicious and doesn't want to leave. She knows they barely made it back from Pallen alive, and she thinks we're bringing more trouble."

"Well, she's not wrong about that," Alissia muttered.

"Mia needs help now," Luke warned. "We can't wait." He set his drink aside and bent down to reach into the compartment.

"How's she doing?" Lita asked. When he straightened with Mia's body draped over his left arm, she rushed toward him and grabbed his flask. "She needs water."

Alissia felt tears surfacing, and she lifted her drink and took a few sips. Quick to numb her pain, she set the flask aside as Luke and Lita sat down at the front of the carriage, near the driver's seat.

Their unusual display of compassion intrigued Alissia, and she watched as Lita whispered soothing words while trickling water onto the back of Mia's head. As she massaged the cool liquid into the fur, Luke stared down at the large, open wound.

Alissia noticed how he rubbed one of Mia's tiny hands between his fingers—absentmindedly, yet tenderly. His grave expression worried her.

Lita asked him to help her wet the inside of Mia's mouth, and he carefully tilted her head and held it in place. Seeing no sign of life, Alissia dropped her gaze as the thought of death came to mind.

She soon began to look around for a distraction and noticed the open hatch. After closing it, she rolled out the rug and arranged the beanbags over it. Then, with nothing else to do, she sat down in one of them.

Leaning back, she stared up at the trees through the screening. Then she closed her eyes and clasped her hands over her chest. Hoping to clear her mind, she inhaled deeply.

"You can wake up now," Lita whispered, to Mia.

Alissia slowly exhaled and took in another deep breath.

"What's taking so long?" Luke complained. "We're just sitting here."

She exhaled through her mouth and inhaled through her nose.

"I haven't changed yet, so I can go in and help," he added.

Alissia's breath came out as a sigh, and she opened her eyes and frowned. She began to tap her fingers on her chest, focusing on a rhythm to keep her mind busy. Although slow at first, the pace soon quickened, and her knees began to bounce along.

After a while, she sat up and looked around, hoping to find something to do. However, the carriage looked the best she had ever seen it. Lita, Duff, and Santo must have stripped the carriages down for deep scrubbings during their time off in Allure. They polished all the wood and leather, washed the covering materials, and bought new rugs. The smell of citrus still lingered in the air, and all of Lita and Duff's belongings and gear were properly stowed.

"That's it!" she whispered harshly, turning around to face the others. "One of y'all need to go in there and kick—"

Salvatore's two dogs began to bark outside, and Lita rushed out the back of the carriage. Seconds later, the dogs stopped barking, and her head popped through the flaps.

"You can come out now."

Alissia bolted from the beanbag and jumped out of the wagon. She pulled one of the flaps back and watched as Luke stepped down with Mia still draped over his arm. With wet fur, she looked worse than before.

"I brought someone to care for Mia," Duff announced.

She let go of the flap and turned around, only to find Lita and Duff at the back of the wagon.

"Hello, Alissia."

Recognizing the feminine voice, Alissia's eyes grew wide before Emera even stepped around the corner of the wagon. When she found her breath again, her face twisted in confusion. "What? What are—"

"We don't have time," Luke said, rushing past her. "I'll explain later."

"You knew?"

Ignoring her, he stopped in front of Emera and lifted Mia. "It's bad."

Alissia could only stare in disbelief. Her mind filled with questions, and her emotions plunged into chaos. She wondered if Luke's comment meant he had known Emera would be there. But how? And how did she get from Pallen to Allure? Why was she even in Allure? And not just Allure—what was she doing on Langley's ranch?

A light shove from behind interrupted her thoughts, and she stumbled forward.

"I told you to go," Lita responded, to Alissia's glare.

"Well, *obviously*, I didn't hear you."

"Obviously." Lita motioned to the others walking toward the house. "We can go in now."

Alissia nodded and started forward. After a few steps, she let out a sigh and said, "I killed her brother, Lita."

"That's what I heard."

"I didn't just kill him. I mean, I *literally* stabbed him to death."

"Heard that, too."

Alissia stopped walking and turned to face Lita, who stopped as well. "I don't think you really know how bad I killed him."

Lita's expression softened. "Does it really matter?"

"Yes!" She glanced toward the house, where the others were already inside. "You attacked Luke when you heard about it, cause you thought he was the one who did it." She lifted her hand to her forehead and gave it a squeeze, as if it would help her to remember. "What all did you say? Didn't you call him a monster? Said he mutilated the body?"

Dropping her hand, she met Lita's gaze, her expression troubled. "What's she even doing here?"

"I don't know," Lita answered softly. "But I do know, it's probably the best thing for Mia."

"And why's that?"

Lita's brows lifted, and she stared expectedly at Alissia for a moment. Then a smile crept to her face. "You don't know, do you?"

"Know what?" Alissia frowned. "It seems I don't know anything anymore. In fact, I've been clueless since landing in this reality. And it's beyond frustrating!"

Lita chuckled. "You're the one who said Emera didn't like her father."

"Yeah. And?"

"You said she blamed him for the death of the man she loved." Lita paused, causing Alissia's frustration to grow. "You also said her family considered that man nothing more than a stable boy."

"Oh, for goodness' sake! What are you trying to say?"

Lita grinned, seemingly pleased with Alissia's outburst. "What better way to get back at her father than to go to school for something related to horses, or animals in general? And since she came from wealth, she easily chose one of the best schools and got the highest degree available as an animal doctor."

Alissia scowled and started walking toward the house. "You could have just told me that in the beginning."

"Oh, but what fun is that?" Lita ran past her, laughing. "And hasn't Luke told you how cute you get when you're angry?"

Chapter 22

*I*nside, Alissia slipped past Lita as she leaned against the doorframe of the kitchen, and she found a place to stand in a corner of the room. Except for the sound of Anika hastily washing large pots, bowls, and strainers, a tense silence filled the air.

A blanket covered the kitchen table, where Emera sat hunched over Mia. She wore a strange pair of magnifying glasses, with a small glow stone on the end of a thin rod protruding from the middle. Luke and Duff stood nearby, both watching.

When Emera pulled a pair of tweezers from her bag on the table and inserted them into the wound, Alissia cringed and turned away. She closed her eyes and waited a while before looking back to find Emera scribbling in a small, leather book, no longer wearing the special glasses.

Santo rushed into the kitchen and set a wooden crate on the table. "Here's everything you said you needed. Langley's still gathering the other supplies."

Emera stared at the crate for a moment, her face deep in thought. Looking up at Santo, she shook her head. "Tell Langley I need the other med room in the barn. She needs fluids and surgery, and I'll need the equipment."

She ripped a page from her book and held it out. "I'll also need everything on this list. And he needs to hurry. She doesn't have much time."

Santo nodded as he accepted the paper, and then he turned to Duff. "We'll probably need you, too."

The two of them bounded out of the house, and Emera stood and began to sort through the contents of the crate, placing various items on the table.

"Will she wake up soon?" Lita asked.

"We don't want her to wake up," Emera answered, not looking up, "and I'm about to give her something to keep her asleep. I don't know anything about this type of animal, and I don't want her to go into shock."

She stared down at three face masks, each sized differently. After she made her selection, she fastened it over Mia's face and attached a breathing bag to it.

"I need you to pump this," she said, looking up at Luke. Her gaze landed on Alissia, and she frowned. "And I need you to leave the room."

Alissia's surprise only lasted briefly before she crossed her arms. "And why would I do that?" she challenged.

Emera turned to Luke, now standing at her side, and passed the pump to him. "I promise to do all I can for Mia," she vowed, "but at this moment, Alissia's presence is distracting."

Luke met Alissia's gaze. *"Give her this, Alissia."*

His mental voice sounded firm, and she stared defiantly into his eyes, forcing herself to appear calm as the feeling of betrayal slammed into her.

"Please," he added softly. *"We can sort this out later. Right now, we need her to save Mia's life."*

"Your clothes are still here," Anika said pleasantly. Alissia turned to see her standing next to Lita in the doorway. She took off her apron and hung it on a nearby hook. "And we have much to talk about," she added, urging Alissia to follow.

Alissia glanced at Emera, still facing Luke, and after giving him a quick, dirty look, she nodded and followed Anika out.

"All the clothes you didn't take to Pallen are still here," Anika said, opening the door to the guestroom. She stepped aside, allowing Alissia to walk past.

Alissia glanced around the room before her eyes locked on the four-poster bed. The memory of waking to Langley and Grady's voices outside the door came to mind, and she recalled how strange their accents seemed at the time.

"Remember your first night in this reality?" Anika asked, taking a seat on the bed.

Alissia nodded. "You were the first person I saw." She lightly touched one of the glowing, blue flowers wound around the nearest column of the bed. "And these were the first bella flowers I ever saw. Seems like forever."

Dropping her hand, she pushed her nostalgic feelings aside and looked at Anika. "What's Emera doing here?"

Anika chuckled. "I knew that would be the first thing you'd ask." Using her feet, she removed her slippers and let them drop to the floor. Then she lifted one of her legs onto the bed and twisted in her seat. She patted the spot in front of her and waited for Alissia to sit down.

"She came here looking for you."

"Me?" Alissia frowned worriedly. "Anika, I stabbed Ian to death."

"Yes," Anika replied, nodding, "but she said you also left behind a mysterious note."

Alissia's mind drifted to the night they escaped the palace in Pallen. Although she recalled placing a note in the stall of Emera's horse, she forgot her exact words. She remembered, however, the beautiful horse, thinking Emera took excellent care of it.

"Do you know what the note said?" she asked.

"You're the one who wrote it. I was planning to ask you."

"Yeah, but that night was crazy. I mainly remember Luke almost dying." Averting her eyes, she looked at the closed door. "And I can still see Ian's body, covered in blood. Honestly, I try not to think about that night."

She forced a smile and turned back to Anika. "I only remember wanting to let Emera know that her father wasn't the one who killed her boyfriend, but I don't know what all I wrote about it. How angry is she?"

"I don't think she's angry," Anika answered, her voice lacking confidence. "She doesn't seem like an easy person to get close to, and she's never really confided in me."

She lifted the bottom of her long, auburn braid and stared at it, as she added, "Besides, we haven't had much time for friends lately. Since our release from the palace in Allure, Langley's family stays close, as well as mine."

"Release?" Alissia asked in surprise. "Y'all weren't in trouble with the Eldership here, were you?"

"Not really in trouble, but we did have a lot of explaining to do." Anika let go of her braid and dropped her hands onto her lap, giving Alissia her full attention.

"When we got to Allure, Grady immediately went to the Elders to tell them what happened in Pallen." She paused before clarifying, "Well, just not the hidden details about you." She frowned. "Although, he did have to tell them about you."

She waved her hand through the air, shaking her head. "Anyways, Morton's family had already arrived and talked to the Elders. Grady filled in more details, and Langley and I had to tell them what we observed. We also had to answer questions about you. We were treated as witnesses, and once the Elders finished questioning us, we were allowed to return home."

Anika let out a deep breath and rolled her eyes. "Then," she stressed, "we had to explain things to our families. They had been extremely worried about us when we didn't return in the spring or send a message." Shaking her head, she added, "It was a mess. They actually thought we were dead."

After a moment of silence, Alissia asked softly, "How's Grady? Is he in trouble for not taking me to the Eldership?"

Anika frowned. Her worried expression matched Alissia's as she seemed to consider her answer.

Dropping her gaze, Alissia began to chew on her bottom lip while twirling her wedding band around her finger.

"He's doing better," Anika replied, causing Alissia to look up. "At first, we thought the poison was the main reason for his silence and withdrawn behavior. However, we eventually began to worry it was more." She smiled slightly. "For a while, I even blamed you for choosing Luke over him."

"And now?"

Anika shook her head. "No, I don't blame you, and I think Grady has more to deal with. It took a while for me and Langley to recover from everything that happened, and we're still not the same."

She paused before continuing thoughtfully, "I could tell Grady had strong feelings for you the moment he brought you here. So much blood. We all believed you were dying." She met Alissia's gaze and held it. "I'd never seen that much emotion from my cousin. He was desperate. And after I cleaned you up and told him I didn't find any wounds, his face filled with hope."

Her gaze turned distant as she continued softly, "I watched him gently scoop you into his arms and carry you to this bed. His hands trembled as he pulled the covers over your body. When I left to clean the mess in the bathroom, he didn't even notice when I returned. I stopped in the doorway and watched him for a while, not quite believing my eyes."

Anika looked at Alissia and chuckled lightly. "It's not that I believed him to be incapable of affection. It's just not something I had ever seen from him. He's always seemed somewhat reserved, and he's known for his brain—not his heart."

She held up her hand and shook her head. "I said that wrong. No one thinks of him as heartless. It's just that he's more of a thinker, not a lover."

Alissia nodded. "I know what you mean. He loved his work. He was ambitious."

"Exactly!" Anika's expression turned serious. "But when I watched him from the doorway, he was sitting on the bed, leaning over you and whispering. He held one of your hands up to his chest, while his other hand stroked your forehead." She met Alissia's gaze. "He was smitten—before you had even met him."

Alissia looked down at her hands, welcoming the guilt rising within her.

After a moment of silence, Anika asked softly, "But that wasn't fair to you, was it? I mean, you'd never even met him, and your entire life was taken from you."

Alissia's body stiffened. She could feel Anika watching her. Hating the attention, she quickly clasped her hands together and looked up.

"Is Grady in trouble with the Eldership?" she asked, changing the subject.

"That's one of the things I believe is bothering him. Langley and I don't think he withdrew so much just because of losing you. We believe he lost some of his respect for the Eldership." Anika shifted her body weight on the bed. "You see, he was raised by the Eldership."

Alissia nodded, reminding her friend she already knew this.

"Well," Anika continued, "he's always believed in the system. Held it to high standards and could easily defend any faults. But after seeing the corruption in Pallen, along with all the conversations he shared with Luke—before the felium bit him—he can no longer justify a lot of what the Elders do here in Allure."

She paused, staring at Alissia with raised brows, and Alissia nodded to let her know she understood.

"He not only lost the only woman he ever loved," Anika replied, "but he also lost his identity, which has always been tied to the Eldership." She waved her hand through the air, adding, "Not to mention he was poisoned and almost killed."

"So he's leaving the Eldership?"

Anika shook her head. "No, we're on the verge of war, and I think he's trying to get the Elders to change some of their ways."

"Are they listening to him?"

"Not like before. He's lost some respect within the Eldership since his return, and things don't seem to be as easy for him as it used to be."

"Because of me?" Alissia frowned, seeing the answer on Anika's face. She crossed her arms. "Seriously? So, they don't trust him as much, because he didn't take me to them?"

"That's part of it, but I think some of his peers are making things worse."

Alissia uncrossed her arms and gave Anika a questioning look.

"Don't tell him what I'm about to tell you," Anika warned. She waited for Alissia to nod before divulging, "Well, I haven't talked to Grady much lately. This is our busiest time of the year on the ranch, and Langley and I've both been working a lot. Grady doesn't visit us as often as he did before, but some of the women in our family have been here to help with this season's food prepping. I don't know specific details, and the only reason I even know any of this is because some of the men in our family work at the Eldership. Their wives overhead some of their conversations, and they told my mom."

Alissia nodded again when Anika paused.

"Well, the Elders weren't happy at all with him for taking you to Pallen, and they spent a lot of time deliberating on his punishment. If it had been someone else, I think they would have dismissed him from the Eldership, or even had him arrested."

"How bad is it?" Alissia asked, expecting the worst.

"Luckily, Grady didn't have a single mark against him on his record, and he's always been a favorite with the Elders. With his family here in Allure, he's never taken off much time, and he's always doing some kind of training."

"I know. He's a workaholic and was on his way to becoming an Elder," Alissia replied, wishing her friend would get to the point.

"Well, in the end, the Elders decided to leave him in his position, and when some questioned their judgment, they said the Eldership needed his input, since he observed the corruption in Pallen. Some people saw that as favoritism and unfair, while some just wanted his position."

Anika's face twisted with displeasure, and she added, "You've been around enough of the Eldership women in Pallen to know the greed and jealousy in that environment. It's the same with the men. It just comes out differently."

"So a lot of Grady's peers have tried to discredit him," Alissia replied.

"Not just any of them," Anika answered sadly. "He considered some of them close friends."

Alissia let out a frustrated sigh, staring at the door. "Any good news?"

"Yes."

She looked back at Anika in surprise.

"If we hadn't gone to Pallen, Alrik's plan may have worked."

"But I thought you just said there's still a threat of war," Alissia responded, confused.

"Yes, but I don't think Alrik's in charge anymore. He was able to stir up the tension that was already building, and he succeeded in planting the idea of war. But . . ." Anika paused, smiling slightly. "Now that the Elders are aware of the threat, they've been holding conferences to address the situation. That may be one of the reasons we haven't seen Grady lately. He's been extremely busy."

Alissia stood from her uncomfortable position on the bed. Unlike Anika, she still wore shoes and had been sitting with her feet dangling, too short to reach the floor. As she clasped her hands behind her back to go into a stretch, her worry returned.

"How's Mia?" she mentally asked.

"Emera's still working on her."

"Is she going to live?"

"I asked that question earlier, and Emera said she couldn't commit to an answer yet."

"Then ask her now."

"No, she's trying to concentrate right now. I know you're worried, but I need to focus, too. She's got me helping. I'll let you know as soon as I know something. I love you."

"What's wrong?" Anika asked.

Alissia smiled and shook her head before going into another stretch. "What's Emera doing here?"

"She offered updated training to the medical staff on the biggest farms and ranches in the area, and Langley's father hired her to teach our animal doctor some things. She's been coming out here for the past two weeks, but I've been busy and haven't really seen her."

Alissia ended her stretch and put her hands on her hips, giving Anika her full attention. "Should I trust her with Mia's life?"

"Yes."

"Why do you sound so sure, yet you said you don't even know her that well?"

Anika smiled. "Because Langley has seen her with animals, and he said it's obvious she loves them. He also said she knows what she's doing and wished they could hire her permanently."

Alissia sat down on the bed again, facing Anika with her legs up and the soles of her boots off to the side. "Why can't y'all hire her?"

"Her level of education is beyond our budget, along with most other ranchers. She could take a lead position at an Eldership palace, or she could continue to offer her services for emergencies and training." Anika gave a half shrug. "With her family's money, she could even start her own animal hospital in any big city in the land."

She grinned and reached out to tap the new star on Alissia's hand. "You met another one?"

Alissia returned the smile. "Yeah, I can now make flowers grow really fast."

"And you can revive them if they're weak?"

Alissia nodded.

"Oh, I need you," Anika said eagerly, while glancing around the room at the many plants. "How about crops? Can you make them produce more or grow faster?"

"Definitely. I can grow a melon from seed to fruition."

Anika beamed with delight as she clapped her hands and rubbed them together. "I should give you some evening tours of the family property."

Alissia chuckled. "Yes, and now I know how I can make up for barging in on you today."

"You don't owe us anything," Anika replied, suddenly serious. She looked down and rubbed her hand across a crease in the bedding. After a quick, futile attempt to smooth it out, she set her hand in her lap and looked up.

"That was a lot of money you gave us."

Alissia shrugged. "I don't need it. Besides, y'all spent a lot of money on me."

"That was Grady," Anika responded, shaking her head.

"Was it enough to pay him back for everything?"

"It was more than enough, but he refused to accept any of it. He . . . uh . . . told Carlo to give everything to Langley and me."

Alissia smiled instinctively, masking her sadness. "Well, hopefully, it will help with all the chaos I caused y'all."

"It's not like that." Anika's gaze dropped to her lap, and she picked at her nails for a moment before looking back up. "I know things were slightly strained between us when we last saw each other, but I don't want you thinking you were the cause of everything that happened."

She let out a small sigh before saying, "It hurt my feelings when I found out you didn't tell me about saving Luke's life in the castle, but that doesn't mean I don't care or love you anymore, Alissia." Leaning forward, she grasped Alissia's hand with one of hers and stressed, "We're still friends. I want you to find happiness and safety in this new life forced upon you, and Langley and I will always be here for you."

Alissia felt herself swallow as heat rose to her face. Although her calm expression hid her body's internal chaos, she glanced at the door, longing to escape her friend's hand and firm gaze. Each second felt like a minute as she struggled with a proper response.

"Thank you. You're a great friend."

She cringed as the words left her mouth, wishing she knew how to say more and hating the lack of emotion in her voice. When Anika smiled and pulled her hand away to straighten, Alissia's body relaxed.

In an effort to steer the conversation away from the subject of feelings, she quickly smiled and asked, "Did y'all have any problems getting home?"

"No, it was quite easy after we boarded the boat. Once we arrived in the southern territory, Grady went to the Eldership and got a military escort for us."

"What about Carlo and the others?"

Anika shook her head. "They knew we'd be safe and didn't go with us. Edda's pregnancy was making her miserable, and Bruna was expecting as well."

"What?" Alissia asked, her eyes wide. "Salvatore didn't tell us that."

"He didn't know." Anika chuckled at Alissia's surprise. "It seems Bruna and Edda wanted their children close in age. It just took Bruna a little longer to get pregnant."

Alissia wondered if the pregnancies bothered Anika, since she and Langley seemed unable to have children.

"I want to hear about you," Anika said eagerly. "I got to meet Lita's new husband a couple of weeks ago. They stopped by with Santo and told us a lot. I want to hear about the underground creatures and the Medicians. What were they like?"

Alissia let out a long breath and reached past Anika for a pillow. "Might as well get comfortable. If I know you, you're gonna want details."

Anika lowered onto her side, grinning. "Of course! Tell me everything."

Chapter 23

*N*ot wanting to leave out anything, Alissia started with her swim with the dolphins. The two of them giggled as she gave details on Lita and Duff's courting days, and Anika laughed heartily, while Alissia felt guilty, about her fight with Lita that ended with Duff and Salvatore bleeding.

After hearing what happened in the forest with the underground beings, Anika began to speculate where else other creatures could conceal themselves in the land. Her ideas quickly escalated into the notion of creatures secretly living among them, and she began to describe various quirky people she knew before conjuring up strange creatures to match their ways.

Alissia continued recounting the recent events of her life, but when she began to talk about returning Selona to the bog, she stopped abruptly in midsentence, her eyes wide with sudden understanding.

"What is it?" Anika asked. "What's wrong?"

"Oh, my goodness," Alissia breathed, shaking her head. "I can't believe I didn't get it." She gave a sarcastic laugh as she sat up on the bed. "I mean, I knew something wasn't right, but . . ." She clenched her teeth.

"What's wrong?" Luke mentally asked. *"Why do I suddenly feel like killing someone?"*

"Remember Selona's last words? She knew they were going to attack. It was their plan the entire time." With an unconscious sneer, Alissia mimicked Selona's raspy voice in her head, *"I want to thank you. Your name will go down in all the scrolls as the one responsible."*

Alissia jumped from the bed and turned away from Anika, feeling tears of fury coming to her eyes. Her hands trembled, and in that moment, she desperately wished Selona stood in front of her.

"I need you to calm down, Alissia. I'm supposed to be focused right now. Where's Anika?"

Alissia closed her eyes and took in a deep breath before slowly exhaling through her mouth. She turned around to find Anika sitting up on the bed, staring at her with wide eyes.

"Seriously, what's wrong?" Anika asked gently.

Alissia frowned and sat back down on the bed. "I didn't even think about it on the way here. I was too busy worrying about the Medicians and didn't even think about it."

"Think about what?"

Alissia let out a sigh. "It all makes sense now. Remember Gafeen's last words? He said he'd see me again."

"And did you see him?"

"No, but he was there when the Medicians were attacked." Alissia paused before explaining, "When we dropped Selona off near the bog, she said some things that worried me, but I didn't know what they meant until now."

"She said a lot of things that worried all of us," Anika muttered wryly.

Alissia smiled slightly and nodded. "This was different. She actually thanked me, and she said all the great races would write my name in their historical records as the person who made all this possible. She made sure to let me know none of this would have been possible without me."

"She thanked you?" Anika stared back at her in disbelief. "She actually said the word?"

"Oh, yeah. But think about it. She wasn't being nice. It was her way of letting me know they couldn't have attacked everyone without me."

Anika shook her head adamantly. "This isn't your fault. You even said you warned everyone about them. They're the ones who chose not to listen."

"This was Gore and Gafeen's plan the entire time," Alissia replied. "It was never about starting a trade route, and Selona knew it. She left the bog and gave up her health—not for trade. It was always about taking control of the other great races. I can't believe I didn't see it coming."

Before Anika could respond, Alissia waved her hand through the air. "Anyways, let me tell you about the Medicians in the valley. They're a lot different than the ones on the island."

Behind the mask of a smile, Alissia detailed her time in the valley. Although her mood grew dark as she talked about her new family of Medicians, she never allowed her pain to show.

Not wanting any pity, she tried to avoid mentioning that today marked her and Luke's first day of marriage. Anika listened eagerly as she described the wedding, but a confused expression soon filled her face.

"Wait," she interrupted. "He hasn't changed. I thought he would turn once the two of you . . . you know."

"Yeah," Alissia replied slowly, "but it takes a little time."

"When was the wedding?"

Alissia frowned, dreading her friend's response. "Last night."

Anika gasped. She looked horrified as she took Alissia's hand. "Oh, no, Alissia. Today's your first day of marriage. I'm so sorry."

"It is what it is," Alissia replied, shrugging. She stood from the bed and walked to the standing mirror. "I look horrible." Although her words were only meant to change the subject, she lifted her hand to her rain-induced, frizzy hair and frowned. Indeed, she looked dreadful.

She turned back around. "How long do you think before I can see Mia?"

"I don't know." Anika stood and walked to a corner of the room, where she picked up one of two drawstring bags. "But if I'm going to feed everyone tonight, I need to start cooking." She placed the bag on the bed and turned to Alissia. "I haven't had a chance to do anything with the clothing you left behind, so both of these are yours. You can bathe and dress while you're waiting."

Alissia smiled, pleased with the change in subject. If not for having to cook, she knew Anika would have continued her efforts to console her, and after talking about the Medicians in the valley, she felt drained and desperately wanted some time alone.

"I brought a pack," she said. "Luke filled it, so I don't know what's in it. I think it may still be in the hidden compartment of Salvatore's carriage, unless someone got it out for us."

"Don't worry about it," Anika responded, waving her hand through the air. "There's plenty here, and they're yours. I meant to have Lita take them to you with your other belongings, but I forgot."

She walked to the door and placed her hand on the nob. "Let me see who's out here while you find something to wear."

Alissia nodded and opened the bag on the bed. By the time Anika returned, she had an outfit picked out.

"No one's here, but don't linger in the sitting room," Anika warned. "This is our busy season, and some of Langley's family walks in without knocking. I'll start locking the door tomorrow, but that'll make them even more curious."

"Where's everyone at?"

"They probably slipped Mia into the medical room at the barn, since it has better lighting and equipment."

Alissia picked up the legging outfit from the bed and followed Anika out of the bedroom. "Do you want help in the kitchen after I dress?"

"No, don't worry about it. During this time of year, it's the men's job to cook the meat, and they make a big show of it. I only need to prepare some vegetables, and I have plenty of those."

Once alone in the bathroom, Alissia gave a weary sigh and set aside her fresh clothing. Staring at her reflection, she frowned.

"It's amazing how you can go from looking like a princess to a circus clown," she mumbled. Her frown deepened at the thought of Emera seeing her so disheveled, as the younger woman managed to somehow always appear sophisticated and elegant, even while working with animals on a ranch.

Alissia recalled the moment they first met at a ball in Pallen. Tall and slender, with silky, black hair, Emera had walked toward her and Ian with the poise of royalty. Confidence exuded from her as she spoke flattering words to Alissia, only to follow them with subtle, unnerving jabs.

She had toyed with Ian that night, leaving him flustered, which had intrigued Alissia. When Emera stared at her father, Alrik, like a cat playing with a mouse before devouring it, Alissia thought she had found an ally in the woman. However, that hope faded the moment Emera decided to toss aside her date for the night, so she could flirt with Luke and Grady—just to provoke her father.

Later, during a brief lunch together, Emera incited Alissia's rebellious spirit within the first few minutes. Bold and defiant, the younger woman ended the meal early and left Alissia sitting at the table, feeling unsettled and confused.

"And then you had to go and kill her brother," Alissia muttered, massaging the back of her neck. She dropped her hand and shook her head. "There's no way this is going to end well."

She removed her dark glasses and began to turn her face from side to side. The remaining glitter around her eyes still sparkled, and a memory from the night before came to mind.

With Luke's body on top of hers, she stared into his eyes and trailed her fingers down his back, beneath the covers.

"I could stare at you all night," he said, his eyes mirroring the overwhelming peace and happiness she felt.

Alissia gave a sheepish grin and turned her head. He began to rake his fingers through her hair, pushing it back onto the pillow. She closed her eyes when his thumb went to the paint near her brow, and he lightly traced his fingers down her face, stopping at her throat.

"I can't believe this is real," he whispered.

A tear escaped and trickled down Alissia's cheek as the memory faded. She quickly wiped it away, and her expression hardened. Staring at her reflection, she whispered harshly, "There'll be none of that."

Knowing Luke could feel her emotions even more than before, she vowed to get control of herself. The last thing she needed was for someone to see her weak—including Luke.

"Tears don't fix anything," she reminded herself. "You know what you need to do." She let out a weary sigh before closing her eyes. "It's the only way you're going to survive this, and with Luke distracted at the moment, you need to do it now."

Unlike most of the times, when her memories forced their way into her mind—bringing pain and chaos—Alissia controlled her thoughts, pulling the exact memory she needed.

She rarely allowed her mind to revisit the night her father almost killed her, and even then, she usually focused on the aftermath, not the actual stabbing. By now, she knew which memory had enough strength to help deaden her emotions over time, but the act of numbing her feelings usually brought guilt with it. It always reminded her of what she had done.

Although her father had failed to kill her in his drunken state, deep down, she knew she dealt the final blow that night. She had always been harsh with herself, but at some point during her youth, she began to believe many of the words he often screamed at her. Part of her grew callous, creating a division within her.

After dressing her wound and cleaning up all the evidence of her blood, she locked her bedroom door and walked to her mirror. Glaring into her swollen, red eyes, she swore she would never be a victim again, and in that moment, she stifled her true self into perpetual silence. A harsh spirit settled in, leaving no trace of fear and vulnerability—even of death itself. All of her sweet innocence died that night. She made sure of it!

Her bloody hands—she locked onto that image. The familiar ache began to set in, and she welcomed it. She knew if she kept that memory close over the next few days, it had the power to numb her spirit. It's a pain she knew well, and unlike the raw agony she now felt, it was one she could control.

Alissia opened her eyes to a changed reflection. No longer sad and defeated, a fighter stared back at her—determined and ready, expecting the worse.

"I will *not* be broken," she whispered.

Chapter 24

*C*raving solitude, Alissia took her time bathing and dressing, but the scent of freshly baked pies eventually drew her from the bathroom. She needed to keep busy, so she ignored Anika's protests and began to clean after she finished eating.

While scrubbing the bathroom sink later that evening, she heard the others enter the cottage, and she quickly finished the chore before joining them. She stopped in the kitchen doorway to find Lita and Duff washing their hands at the sink, and Anika pouring drinks at the table. Langley, Salvatore, Santo, and Luke eagerly filled their plates at the counter.

She almost asked about Emera's absence, but she stopped when she noticed Luke standing by a large pan of meat. With his fork raised, he stared down at it.

"I wouldn't do it, if I were you," Langley warned, standing beside him.

Luke glanced at him before looking back down.

"Well, I can," Santo replied. From the other side of Luke, he stabbed his fork into the meat and loaded it onto his plate. Using his fingers, he ripped a large chunk from the pile left on the pan and stuffed it into his mouth.

"Mmm, it's still warm," he murmured, setting his fork onto his plate. He smacked his lips as he tore off another strip and plopped it into his mouth. "Mm-mm. This tastes amazing! You can really tell they took their time cooking it." He began to lick his fingers.

Luke set his fork on his plate and reached out to grip Santo's shoulder. "Thank you."

"For what?"

"For volunteering." Santo's brows bunched together, and Luke grinned. "It takes a brave man to offer a challenging spar to a member of the league—especially a highly ranked one dealing with repressed aggression."

Luke released Santo's shoulder and gave him a pat on the back as he began to walk toward the table. "I'm sure we can find time tomorrow. Oh, and you'll want to arm yourself with plenty of knives for when I take your sword."

Alissia laughed at the look of regret on Santo's face, and Langley turned around with a grin. He set his plate on the table and rushed over to pull her into his arms.

"Didn't know if I'd ever see you again, little one," he said, lifting her from the ground. She nodded, barely able to breathe, and he spun her around before setting her back down. "I hate that it's under such circumstances, but . . . uh . . . you know you're always welcome here."

Following Langley's distracted gaze, Alissia turned to see Grady closing the front door behind him and Emera. No longer looking weak from the bite of the felium and dressed in a formal suit, he looked like his true diplomatic self. His neatly cropped, chestnut brown hair and natural skin tone had returned, replacing the look of the tanned, shaggy-haired fugitive he had become while hiding from Pallen's soldiers.

Although Emera had just emerged from long hours of treating Mia in the barn, none of that showed in her appearance, and she naturally looked elegant, even while standing next to Grady in his formal clothing.

Not a single strand of her black, silky-straight hair appeared out of place from her ponytail. No longer wearing her loose, apron jumper, the grey, fitted and sleeveless dress that had been hidden beneath the jumper now emphasized her sleek, model's figure. With her Victorian-styled boots perfectly matching both fashions, Alissia felt a tinge of jealousy at how effortlessly she went from daytime, animal doctor to evening casual, just by simply removing one item of clothing.

Grady took Emera's hand and started across the sitting room, and Alissia glanced up to find Langley staring at Grady with raised brows.

"This is a bit unexpected," Luke mentally said, placing his hand on her shoulder from behind. She guessed her clenching stomach had pulled him away from his food.

Grady smiled and answered Langley's unspoken question with a nod as he stopped in front of them, while Emera turned her body toward Grady and tucked her free hand around his arm, as if asserting her claim on him.

Alissia ignored her shock and blurted out, "How's Mia? Will she live?"

"I've done all I can for now, but her recovery will take time," Emera replied, her voice smooth and silky. "Although I believe she'll survive, she'll live the rest of her life with a great scar, but I believe she'll be able to walk again. The burn is deep, but it missed her spinal tissue—barely."

"When can I see her?"

Emera looked to Langley, and he answered, "I can slip the two of you in after I eat."

"She needs to eat as well," Grady replied.

Emera nodded, and as they entered the kitchen, Alissia walked to the sink and started washing dishes. Wishing she could disappear, she quietly listened to the chatter in the room and immediately noticed the conversation seemed light and somewhat strained. With Emera around, too many secrets lingered in the air—unspoken, yet noticeably on everyone's minds.

Later, while walking to the stables with Langley and Emera, Alissia listened to their discussion about the extra supplies needed for Mia's care. Langley feared the secrecy surrounding the medical room would rouse his father's curiosity, and since he had a key to the room, Langley found it difficult to keep him out. Nonetheless, Emera insisted she needed the room for Mia's survival, and there seemed to be no other way.

When they neared the stables, Langley told Alissia to stop and wait for Emera's signal. With her presence concealed by the night sky, she watched Langley and Emera enter the stables, and after a brief wait, Emera appeared from the opposite side of the building and motioned.

Alissia ran to her, and the two women walked around the corner and entered through a closed door.

"Try not to touch anything," Emera warned.

Alissia stopped about a foot away from something resembling an incubator. Attached to a small generator, she assumed the clanking machine next to it pumped fresh air into the box.

Seeing the line of stitching along Mia's shaven back pulled at Alissia's emotions, and she looked away and began to scan the room.

"Don't let this room scare you," Emera replied. "It's used for horses, and I had to borrow and rent much of what I'm using from an animal hospital in Allure."

"I'll pay you back." Alissia turned and regarded Emera for a moment. "Why are you here?"

Dropping her smile, Emera answered, "You killed my brother."

"So, you're here for revenge." Alissia's body tensed, ready for a fight.

"I'm not here for vengeance. Our family's never been that close."

"Then why did you come to Allure? To Langley's ranch?"

Emera picked up a hand towel from a table beside her and folded it before setting it down. Turning her attention back to Alissia, she said, "You left me a message the night you left. Why did you do that?"

Recognizing pain and confusion in Emera's eyes, Alissia's expression softened. "When I met Ian, I thought he was working with your father and was only trying to court me because of that, but he soon began to tell me he didn't trust Alrik and wanted to protect me from him. The night I . . . uh . . . Well, he died. He had proposed to me, but I declined. Then he tried to get me to run away with him—even if I didn't want to marry him. He had been talking about getting me away from Pallen for a while, and that night he told me it was time. He had a plan and could even get Langley and Anika out with me."

Alissia shook her head. "But, I told him no. I wouldn't leave." She paused before continuing, "Later that night, a man knocked on my door and said he was with Luke, and it was time for *us* to leave." Looking into Emera's eyes, she stressed, "All of us. Langley, Anika, Grady, Luke, and me."

Emera nodded in understanding.

"So I followed him to the dungeon," Alissia explained. "But when I walked in, Luke was chained to the wall, and he was severely beaten."

To help with the pain of the memory, she clasped her hands together and began to massage her palm with her thumb. "By now,

I thought Ian was a good man, and I wasn't expecting it when I turned around to find him in the dungeon."

Alissia dropped her hands and met Emera's gaze. "He was a completely different person that night. Angry and bitter. Not the sweet and kind Ian I knew."

"Angry about what and with whom?" Emera asked.

"He was furious with me for turning him down, and he somehow figured out that I had feelings for Luke. He was also bitter at your father for not giving him more of an inheritance. Something about the oldest brother getting more."

Emera nodded, and Alissia continued, "He went on about how he had tricked Alrik into signing documents, and he ran more of the business than Alrik knew about. He planned to kill Luke and take me away that night."

"And what did he say about me?" Emera asked. "You said in the note he confessed to something."

Alissia nodded. "He did. He compared my feelings to Luke with your feelings to a young stable boy. Just like with you, he planned to kill the man I loved, and your father would take the blame. He wanted to take my obsession away for the greater good, just like he did with you."

"Did he admit he was the one responsible for the killing?"

Alissia locked eyes with Emera. "Yes, I heard it from his mouth. He was the one who killed your boyfriend, not your father."

Emera turned and picked up the hand towel she had just folded. As she began to refold it, she asked, "And you're the one who killed my brother?"

"Yes, when he tried to rape me in front of Luke—who was chained to the wall."

Emera set the towel down but continued to look at it, and Alissia began to chew on her bottom lip. When Emera turned back around, her expression seemed void of emotion.

"I'm not here for revenge and would probably have done the same thing in your place. I apologize for the trouble my family has caused you. Thank you for taking the time to leave the message. You've given me the truth behind a lie I was led to believe for many years."

Alissia gave a nod, not really knowing how to respond, and Emera walked to the door leading outside. Turning back around, she said, "I've had a long day and will need to check on Mia throughout the night, so I hope you don't mind if I end our conversation. Did you have any other questions concerning Mia?"

"Not about Mia." Alissia paused, staring at Emera. "But, I am concerned about your intentions with Grady."

Emera's expression hardened. "And what business do you have with Grady's personal affairs, now that you're married to Luke?"

"None. But he's had a rough year, and I don't want him to get hurt."

"You don't want him to get hurt?" Emera sneered. "It's a bit late for that, don't you think?"

"What's that supposed to mean?" Alissia challenged.

Emera stared back at her for a moment, looking incredulous. "You nearly destroyed Grady's life and practically ripped his soul from him. Oh, but now you're worried about him getting hurt?"

"I never intended to hurt Grady," Alissia responded, her pulse growing faster.

"But you did," Emera replied matter-of-factly. She crossed her arms over her chest.

"I did by accident. He's a great man and doesn't need to get hurt again."

"I agree."

Alissia regarded Emera for a moment before her expression softened somewhat. "Look, if this has anything to do with me, I ask that you leave Grady out of it."

Emera's arms dropped from her chest. "My relationship with Grady has nothing to do with you, Alissia—or anyone else, other than Grady." She turned to the door and put her hand on the knob. "Now, if you'll excuse me, I do need some rest."

"How much has he told you about me?" Alissia asked, not moving.

Emera let out a harsh breath as she turned back around, leaving her hand on the knob. "He doesn't talk about you anymore, and he never betrayed your secrets, since that's what you're really asking. Other than what he knew about your note and Ian's death, I didn't ask questions about you, or the two of you."

She seemed to consider her words before adding, "I wouldn't think so highly of him if he confided your secrets to me. That's not what I want or care about."

Turning back to the door, she said, "I'll check to see if anyone's outside. Then you can go out. I'll let Langley know you're gone, so he can meet you on the trail."

Emera opened the door and walked outside. She returned shortly to let Alissia know it was clear.

When Langley joined Alissia on the trail, they began to walk, and she asked, "Do you trust her?"

"With the animals and Mia, I do." Glancing at her face in the light of the glow stone in his hand, he added, "With Grady, I don't know."

"Did you know they were together?"

"Not until tonight. I haven't seen him much lately, and Emera and I only talk about work."

Lines creased Alissia's forehead as she frowned. "I'm worried he's going to get hurt again. I thought y'all said he didn't date much."

"He never has, but maybe he has a liking for stubborn women with father issues."

"*What?*" Alissia stopped walking and stared up at Langley in disbelief.

He stopped and turned to face her. "I thought about it just now in the barn, and it makes sense somewhat. She seems like a strong-minded woman, has a dark past, and she's not close to her family. Who does that remind you of? Oh, and she doesn't seem pretentious and shallow like most of the women Grady often meets at the Eldership."

"Everyone's so quick to believe she's not close to her family," Alissia grumbled, as she resumed walking. "How many times have we been lied to since I've been in this reality?"

Langley continued beside her. "I didn't say I trusted her. I can just see how Grady could find her interesting. He's also lost a lot of friends at the Eldership. I don't know if Anika told you anything, but right now, he's the loneliest I've ever seen him."

Alissia nodded. "We talked about it."

"Emera's either the best thing for him right now, or she's going to turn on him like everyone else. But if I know anything about Grady, you can't tell him who to care for. He's a grown man, and he's smart. I'd leave it alone, if I were you." He looked worried as he glanced her way. "Things are going to be hard enough, now that he's going to witness Luke changing. That's another blow."

They continued in silence, and as they neared the cottage, Alissia said, "You know I never intended for any of this to happen. I never wanted to hurt him."

Langley took her by the hand and stopped.

"If Anika had done what everyone wanted, she'd be married to someone within the Eldership, and I believe she'd be miserable. Instead, she followed her heart and made me one of the happiest men alive."

Squeezing her hand, he smiled. "Luke's a good man, and you chose from your heart. I'm just happy you found someone to love and share your life with, even if it wasn't Grady. I'm truly happy for you."

Chapter 25

*A*lissia took a sip of her warm drink and set it on the table, suddenly regretting her decision to sit down beside Luke and across from Grady. Placing her hands in her lap, she scanned the faces of everyone at the table, and Salvatore gave her a comforting smile.

Luke, engrossed in Grady's words of tension and distrust growing within the Eldership, barely seemed to notice when she sat down. Looking at his face, Alissia recognized the warrior, not the carefree man she had recently come to know, and she felt a pang of sadness.

"Isn't that right?"

Alissia blinked at Luke, suddenly aware of everyone staring at her. "What right?"

"You met them, and you said you trusted them." Seeing her confusion, he added, "The glowing creatures in the forest."

"Yeah." She straightened in her chair and looked around the table. "I'm sorry. I'm tired and guess my mind drifted. Why do you ask about them?"

"There have been fires in that area," Grady answered, "and the Elders are getting blamed for it."

"Why would they get blamed for it?" Alissia asked.

Grady responded, "The southern and northern lands border in that area, and someone's setting fires on the northern side, destroying a lot of property. There has also been a death."

Alissia's face twisted in confusion. "But, I thought y'all don't like fires and property destruction, even in war. Y'all are tree huggers and nature lovers."

"That's what makes it so bad," Luke replied. "It'll turn people against the Northern Eldership. It's discrediting the Elders."

"It's starting a war," Grady asserted.

"So the threat of war is higher now?" Alissia asked.

Grady rubbed his hand over his face and clasped his fingers together on the table. He looked exhausted. "The Elders have been doing a lot of negotiating, but with the recent fires, things aren't going so well."

"What's this got to do with the creatures?"

"I think they're the ones starting the fires," Luke answered. At her look of disbelief, he said, "Think about it. The Medicians on the island said those creatures were inventive, and do you think Gafeen's people designed the weapon we saw this morning?"

Alissia stared down at her hands, now wrapped around her mug. When she looked back up, she shook her head. "I have a hard time believing they'd do that. They wouldn't just venture out of their forest and start destroying things."

"Anything's possible, given the right circumstance," Luke replied. "I don't know why they'd do it, or what they'd have to gain, but I'm guessing they're the ones behind the fires, as well as the designers of the weapon."

"I need to contact my people," Salvatore said. "Does anyone have any ideas of what we should do?"

Everyone seemed to look around the table for someone else to answer.

"It's late," Luke replied. "I suggest we think about it and meet again tomorrow night." When everyone nodded in agreement, he stood, and the meeting ended.

Alissia went to the sink and washed the remaining dishes before walking to the guest room, where she found Luke with their packs. She sat down on the bed and watched as he pulled fresh clothing from his. He looked deep in thought.

"Langley should be out by now," he said, turning to her. "I'm going to get a bath."

She nodded, and he walked out, shutting the door behind him.

Alissia fell back onto the bed and let out a heavy sigh. "Back to reality," she mumbled, staring up at the night sky, through the clear ceiling. Luke's smile, the first thing she saw that morning, came to mind, and she quickly pushed it away and sat up.

After cleaning her teeth in the kitchen, she walked back to the bedroom and closed the door. The thought of her diary came to mind, and she began to search beneath the mattress.

She soon sat on the edge of the bed, staring at the book containing her darkest secrets from her youth. Although worn and faded, the art on the cover still evoked an emotional connection, drawing her in.

It was while browsing a gift shop in Savannah, Georgia, with one of her aunts, that she spotted a blue eye peering at her from a shelf. Intrigued, she picked up the thick book and opened it to discover its blank, lined pages.

"There's a green one, too," her aunt said, stepping beside her. "They're a bit eerie looking, don't you think?"

"They're beautiful," Alissia responded. She exchanged the book in her hand for one matching the color of her eyes. Flipping it over, she cringed at the price.

Her aunt continued down the aisle, leaving Alissia alone to consider how much of her Christmas money she should spend on a book. In the end, she could not resist the green eye staring at her from the dark background—looking trapped, mysterious, and full of secrets.

By then, she had already pushed her friends away and become a loner, and although she had never kept a diary, she desperately needed an outlet. That very night, she began to pour her soul into the journal, filling the pages with her secret pain and desperation.

Alone in the guest room, Alissia traced her fingers along the raised design of the eye. Although she wanted to open the book, she suddenly feared it would pull her back into her former reality, even though she knew otherwise. The thought of losing Luke and leaving the Medicians in peril scared her.

Chuckling at the irony of wanting to stay in a life full of danger and chaos, she whispered, "I guess I'm home now."

Her body tensed when Luke opened the door and walked in. Stopping in front of her, he stared down at the book in her hands.

Acting casual, Alissia smiled up at him and stood. "You smell nice." She slipped past him and tucked the journal into her pack.

"Did you open it?"

She cringed, as the tone of his voice let her know he would not let it go. Still smiling, she answered, "No, I just found it."

"What do you plan to do with it?"

Alissia shrugged and walked back to the bed. "I don't know," she responded, taking a seat.

Luke set his clothes and boots down beside his pack and walked back over to stand in front of her. "Do you plan to read it?"

Giving up on her fake smile, she frowned up at him in frustration. Then a smile crept to her face, and she put her hand under his loose shirt. Rubbing her fingers along his side, she gave a seductive look and said, "I don't know."

She tried to pull him onto the bed, but his body refused to budge.

"Do you plan to read it?" Luke asked, looking unfazed.

Alissia fell back onto the bed, groaning in frustration. Propping herself onto her elbows, she frowned up at him. "I don't know, Luke. I'll either read it, or I'll burn it so that no one else can get to it."

"You'd burn it?"

"I could burn it," she said nonchalantly.

Luke walked to his pack and pulled out a small, black bag. Holding it up for her to see, he held out his hand. "Ready?"

Alissia blinked, staring at the bag of fire rocks in surprise. She quickly regained her composure and said, "We can't burn it tonight. Everyone's going to bed."

"Perfect time to burn something you'd rather no one see," he countered. Stepping closer, he held out his hand.

She pulled her bottom lip between her teeth and considered her choices. Although she knew visiting her past could only bring heartache, the writings contained the thoughts and fears of the person she forced into oblivion long ago. Burning the journal would destroy the only evidence of that existence. It would be the ultimate death—nothing left behind.

Luke sat down beside Alissia and took her by the hand. "We're fighting hard for our future. Do you really want to revive your past?"

"No," she mumbled, staring down at their hands. She looked up and gave him a weak smile. "Let's burn it."

He leaned in for a slow and gentle kiss. After pulling away, he caressed her cheek with his thumb. "Ready?"

Alissia nodded, and Luke stood and pulled her beside him. As she retrieved the diary, he sat back down to put on his boots. When he stood again, she held out the book.

"Here. I was scared if I opened it, I'd get thrown back into my reality."

"I thought that wasn't possible," he said, staring down at the cover.

"It's not supposed to, but I didn't want to risk it."

He looked up with a smile. "Don't want your old life back?"

"You know the answer to that."

Luke took Alissia's hand and kissed it. "I'm afraid you're stuck with me, Pixet."

"I think I can live with that," she teased, leaning into him.

He opened the door and led her to a fire pit in the back yard. After setting her diary in the pit, he pulled out the fire rocks.

"Sure you want to do this?"

She nodded. "Do it!"

Luke struck the rocks together and started a flame along the edge of the book. He added some tinder from a nearby bin before stepping back and taking Alissia's hand.

"It really was a pretty book," she said, watching the fire.

"It was."

"You weren't curious what a book would look like from my reality?" she asked, still watching the flames.

"A little."

"The paper looked different."

"I'm sure it did." Luke continued to hold Alissia's hand as he picked up the poker and stirred the fire, opening the book as he did so.

Although she hated destroying the only evidence of her former self, peace filled Alissia as she watched the pages burn. When Luke began to lead her back to the house, she looked down at their hands and smiled.

In that moment, she easily accepted the pains from her past and would change nothing, if given the chance. She knew every tear and struggle she had ever endured in life led her to that very moment—to Luke.

Chapter *26*

*A*lissia woke to the sound of thunder and rolled onto her back to find herself alone in the bed. Barely aware of the rain pounding on the tinted ceiling, she let out a harsh breath as memories from the night before came to mind. Her frown grew deep when she recalled making love to Luke before falling asleep.

The bond they shared heightened their senses even more during physical intimacy. While feelings of passion, love, and happiness had gushed between them on their wedding night, immense desperation and sadness had surged between them last night.

She placed her arm over her eyes and sighed, never wanting to feel vulnerable like that again.

"This bond's a problem," she whispered.

Alissia's thoughts turned to the Medicians in the valley, and her mood darkened even more, as she began to imagine the worst. "They need a miracle. There's nothing we can do."

Moving her arm to her forehead, she stared up at the rain. "They need Your help. Can't the guardians do something?"

She ended her prayer in silence, relying on her faith.

After a while, Alissia pulled herself from the bed and dressed for the day. She joined Luke and Anika in the kitchen, with Salvatore and his family. After scooping some warm oats into a bowl, she placed her breakfast on the table next to Luke.

"Oh, my goodness! It's starting to happen!" Alissia snatched a cluster of Luke's hair, leaning close for a better inspection. Releasing his hair, she grabbed his chin. "Let me see your eyes."

She giggled at the sight of purple flecks mixing with his dark eyes. "I think your eyes are going to match the plum color of my hair, but your hair will be darker. Kind of a deep, winish color."

She let go of his chin and turned to the others. "Did y'all notice it?"

"It's noticeable," Salvatore replied, nodding along with everyone else, "but only slightly."

"What's the usual color for the Medicians?" Anika asked.

"Oh, there's a variety," Alissia answered, as she sat down.

Salvatore nodded in agreement. "There's everything from pale lilac to a deep plum, but I don't think I've seen anyone with a dark wine color."

"No, I think mine will be darker than any of theirs," Luke said. "I thought about that while in the valley."

Alissia's thoughts returned to the Medicians, and she looked down and took a bite from her breakfast. Silence lingered in the air as she chewed her food, and after swallowing, she looked up and asked, "Anyone know what we're gonna do yet?"

Luke leaned back in his chair and crossed his arms over his chest, looking thoughtful. "I believe we need to go back to the forest."

"But that'll take forever," Alissia complained.

"I've thought about our options, and that's our best chance," he responded.

Across the table, with his hands clasped in front of him, Salvatore looked at Alissia. "No matter what we decide, it's going to take time before we can act. We can't fight this on our own, and we'll need help from my people."

Sitting next to her father, Lita asked Alissia, "Do you have any suggestions?"

Alissia shrugged. "I've got nothing. I'm just worried, and everything looks hopeless."

"I don't believe they're going to kill the Medicians," Salvatore replied.

"This is much bigger than the valley," Luke said, uncrossing his arms. He ran his hand through his hair before dropping it in his lap. "Gore asked about the possibility of a human war, and I believe they're trying to start one. Right now, they could have control over the greater races, and we need to know more before we battle them. What if they have more weapons we don't even know about? They could even have an army ready to fight against humans. Has anyone considered that?"

Alissia cringed at the thought of countless feliums swarming the land, biting every human in sight. Then she remembered they would die if they left the bog.

"We know the warriors need their bog to survive" Luke continued, "so I doubt they're building a permanent residence in the forest—or even the island or valley. They're probably setting up posts of some kind near the portals, and with all the toxic vegetation in the forest, I'm wondering if they're even venturing that far into it."

Luke gave a half shrug. "However, their bodies may be immune. We just don't know." After a quick sip from his drink, he looked at Salvatore. "How soon can your people get to the forest?"

"I don't know, and now I'm beginning to worry about our families living on the island. With the fresh jade I received in the valley, I can use the orb again, but I don't think it's a good idea to contact the ancients. I need to change the settings."

"Can you get that done today?" Luke asked.

Salvatore nodded. "I'll contact my people and see what they know."

"How soon before we leave?" Lita asked.

"I don't know," Luke answered. "Grady's checking into some things today at the Eldership, and I'll know more tonight."

"What's Grady and the Eldership got to do with this?" Alissia asked, pushing aside her bowl of half-eaten oats.

Luke let out a sigh and leaned forward, resting his elbows on the table. "We may have some trouble getting to the forest, now that there's a heightened threat of war—especially in that part of the land. The area's full of military, and they're starting to evacuate people."

"It's that bad?" she asked, lifting her drink from the table.

"Yes. You were with Emera when Grady talked about it." Luke looked up at the ceiling and frowned. "I'm hoping this storm will pass so that he can stop by tonight. I don't want to waste any time getting a plan together."

Alissia swallowed a sip of chet and set the mug back down. "What will we do with Mia when we leave?"

Staring down at his hands, Luke fidgeted with his wedding ring for a moment before looking up to meet her gaze. "I don't know yet, Alissia. I'm still trying to put everything together."

Frustration, doubt, sadness, and anger—overwhelming anger—flooded into Alissia. The feelings only lasted for a moment before Luke's expression closed off, taking his emotions with it.

Surprised by the sudden emotional overload, Alissia ignored Luke's words when he turned to Salvatore and spoke. When the two of them rose from the table, she gave Luke a questioning look.

"You don't have to come," he said. "It's storming out there."

She nodded and watched the two of them as they walked out of the kitchen.

Duff gave Lita a playful smack on the thigh. "It's too wet to do anything. Want to spend the rest of the morning with me in the carriage?"

Alissia turned to Anika and snickered.

"Something wrong?" Lita questioned, her brows raised.

"Nothing." Alissia smiled innocently.

Lita stood, and Duff followed her lead. "You know," she said, grinning down at Alissia, "Duff and I aren't the newlyweds anymore. You and Luke are."

"Yeah, but me and Luke aren't anything like you two." Alissia leaned forward and knocked on the table. Doing her best Duff impersonation, she whispered, "Let me in. Hurry! My dad's almost here!"

Santo laughed out loud, and Lita punched his shoulder before bounding out of the kitchen.

"I didn't sound anything like that," Duff asserted. He turned and started after Lita.

"Yeah, keep telling yourself that," Alissia called out. She took the last sip of her chet before getting up and placing her dirty dishes on the counter.

"What do you want me to do with your flowers?" she asked, turning to Anika.

*****

Restless and forced to stay inside, Alissia refused to sit down, and she spent most of the day leading Anika through a series of tasks.

The storm eventually ended, and by the time Langley arrived home for dinner with Grady, flowers bloomed abundantly in every room. The smell of freshly baked bread and pies pervaded the small cottage, and compliments abounded as everyone helped themselves to the generous buffet arranged along the counter.

"I really don't see any other choice but to inform the Elders," Grady said, during the meal. "We could get you an escort, while at the same time, put an end to the conflict in that area."

"I'm listening," Luke replied.

"There's just too much military to get you near the forest, and I fear the war will soon start there." Grady set his fork in his plate and looked at Alissia. "You could possibly put an end to the war before it even begins."

"Explain yourself, before filling her head with ideas!" Luke chided, a bit harshly.

Surprised by Luke's tone, everyone looked at Grady, waiting for his response. With a tight smile, he gave a nod to Luke.

"The Eldership already knows about the creatures in the bog, as I informed them of the bite I received. They also know the two of you were kidnapped by them, and in my report, I stressed the evilness of the creatures. In fact, there's now talk of closing off the roads in that area, now that we know what exists beyond those skull trees."

Luke nodded in understanding, and Grady continued, "They already know about Alissia and believe she's trying to find a way back to her reality. If she goes to the Eldership, she could say she believes the creatures are the ones behind the attacks—not our people. The ambassadors leaning toward war may then put a hold on the battle in that area, and you'd get an escort to the forest."

Grady picked up his fork. Holding Luke's gaze, he stressed, "You know this would save lives and give the Elders more time to negotiate a way out of this war."

Luke frowned thoughtfully, and Grady continued eating. Silence filled the air, as everyone seemed to wait for Luke's response.

"And what would be our reason for going to the forest?" Luke asked. "Shall we tell them the location of a race that's been hidden for nearly two thousand years, or have you already done that?"

Grady shook his head and swallowed a bite of food. "I did not." He gave a half shrug. "You're the military man. Can't you think of a reasonable explanation?"

"We could say some of the bog creatures found their way to the forest," Alissia interjected. Everyone looked her way, and she shrugged.

"I've already told the Elders the creatures can't leave their bog," Grady replied, "and I promised they held no threat outside that area."

"Then we can just say some of them followed us to the forest," Alissia suggested. "Maybe they even traveled there with me. What did you tell them about our kidnapping? Why did you release us?"

"That's where my memory went blank," Grady answered. "I used the felium's bite as a way out of explaining some things to the Elders."

"But we couldn't use that excuse," Anika said. "Langley and I told the Elders that you and Luke withdrew and didn't talk much after the kidnapping. That it really upset you both. You seemed completely focused on returning back to your reality."

"And how did Grady explain his recovery from the felium bite?" Alissia asked.

"I told them I received a temporary poisoning, and I recovered slowly."

Alissia's face twisted in thought. "Maybe we can say they released Luke and me, but we had to agree to take some of them with us." She shook her head. "No, that wouldn't work."

"I think I may have an idea," Salvatore announced. Everyone looked his way expectantly. "When Alissia first told me she was from another reality, I believed she was searching for a way to get back home. I didn't know how she'd get there, but she sounded desperate."

He paused, looking around the table. "What if a few bog creatures followed her hoping to find her reality—or maybe a power source of some kind? Call them martyrs, since they knew they'd die for leaving their home. The forest creatures are supposed to be inventive. Maybe, once this is all over, they can build something that looks intricate, and you can give it to the Elders, with some kind of excuse about it being what the bog creatures were searching for."

"And what if the forest creatures aren't on our side?" Lita asked.

"Then we unite the land in a war against them," Luke declared.

Alissia turned to him in surprise. "They're on our side." Although she sounded confident, she felt a tinge of doubt for the first time. "Are you really considering that we go to the Eldership? How'd that work out in the past?"

"This will be different," Grady replied. "Pallen's corrupt, and the Elders are desperately trying to avoid a war right now."

His face softened, and he added, "I know I was scared they'd lock you away, but things have changed since then. If you go in there with the story of the bog creatures setting the fires, I'm certain the Elders will get you to speak in front of the ambassadors. You could stop this war, and they need that."

Alissia chewed on her bottom lip as she stared back at him for a moment. Then she frowned and let out a resigned breath. "If it's what we need to do, then I'll do it. But I'm not acting shy and timid this time round. Ain't nobody got the patience for any of that!"

"I agree."

Alissia jerked around in her seat and stiffened at the sight of Emera smiling confidently from the kitchen doorway. She could barely breathe as she wondered how much of the conversation had been overheard.

Everyone watched as Emera crossed the room to stand behind Grady. Looking unfazed, she began to lightly massage his shoulders.

"My father and most others in Pallen didn't believe Alissia was weak minded, and after the way she escaped the palace, I'm certain her reputation precedes her." Locking eyes with Alissia, she stressed,

"If I were you, I'd walk boldly into the palace and act like you have all the answers, even if you don't."

Her fingers stopped moving, and she leaned forward slightly, still staring at Alissia. "If you recall, I didn't believe your ruse."

Alissia stared back in silence, not knowing how to respond. Although pleased someone agreed with her, she feared Emera knowing her plans. Glancing at Grady, she desperately wanted to talk to him alone.

He stood and turned to Emera. "I'll get you a drink, while you prepare your plate."

"Did you ask him about her last night?" she asked mentally, as she watched Grady lead Emera to the food on the counter.

"He swears by her loyalty, but I still don't trust her," Luke answered. *"We need her for Mia, so it's a delicate situation. Be nice!"*

"How will Luke's changes be explained?" Duff asked.

"That's easy," Alissia answered. "I can only bond with one person, and since I'm already bonded to him, that should help against anyone trying to . . . uh . . ." She glanced at Emera's back. "Take advantage of me."

Looking around the table, she added assertively, "We're married, and there's no reason to hide that."

"There's no point to hiding it," Luke agreed.

Alissia smiled, surprised no one objected. "So, I finally get to be myself and talk with my own accent in public. And now that I'm married, I won't have to deal with the mess I had to in Pallen."

"It'll be much different," Grady affirmed, setting Emera's drink down where he had been sitting.

"When do you think the two of you'll be leaving for the palace, and what are your plans for Mia?" Langley asked, looking at Luke. "I can't keep my father out of that room much longer. I'm already getting questions."

"It'll need to be soon," Luke answered. "We can't waste any time." He looked up at Emera as she set her plate on the table. "What can you tell us about Mia?"

After sitting down, she placed her hands and cloth napkin in her lap before answering, "Her recovery won't be quick. I could try to wake her tomorrow, but she'll need someone she knows in the room to help keep her calm."

"She understands the ancient language," Alissia said. "We can tell her what's going on."

Emera's eyes widened with surprise. "She comprehends a complete language?"

Alissia nodded. "She's not like a dog. She's not a pet."

Taking a bite of her food, Emera's expression appeared thoughtful as she chewed. After swallowing, she said, "If you're planning to go to the palace, it may be better if Mia goes as well. That way I could use their equipment and have some things readily available. That would help immensely." She looked over her shoulder at Grady, now leaning against the counter. "What are your thoughts?"

He crossed his arms over his chest and considered the question for a moment. "I don't see a problem with that." Looking at Luke, he said, "I've already had to tell the Elders about her because of the bite marks on the body in Pallen."

"And what do they know about her?" Luke asked.

"I actually had to do a lot of thinking, when it came to her." Uncrossing his arms, Grady straightened from the counter. "I told them she entered this reality with Alissia, but they were separated until in Pallen—that I didn't even know about Mia until Pallen."

"Why'd you tell them that?" Alissia asked, confused.

"Well, think about it. If Mia had been with you before Pallen, could you really have been kidnapped and needed Luke's help to save you?" Grady paused, giving Alissia a questioning look. "The amount of destruction she left in the dungeon proved she's viscious and capable of extreme damage."

"He did the right thing," Luke stated, looking thoughtful. "I'm sure the Elders will ask about that night in the dungeon, and if Mia had been around earlier, things would have worked out much differently the night you first left Pallen."

To Grady, he said, "Alissia and I need to sit down with you to hear everything you told the Elders. Our stories need to be aligned."

Grady nodded, and the discussion turned to what he would tell the Elders about Alissia and Luke's arrival.

Alissia waited for a break in the conversation before she left her seat and put her dishes by the sink. Behind Emera's back, she stared expectantly at Grady as he spoke, hoping to get him alone for a moment.

Thankfully, Luke and Salvatore took control of the conversation, allowing her to subtly draw Grady out of the room. After leading him to the bathroom, she shut the door.

Chapter 27

"How have you been?" Alissia asked, walking past Grady. With a smile, she turned to face him.

"I'm well."

"You look healthy." Her smile faltered, and she added, "Sorry to drag you back into this mess."

"You're not dragging me into anything, Alissia."

She tucked her hair behind her ear, hating her awkwardness.

"You want to know about Emera," Grady replied knowingly. She nodded, and he said, "I actually believe you'd like her. She came to me hoping for more details about what happened in the dungeon." He paused before stressing, "You know, you did the right thing in leaving her that note."

Alissia frowned but nodded in agreement.

"She's nothing like her father or brother. She has emotions, and she feels them deeply." Looking troubled, Grady lifted his hand to the back of his neck and began to massage it. "I know nothing I say will get you to trust her, but I ask that you give her a chance." Dropping his hand to his side, he added, "Her family nearly destroyed her. And you, of all people, should understand that feeling."

"And how do you know she's not spying for Alrik or out for revenge?"

With pleading eyes, Grady met Alissia's gaze. "Because I know that's not who she is, and if you get to know her, you'd feel the same."

Alissia closed her eyes and frowned, rubbing her temples. With a sigh, she looked back at him. "I thought you weren't into relationships and was a workaholic. You know what she did at the ball. Did she seduce you or something? I mean, what's happened?"

"It's not like that," Grady answered, shaking his head. "She only acted that way because of her father."

"Well, it could have gotten you killed."

"But it didn't. Give her a chance."

Alissia crossed her arms. "It doesn't seem like I have a choice, if I want her to save Mia."

"She would help Mia, either way."

"How much did you tell her about me?"

"She knows what I told the Eldership. I never mentioned the Lamians living in this reality, and like everyone else, she believes they sent you here."

"So she thinks I'm trying to find a way home?"

Grady nodded, and Alissia uncrossed her arms, her expression still troubled. After a brief silence, he said softly, "You know I would never do anything to hurt you or the Lamians, don't you?"

She studied his face, not responding.

Stepping closer, he placed his hand over his heart. "I would *never* do anything to hurt you, Alissia, and I'm not angry with you for choosing Luke." His hand fell away as he continued, "I know you have reasons to be suspicious of Emera, but I ask that you trust my perception of her. Like you, she moved away from her family and found her own way in life."

Alissia let out a sigh. Staring back at him, her expression softened.

A smile crept to Grady's face, and he said hopefully, "She could even help you at the Eldership."

"And how's that?" Alissia asked skeptically.

"When she first arrived in Allure, she went to the Elders and gave details about Alrik. She's earned their respect, and she could help you adjust while at the palace."

Alissia frowned. "I thought we weren't going to be there that long."

"You're not, but it would still be nice to have someone to talk to while there. Anika won't be there this time, but Emera will need to stay with Mia."

Although her face twisted in disapproval, Alissia conceded. "I'll do this, but only for you." Pointing into the air, she emphasized, "But, if she gives me any reason not to trust her . . ."

Grady chuckled, looking somewhat relieved. "And I'm sure you'll be looking for something."

"Of course!" Alissia's expression softened, and she stared back at him for a moment.

"Are you happy?" she asked softly.

He nodded. "I'm getting there. Things aren't the best at the Eldership right now, but we both know it could be much worse. How about you? How's life with the Lamians?"

"Medicians," she corrected, with a smile. "Although, we'll need to call them Lamians from now on—now that I'm hanging with humans again." Blinking back her emotions, she looked down. "They were much better than I expected. I'm worried about them."

Feeling Grady's hand on her shoulder, she looked up into his eyes.

"You have a lot of people by your side, Alissia, and with Salvatore's resources and Luke's skills, there's hope. I'll get the Eldership to do all I can, without giving up your secrets." He squeezed her shoulder and gave a reassuring smile. "Have faith."

She smiled slightly and nodded. "We should probably get back to the kitchen, before you get into trouble with Emera."

He shook his head, letting his hand drop from her shoulder. "She'll understand, but we should get back in there to help finalize the plans. We still have a lot to figure out."

Alissia followed Grady back to the kitchen. When they entered, she noticed Emera give him a private, encouraging smile. Alissia quickly turned away and began to help Anika put away the food.

The planning continued into the late evening hours, and by the time everyone stood from their chairs, Grady knew exactly what to tell the Elders the next morning.

Luke and Alissia received a quick update on Mia before going to bed, and in the light of the blue bella flowers, Alissia stared up at the stars, considering the plan.

"I don't like this idea," she mumbled, turning to face Luke. "We need another one."

He rolled onto his back. With a sigh, he clasped his hands over his chest. "I don't like it either, but it's our best option."

Alissia stared at the glowing specks of purple in his eyes when his face turned her way, and he said, "We have the opportunity to stop a war, and we have to think of everyone."

"I thought you wanted a war when I first met you."

"I never wanted a war," he said gravely, "and I don't believe many people actually do. We just want the Eldership to make better decisions. They're funneling money into the South, and things need to change."

He paused before adding, "I don't regret leaving my life behind, but as a member of the league, I can't just walk away from this when we could stop it. It's the right thing to do."

Luke rolled onto his side and took her hand, pulling it to rest between them. "Do you trust me?"

"I guess so," Alissia mumbled.

He chuckled. "Then trust that I can make this work. It won't be easy, but we can do this."

Although he appeared confident, Luke's fear and worry seeped into Alissia. She sat up and leaned down for a kiss. Dreading the vulnerability she had felt the night before, she kept it short and sweet.

"Goodnight," she whispered, nestling her back against his chest.

He wrapped his arm around her. "I love you."

A lone tear escaped from Alissia's eye. "I love you, too."

Dear reader,

You're almost there! Get ready for *Unexpected Legends*, the fifth and last book in the Alissia Roswell Series. Full of action and adventure, the end of her journey will leave you astounded.

I pour my heart into my writing and would love to hear if it connected with you in some way. Please consider leaving an online review—even if only one sentence. I would greatly appreciate it.

To get updates or check out the Pinterest boards I've created for each book, you can connect with me at:

www.tiannaholley.com
www.facebook.com/authortiannaholley.com
www.instagram.com/tiannaholley/
www.pinterest.com/tiannaholley/
www.google.com/+TiannaHolley
www.twitter.com/holley_tianna
www.goodreads.com/author/show/7140745.Tianna_Holley

Stay tuned! A labyrinth of stories lives within my head, and I can't wait to share them with you.

Tianna Holley
Writer of passionate fantasy romance without the guilt

www.ingramcontent.com/pod-product-compliance
Lightning Source LLC
Chambersburg PA
CBHW031227120726
47905CB00002B/497